# Take Me Home

Karly Lane lives on the mid north coast of New South Wales. Proud mum to four children and wife of one very patient mechanic, she is lucky enough to spend her day doing the two things she loves most—being a mum and writing stories set in beautiful rural Australia.

**Also by Karly Lane**
*North Star*
*Morgan's Law*
*Bridie's Choice*
*Poppy's Dilemma*
*Gemma's Bluff*
*Tallowood Bound*
*Second Chance Town*
*Third Time Lucky*
*If Wishes Were Horses*
*Six Ways to Sunday*
*Someone Like You*
*The Wrong Callahan*
*Mr Right Now*
*Return to Stringybark Creek*
*Fool Me Once*
*Something Like This*

# KARLY LANE

## Take Me Home

ALLEN&UNWIN
SYDNEY・MELBOURNE・AUCKLAND・LONDON

This is a work of fiction. Names, characters, places and incidents are products of the author's imagination or are used fictitiously. Any resemblance to actual events, locales or persons, living or dead, is entirely coincidental.

First published in 2021

Copyright © Karly Lane 2021

All rights reserved. No part of this book may be reproduced or transmitted in any form or by any means, electronic or mechanical, including photocopying, recording or by any information storage and retrieval system, without prior permission in writing from the publisher. The Australian *Copyright Act 1968* (the Act) allows a maximum of one chapter or 10 per cent of this book, whichever is the greater, to be photocopied by any educational institution for its educational purposes provided that the educational institution (or body that administers it) has given a remuneration notice to the Copyright Agency (Australia) under the Act.

Allen & Unwin
83 Alexander Street
Crows Nest NSW 2065
Australia
Phone: (61 2) 8425 0100
Email: info@allenandunwin.com
Web: www.allenandunwin.com

A catalogue record for this book is available from the National Library of Australia

ISBN 978 1 76087 849 8

Set in 12.25/18.25 pt Simoncini Garamond by Bookhouse, Sydney
Printed and bound in Australia by Griffin Press, part of Ovato

10 9 8 7 6 5 4 3 2 1

The paper in this book is FSC® certified. FSC® promotes environmentally responsible, socially beneficial and economically viable management of the world's forests.

*In memory of my ancestors—
long gone but not forgotten*

# One

Elspeth Kinnaird sighed in irritation as she stared at the computer screen and the picturesque image of rolling green Highlands hills that had interrupted her Facebook newsfeed. Normally Elle wouldn't give the ad a second glance, but that was before she'd started to notice the unsettlingly repetitive signs. No, not signs, she told herself firmly. Coincidences. That's all they were.

Ever since her gran's funeral two weeks ago, everywhere she turned, Scotland kept appearing before her eyes.

Elle knew it wasn't really a sign. She'd just been thinking about Scotland so much lately. A similar thing happened when she updated to the new iPhone—she hadn't seen anyone with one, and then suddenly every second person in town seemed to be carrying her model. This was the same kind of thing. She was just noticing the Scottish references more now because of Gran.

Her heart sank a little at the thought.

Gran.

'I miss you so much,' she said quietly.

She had only been gone a few weeks, and already it felt longer. Elle closed the laptop and stood up, grabbing her keys and handbag before heading out the door to work.

Jessup's Creek had been her home her entire life. Population three thousand two hundred and fifty-three. Tucked away in the New South Wales hinterland, their sleepy little town had been bypassed by the tourist trade and highways for most of its life, which had never been a problem for a tightknit farming community. Not until the past few generations, when working farms began to dwindle as kids moved away to start their careers, and parents running properties got too old and tired to continue working them.

Then, a miracle of sorts happened. Over the past two years, the grey-nomad trade had come to the rescue, saving Jessup's Creek from becoming another dying country town with more closed shops than residents. The retirees and their caravans, motorhomes and campervans were an almost constant stream driving through. More shops had opened, filling the main street with all kinds of quirky businesses, drawing not only the travellers but weekend tourists from the coast and inland as well.

There was a chocolatier, two antique stores and a pottery-and-craft barn, which sold local handmade items and ran workshops, where Elle had taken a few art classes. Cafes were springing up left, right and centre, and only a month ago a boutique brewery had opened its doors, bringing quite a few beard-sporting, man-bun-wearing men to town on weekend beer-tasting sessions.

As a result, property prices had begun to climb, and new people were moving to town. The downside to this was that the once-quiet village was changing. It looked the same, with verandah-lined shops running along both sides of the wide main street, but there was a very different vibe about the place. Where Elle once knew every face in town, nowadays, more often than not she could walk into a shop and not recognise a single person. It wasn't like newcomers were overrunning the place, but it was still strange, and a lot of the older residents were finding it a tad confronting.

Elle turned her old VW Beetle into the carpark at the back of the independent supermarket and headed inside to work.

'Morning, Elle,' Pat called as Elle walked past with a smile.

Pat was in her late fifties and had been working in Brown's Grocer ever since she left school. She was about as permanent a fixture as the business itself. She was also the example Elle's parents liked to use whenever they tried to discuss their daughter's future . . . or lack of one.

*'Do you want to end up like Patricia Adams?'*

Elle didn't think ending up like Pat was the worst thing that could happen to a person. Pat was single, she had a steady job and a cat she adored, and everyone loved her. But to Caroline and Alister Kinnaird, it was a fate worse than death; to them, Pat was a lonely old spinster who had never left Jessup's Creek and was doomed to die alone alongside her cat.

Caroline and Alister were a Jessup's Creek success story. They were high-school sweethearts who left town to go to university. Alister became a doctor and Caroline an accountant. They married and returned to their hometown to set up businesses and raise a family.

They'd had three perfect children who followed in their footsteps: first Lauren, who went into law; then Lachlan, an engineer; and Malcolm, who was studying biomedical science . . . and then there was Elspeth. She had never really fitted into the family mould. For starters, she was the only redhead. It was some kind of throwback, apparently. Gran had always said Elle was lucky—that inheriting her Scottish genes was a blessing—but as a kid Elle considered her red hair and freckles a curse. She was so different to her siblings that growing up she often wondered when her parents would sit her down and break the news that she was adopted. They never did, and now that she was twenty-four she assumed they would have done it by now if they were ever going to.

It wasn't as if Elle hadn't tried to fit in. She'd done her best; she'd even gone to university, partly to keep the peace but mostly because, more than anything, she wanted to make her parents proud. Unlike her siblings, though, she had no career in mind, and it only took two semesters for her to realise that being an accountant was *not* for her. Her lecturer suggested changing some subjects, which she did, picking up an art elective, which went a long way to making life bearable. Elle had always loved to draw and paint—it was the one thing she could do to escape everything going on around her.

She had toyed with the idea of switching to art school—she researched it and went as far as presenting the idea to her parents—but in the end she had been talked out of it. 'You need security, Elspeth,' her mother had said. 'A reliable career.'

Gran had been the only one who encouraged her. 'If art is where your heart is, then you should follow it,' she'd argued when a tearful Elle had come home between semesters.

'I can't. Mum and Dad won't let me,' she'd sniffed, wiping her eyes.

'This is *your* life. *Your* decision.'

'They've already said they won't pay for art school.'

'So? Get a job and pay your own way. I can lend you some money if you need it,' Gran had suggested.

The idea had been tempting, but the more she'd pictured herself at art school, the more easily she could hear the arguments and imagine the frosty silences she would have to endure throughout her studies, and probably for a long time afterwards. Elle didn't do confrontation. She liked to keep the peace and not rock any boats. So, she'd kept her head down and did her best to stick with the university course. She'd managed two years before giving up.

Mostly, she'd missed the peace and quiet of Jessup's Creek. She wasn't cut out to be a city girl, and studying was not for her, so she'd come home and listened to her parents' concerned lectures before getting a job at Brown's to think over her options. That had been three years ago.

Elle liked the work, for the most part. The oldies who shopped there had been loyal customers all their lives and there was a tightknit community feel about Brown's. It was more than just a grocery store—more than the soulless big-chain supermarkets she'd visited in the city. This was a place where locals gathered for a catch-up and a yarn. People smiled as they passed each other in the aisles, and waited patiently in line at the checkout—even the carpark was civilised, no horns blaring or arguments over who got a spot first. Elle got to talk to people all day; sometimes she suspected she was the only person some of the elderly people saw. She loved to make them smile and listen to them chat about their grandkids. She shared their excitement when they came in to buy up big in preparation for a long overdue family visit or a party, and she commiserated with them when they went through sad times. It sometimes sounded silly or unimportant when she tried to explain to her parents why she loved her job. They just didn't seem to get it.

'How are you today, Pat?' Elle said now as she set up her cash register.

'Good, love, good.' Pat returned her smile.

Elle braced herself as the first of her regular customers came through her checkout.

'Morning, Mrs Henderson.'

'Hello, dear. How are you?' the older woman asked, eyeing her keenly. As president of the gardening club, Margaret Henderson had known Elle's gran well. Gran had been a member and an avid gardener for much of her life until arthritis took hold and made it too painful and dangerous for her to continue doing what she loved. That was when Elle had moved in to help her.

'I'm fine, thanks, Mrs Henderson.'

'How are your parents doing?'

'They're okay. It's been busy with all the family coming and going.' Elle shrugged.

'I can imagine,' Mrs Henderson said, nodding in sympathy. 'Iona will be missed.'

Elle forced her smile to remain in place as she scanned and bagged the items. She had taken three days off work after the funeral, glad not to be fending off well-meant sympathy from locals when everything was still so fresh, but she'd been back at work for more than a week now and it wasn't getting any easier. She was sure everyone who'd known Gran must have come in to buy their groceries by now, but each day brought a few more customers who would wait and come through her checkout just so they could offer their condolences. It was touching that so many people had loved her gran and wanted the chance to say how sorry they were at her passing, but it was also draining.

Gran had been her rock, always. The two had been inseparable. They shared a love of reading and history, and Elle had sat for countless hours listening to her grandmother tell stories about her childhood in Scotland. Gran had always had a deep love for her ancestral homeland, which Elle found infectious. Her Scottish brogue—which she'd managed to hold onto despite having emigrated to Australia with her father when she was fifteen—added a colourful tone to the stories she passed down, and Elspeth, who was named after Iona's mother, loved everything about the world Gran brought so vividly to life.

Elle's favourites were the tales of Stormeil, the once-magnificent castle of Iona's forebears. As a child, Elle had imagined living within its magical walls, as would any kid who ever dreamed of becoming a princess, only to discover when she was much older that the castle no longer existed—it was left to fall into disrepair sometime in the sixteenth century. Her dreams of becoming a princess had been destroyed like the ruins of her ancestors' castle. This, however, never dulled Gran's enthusiasm. To her, the castle was still an important part of her heritage.

It had always made Gran sad that her only son, Elle's father, had never felt the same connection to Scotland. *'He's too much like his father,'* Gran had once said. She had loved her husband dearly, but he was a fourth-generation Australian and a man whose heart and life were firmly rooted in New South Wales.

For years Elle and her gran discussed taking a trip to Scotland, returning to Iona's homeland and visiting the places they had always talked about. But time had run out.

Pa hadn't liked to fly, and even though Elle's parents had offered to take Gran, she had refused to go without him. Years later, after her husband's death, Iona had a series of small strokes that had her doctors cautioning her against flying, and as a result, Gran stopped talking about it. She still had family there, but Elle knew they weren't close. Gran had lost two brothers over the years and had only a sister remaining, but the two had never done more than exchange the odd letter and a Christmas card each year. It was strange for Elle to think that Gran had lived here longer than in her home country—seventy-three years. And yet Australia had never really seemed to be her home. Towards the end, Elle had heard a sad note in her gran's voice when she spoke of

Scotland. Her family may have been here, but her heart was across the ocean.

When Elle had returned from university and moved in with Gran, they'd talked about going again. 'Don't you want to visit your sister?' Elle remembered asking one Christmas as she placed a card from Scotland, with the spidery old-lady writing inside, on the mantel.

'Well, sure, it would be grand to see the family again, but I don't know.' Gran had been a little flustered as she whisked the feather duster over the coffee table, turning away. 'They're like strangers now. It's been so long.'

It had never been easy to bring up her family in conversation, and Elle knew, deep down, that the trip was never going to eventuate. Gran had known it too, she thought. She just couldn't admit it out loud.

Elle frowned, thinking once again about the peculiar things that had happened lately. At first it was subtle—she would absentmindedly pick up a book and it would be set in Scotland, or she would see something on the news. She would spot strange shapes that looked like the shape of the country, or Scottish music would come on the radio. Then it had been other odd occurrences. Things she was trying hard to explain rationally.

Yesterday she had walked past her bedside table and discovered one of her gran's crocheted handkerchiefs that hadn't been there before. She often swore she could smell her gran's perfume throughout the day, only she could never find anything that would explain why. It was clearly some kind of grief-related issue, but it seemed to be getting worse.

Elle had been quietly saving money in a special account that she refused to label *My Scotland Fund*. She wasn't game to tell anyone about it; her parents would disapprove immediately. An overseas holiday would be a frivolous thing to do.

They still hoped she would find her way back into study and a career. As much as it frustrated her, she understood their feelings. They wanted each of their children to be independent, strong people. A career guaranteed security. They were so alike, her parents—both strong-minded and capable—and there was no question they loved each of their children, but they just didn't *get* Elspeth.

Elle knew she lacked her siblings' ambition, and she was okay with that. She didn't feel a need to *want* anything. Sure, she liked to splurge on a new phone now and again, she was always in the craft barn in town on payday buying art supplies, and she couldn't resist a new pair of boots once in a while, but she didn't spend more than she made. Elle paid her bills on time and she had a superannuation account and some savings . . . She was doing all the adult things she needed to do. Her parents just couldn't understand that she simply didn't *need* a house or an expensive car or a fancy job. She was happy doing her own thing—hanging out with her friends, taking her art classes and working at Brown's.

It wasn't as if she were lying around doing nothing and wasting her time. She had a full life—sometimes almost too full. Between work shifts and taking care of Gran, the past few months had been busy. A sadness welled up once more at the thought. She missed the afternoons sketching in Gran's garden after a morning of weeding. Last night, as she flipped through her sketchpad, she came across a few drawings of Gran sitting in her wheelchair, watering her garden. While Elle took care of the more physical tasks, Gran still insisted on doing the watering and Elle had loved sitting out there, capturing those quiet, precious moments. Gran hadn't thought she was wasting her life. Whenever Elle had an argument with her parents about her future, Gran would always comfort her. 'Darling, don't you worry,' she would say. 'Everything blooms in its own time.'

# Two

Pat tried to keep a straight face as she passed on the message. 'Elle, Trudie just called down from the office and said Mr Brown wants to see you.'

Elle always found it amusing to hear her boss referred to as *Mr Brown*. She'd gone to school with the Browns, and it was weird to call Michael Brown, who was only a few years older than her, *Mister*. She still remembered him as the school geek, who used to get picked on by the footy guys and anyone else he might have annoyed, with the pompous air he'd had even as a kid. Having a father who owned most of Jessup's Creek seemed to make him think he was local royalty, which hadn't gone down well with the kids at school. It was unfortunate that her brother, Lachlan, had been on the football team back then. Elle was pretty sure that was why Michael seemed to hold some kind of grudge against her.

'Wonder what I've done this time,' she said with an eye roll as she left her register. Michael had taken over managing the store from his father two years ago, and was always calling one of them up to the office to nit-pick or explain some new procedure he wanted to introduce.

'Elspeth, take a seat,' Michael said, indicating the vacant chair across from his desk as she walked in, without looking up from the paperwork he was signing.

She used the time to study the framed black-and-white photos on the wall of the office of Brown's Grocer through the ages, all the while thinking that if he wanted to go back to the original way of writing out their change slips, she would lose it. They'd just spent the past two weeks changing a perfectly good system to one that involved twice the amount of paperwork, simply because Michael felt the need to shake things up a bit.

'Elspeth,' he began, dragging her attention away from the photo of Brown's in 1901. 'I asked you to come in here today because I have some bad news.'

Elle eyed him warily as his hands tapped on the desk in front of him.

'At our recent general meeting it was discussed that although the town has been growing, the opening of the new supermarket in Hentley has had a significant impact on our profits.'

Elle felt her palms begin to sweat. She'd heard rumours about the new chain store gaining a lot of local business, but hadn't really taken much notice of it until now. They had been assured that Brown's was doing fine, even if the staff had all noticed that they were a lot quieter throughout the day now than they used to be.

'Unfortunately, this has led to us having to make some hard decisions, namely, some staff cutbacks. As you're aware, we're about to install a self-service checkout in the near future and we feel that the service area is the most logical place we can cut back staff numbers.'

Elle stared at him, her mind racing with a thousand reasons why that idea was *not* the most logical at all, but she couldn't get a single word out of her mouth.

'As a result, I'm afraid we'll be giving you three weeks' notice, as of today.'

Michael continued to speak—she vaguely heard something about giving her a glowing reference and holiday pay, but nothing else really registered after that. She was being sacked.

She didn't remember walking from the office and returning to her checkout, but she did see the concern on Pat's face as they worked through an unexpected rush of customers. At her first break, she left before Pat could ask her any questions, heading straight for the restrooms to wash her face with cold water.

She felt sick. She'd never been fired before. Her thoughts instantly went to her parents and she squeezed her eyes tightly shut. Oh God, she was going to have to tell them she was unemployed.

*You didn't need this job anyway, darling,* a voice said from behind her and Elle's eyes flew to the mirror, only to find her lone reflection and an empty bathroom. She spun around, just to make sure she wasn't missing something. But both cubicles were empty. 'What the actual fu—'

*Forget about this dump. Now you have time to go to Scotland.*

Elle let out a small cry, shrinking back against the cold tiles behind her. 'Gran?' She was losing her freaking mind. She had to be.

*Well, I tried to be subtle, sweetheart, but that hasn't been working.*

She *was not* hearing her dead gran's voice in the staff bathroom. It was emotional stress. That was all. Elle exited the restroom and hurried back to her checkout.

'Are you all right, darl?' Pat asked, moving around her register to peer at Elle's face. Her ash-blonde hair, streaked with grey, was pulled back in her usual ponytail, and the creases near her eyes were more pronounced with her concern. 'You look like you've seen a ghost.'

A manic laugh tumbled out of Elle's mouth before she clamped a hand across it in alarm.

'I think you should take yourself off home,' Pat said, nodding firmly. 'I'll call up to Trudie and let her know.'

'No!' Elle said quickly. The last thing she needed was for them to put her off a few weeks earlier. She needed the next three weeks to find another job before her parents found out. 'I'm fine. Just having one of those days.' She tried for a smile and figured by the doubtful look on Pat's face that she hadn't pulled it off. 'Really, Pat,' she added, grateful for her friend's concern. 'I'll be okay.'

'If you're sure,' Pat said, reluctantly heading back to her checkout as a customer came towards them.

*Just concentrate on getting through today*, Elle told herself firmly, but it wasn't easy. She needed a job, pronto . . . and possibly an appointment with a psychologist.

⁂

Elle stopped at the bottom pub to visit Lilly on her way home. It wasn't a normal stop-over, but she really didn't feel up to being alone in Gran's big old house by herself, and the pub seemed the best alternative.

The place was full of its usual clientele of regulars, who had their favourite seats, and thirsty after-work labourers. Music played on a jukebox, a Cold Chisel classic, and loud male conversation rose in competition with the song.

'Hey, what are you doing here?' Lilly asked as Elle approached the bar.

Lilly had been her best friend since kindergarten, much to Caroline and Alister's dismay. Lilly was another example of the 'bad life choices' her parents used occasionally in arguments—pregnant at nineteen and now raising a five-year-old daughter on her own in Jessup's Creek.

Lilly was as small-town as it got—a single mum who worked as a barmaid in the local pub and had a sideline business selling healing crystals and jewellery. Fashion-wise, Lilly had a bohemian love-child kind of thing going on and managed to pull it off perfectly. Her curly blonde hair never looked like the frizzy disaster that Elle's did most days. In fact, it was their hair that had drawn them together as kids in primary school. Elle had been cornered in the playground by Felicity Graham and her pack of mean-girl friends one lunchtime, who were making fun of her wild red hair.

'Look, her hair matches her face!' Felicity had taunted as they all laughed, and Elle's face grew hotter by the minute. It never took much. In class, any time the teacher singled her out for a question she would feel her face go red, then of course someone would draw attention to the fact, and that would make her feel even more embarrassed.

So, there she'd been, her face red and blotchy, verging on tears, when the new kid—a skinny, curly-haired girl named Lilly—marched up and dragged Elle away from them.

'If you wanna pick on my friend, you pick on both of us!' she'd yelled at Felicity.

'Don't worry,' she went on to say quietly as they stormed through the playground, 'it's only scary when you're by yourself. You've got me now.' It was as simple as that. The two had remained best friends ever since. Curly-haired girls had to stick together.

Elle had nothing but admiration and pride for the way her friend was raising gorgeous Rose. Everything Lilly did was for her daughter. She didn't go out like most people their age; she had no interest in dating or drinking. She worked hard to provide for them, without any help from Tommy, who'd been Lilly's boyfriend for almost two years through high school, and the drummer in a local band. Lilly's pregnancy announcement could not have come at a worse time, with Tommy and his band due to leave for Sydney to make their mark on the world. Despite Lilly assuring him a baby wouldn't interfere with his plans—a girlfriend and a baby weren't the kind of image Tommy was looking for—he'd promptly left town when Lilly refused to terminate the pregnancy. Elle found it maliciously satisfying to hear that he was now a roadie for a tribute act who sang Billy Ray Cyrus covers.

'I can't hang out with my best friend when I feel like it?' she said a little too casually as she leaned against the bar.

Lilly eyed Elle silently for a few moments after she handed her a glass of her usual white wine. 'Okay, what's going on?'

Surely, she couldn't be that easy to read? Lilly gave her a look that Elle had seen her use on Rose when she'd tried to talk back, and Elle instantly felt like a naughty five-year-old. 'I was just given three weeks' notice from Brown's,' Elle admitted grudgingly.

'*What?* Why would they do that?'

'Apparently that new supermarket's doing more damage than they'd anticipated.'

'Well, people *had* been trying to tell Brown's they've been getting expensive. Maybe they should have listened before the competition moved in.' Lilly took Elle's hand and squeezed it gently. 'But that really sucks.'

It was true that Brown's had had a monopoly for years, and the recent opening of the bigger chain supermarket in their neighbouring town had been a welcome relief for many in the community. Elle was torn between her dislike of big corporations moving into rural areas, and the fact that a lot of people on minimal wages needed to buy groceries at lower prices than Brown's offered.

'Do you want me to see if Scott can find you a few shifts here?' Lilly asked.

Elle concentrated on not spluttering her sip of wine. Her mother would have a heart attack. 'I haven't started looking yet, but if I can't find anything, that would be great. Thanks.'

Lilly gave her a knowing grin. 'Your mother would not approve at all.'

'My mother doesn't approve of pretty much anything,' Elle said dryly. 'I know you love working here, Lil, and I'd be grateful for any job right now, but I'd like to see what else might be available first.'

'I understand. It's cool. Besides, we'd probably never get put on together anyway and then we wouldn't be able to catch up, so that would suck. Dinner still on for tomorrow night?'

'Of course, wouldn't miss it,' Elle said and took another sip of her wine as Lilly went to serve some more customers.

Elle watched her banter with her regulars and marvelled, not for the first time, at Lilly's easygoing nature. Elle had never been as outgoing as her friend and she doubted she'd make a very good bartender. The two of them had had this discussion before. 'It's all just customer service,' Lilly had protested.

'But there's a difference between serving little old ladies at the checkout and rowdy men who've had a few beers at the bar,' Elle replied.

No, she didn't think bar work was for her. They chatted for a few more minutes once Lilly returned and Elle finished her drink. 'I'd better get going. I'll see you for dinner tomorrow night,' she said, getting down from the bar stool.

Weekly dinners at Lilly's house were a tradition that had been going on since Elle returned from university. They'd missed the last few weeks because of Gran's death and the funeral, but Elle needed a night to catch up with her friend and hopefully get some clarity on all the craziness that had been going on lately.

Try as she might, she couldn't stop her mind going back over the freaky sensation in the Brown's staff bathroom. The voice had sounded so real. She could have sworn Gran had been standing right there next to her. Now that the initial shock had worn off, a tightness began to squeeze around her chest. It was so hard to imagine life without her grandmother. Already it seemed strange not to have stopped in at the nursing home for the past two weeks. Gran hadn't been happy about being admitted for short-term care after her fall, and who could blame her? She'd always been so fiercely independent, holding out doggedly to remain in her own home, and so Elle had visited her there as often as she could.

Elle's return from university had disappointed her parents, but it had coincided nicely with their growing concern over Gran's ability to stay in her house alone. Elle had happily agreed to move in and take over the cleaning and provide company—it was certainly no hardship considering Gran had always been her favourite person in the world. And not living under her parents' roof meant Elle hadn't feel quite so pathetic about moving back home.

She pulled up in the driveway of Gran's house now and let out a small sigh. She had always loved this house, with its square cottage look and wrap-around verandahs. It held so many of her favourite childhood memories—sleepovers with Pa and Gran, school-holiday fun playing with the hose in the garden with her siblings, baking side by side with Gran in the kitchen, and coming here after school every day when her parents were both working. There were memories etched in every nook and cranny of the place.

It had been special to Gran too. She and Pa had bought the house as newlyweds and had raised Elle's father here. The garden especially had been Gran's pride and joy; the abundance of colour and scents always made her smile. A cobbled path led from the front gate to the steps up to the verandah, and on either side grew daisies and delphiniums with their tall, regal spires of purple, blue and pink, along with foxglove, hollyhock and fragrant lavender bushes.

Elle had spent many hours in the garden with Gran, reading or chatting, and later, when Gran could no longer manage it, weeding and listening to Gran's stories and making plans for the big Scottish adventure they had talked about ever since Elle had moved home.

She smiled, as she always did, at the rowan tree that had pride of place near the front gate. When she was little, Gran had told her it was there to ward off any bad spirits and to protect them. It was covered in bright red berries in autumn, and Elle had many fond memories of making fairy rings with her gran, and having picnics with her dolls beneath its shady foliage as a child.

Gran's life had been steeped in Scottish traditions and beliefs. She was always a bit . . . well, odd. She spoke of certain relatives as though they were still around—so much so that

Elle wasn't altogether sure that they weren't and often had to look around and make sure there was no one there. Gran would just smile and say, 'My great-aunt Morag was saying . . .' It became the family in-joke, whenever a door might slam or squeak, that it was 'only Aunt Morag, the friendly ghost'. Elle had always assumed Gran liked to keep talking to the people she'd loved and missed. It was just a quirky thing she did.

Elle unlocked the front door and dropped her handbag on the table, heading for the kettle to make herself a cup of tea. For a moment Elle closed her eyes, bracing her arms on the edge of the sink. It had been a long, horrible day, and she had no idea what she was going to do.

The familiar smell of the house wrapped around her like a warm hug. There had been no drama too big, no problem too complicated, and no hurt too deep that it couldn't be soothed by walking into this house and sharing it with Gran.

Elle's parents had suggested she move home—that staying in Gran's empty old house probably wasn't good for her—but she was reluctant to leave. While she had the house, she still felt as though Gran were around. The mix of smells swarmed her senses: old house, lavender, lemon and biscuits. Elle stopped and blinked uncertainly . . . Biscuits?

# Three

Elle spun around and stared at the plate of biscuits on the table. Biscuits that hadn't been there this morning. Biscuits she hadn't had for a long time . . . the kind Gran used to make.

*Darling, sit and have a biscuit. Everything will be fine.*

Elle shrank back against the kitchen bench and scanned the room. 'This is crazy,' she whispered, looking around the empty kitchen.

*What's crazy is that you still haven't booked our trip yet. You promised me you would.*

Elle's heart raced as she searched for an explanation. It was clear she was losing her mind, but why now? Maybe it was the shock of being sacked. She'd never been sacked before.

*It was the best thing that could happen, if you ask me. You were too good to be working for Michael Brown and his silly family. His grandfather once tried to kiss me, you know . . . brazen old coot.*

'Gran?' Elle shook her head irritably. She was just missing her, that's all.

*Of course it's me. You have no idea how difficult it's been trying to get your attention around here lately. Sit down and have something to eat. You look pale, darling.*

Elle wasn't sure if she sank or collapsed into the nearby seat at the kitchen table—either way, she was grateful for the chair because she wasn't sure how long she could have remained standing. Maybe she'd slipped over and hit her head and didn't remember doing it?

Her gaze fell on the plate of freshly baked biscuits and she once again felt a little lightheaded. She hadn't made these, and she doubted very much if anyone else would have dropped them off. Her mother didn't bake, and there were dishes in the sink from this morning's breakfast—but no baking paraphernalia.

They smelled amazing. Gingerly, she reached out and touched one, certain they would disappear like the illusion they were. But they didn't. The biscuits were still warm. She dropped the round, buttery treat back onto the plate and stared at it.

*They're just the way you like them—crunchy enough for dipping.*

'Gran, what's happening? Why can I hear you?'

*I know it's a wee bit dramatic, but it was the only way I could get your attention.*

'My attention . . . for what?'

*For keeping your promise to me. I want to go home.*

Elle looked around nervously. 'Gran . . . you died,' she said quietly.

*Well, I know that*, Gran said wryly. *It was a lovely service, by the way. The flowers were beautiful.*

The garden club had outdone themselves for the occasion, and it had touched the family deeply that they'd gone to so much trouble.

*And I was chuffed by the Lady of Glencoe bit on the service program*, Gran added.

As a Christmas gift last year, Elle had bought a tiny plot of land through a heritage charity that was selling titles to fund nature reserves throughout Scotland. It was done as a bit of a joke, but Gran had taken the title seriously and from that day forward had addressed all her correspondence using her title, Lady Iona of Glencoe.

*But the fact remains that the last time we spoke, you promised me you'd take me home*, she continued.

'Gran, that was before you had the fall,' Elle started to point out, trying not to feel ridiculous for having an argument with her grandmother who wasn't even there.

*Not that time . . . in the hospital. I asked you to take me to Stormeil.*

Elle felt her breath catch at the memory. Gran had made her promise to take her ashes back to Scotland. But not to just any place in Scotland—back to a place Gran had been told about as a child. It had been the last time Gran had spoken; only a little while after that she'd had another stroke and fallen into a coma and never woken up. Tears once more pricked Elle's eyes and she wiped at them quickly before they could fall.

*Oh sweetheart, none of that now. That time's past. I don't want you sitting about feeling sorry for yourself anymore. I had the best life anyone could possibly ask for. It's time to move on,* she said gently but with a briskness that was oh-so-familiar. *And you can start by booking that trip to Scotland.*

'I can't go to Scotland.'

*Why not?*

'I just lost my job.'

*That makes everything easier. Now you can't use the excuse of having no holiday time accrued,* her gran said triumphantly.

'How am I supposed to go on a holiday when I don't have a job to come back to? I'll need my savings to live on until I get another one.'

*Have a biscuit,* Gran instructed, and Elle, too confused to bother questioning it, reached out and took one, biting into it and savouring the crunchy texture before it melted on her tongue.

*Don't you worry about a thing. It will all be explained tomorrow. You just promise me you'll book that flight.*

'What's happening tomorrow?' Elle asked warily, but her gran didn't reply. 'Gran?' There was no response. She sat back in her chair and stared at the biscuits pensively, wondering how you actually *knew* you were crazy. She took another biscuit and ate it, in case they vanished into thin air or she woke up and realised she'd been dreaming. She wasn't going to give up the opportunity to savour Gran's cooking, no matter how far-fetched the idea was. She just hoped the calories were also a figment of her imagination as she ate the rest of the plate in quick succession. She was too tired to try to figure out what was happening right now—she needed a hot bath, a glass of wine and sleep.

Elle poured a glass of chardonnay as she stood at the kitchen bench after her bath, her head wrapped in a towel and wearing her faded old dressing gown. She caught a glimpse of her reflection in the oven door and gave a snort. All that was missing was a pair of fluffy slippers and she would be the cartoon image of an old spinster stuck at home alone. She could have stayed at the pub longer but she really wasn't up to smiling and accepting any more condolences—well-meaning though they may be. She knew she couldn't mourn forever, but for now she just didn't feel like making small talk out in public and pretending her life was fine. It wasn't fine, at least not at the moment. She was soon to be unemployed. She took another sip of wine, realised her glass was empty and gave a small tsk of annoyance as she went to the fridge and took out the bottle. She poured the straw-coloured wine to an acceptable level, before realising she was home alone and didn't need to be acceptable, then kept going until it reached the very top of the glass. Trying not to giggle, she bent down and slurped a sip so it didn't spill when she picked it up. *See? It was all in my head before—if Gran really had been here, I'd have heard her grumbling about slurping like a sailor on shore leave in a tavern.* She gave a small dismissive snort—again, something that would have earned her a word or two from Gran, and quickly tossed down that glass too. So what if she didn't have a job? Jobs were overrated anyway. She would be *fine.* She picked up the bottle of wine and carried it back to her bedroom.

Later, as she lay her head on the pillow and closed her eyes, she succumbed to the lightness of the wine she'd just finished, floating her into the welcoming arms of sleep. She imagined she felt the comforting weight of a hand on her forehead, brushing back her hair, just like Gran used to do when she was little.

'Tell me the story, Gran,' she whispered, her eyes weighed down by sleep. It was her favourite and it had been such a long time since she'd heard it.

The soft rolling tones of her gran's brogue softly filled her ears. *Once upon a time, in the Highlands of Scotland, a young girl fell in love with a boy. Their deaths would end a war and reunite their clans, but their love would transcend time.*

*Isla from the Clan MacCoinnich and Castle Stormeil fell in love with a boy, Gavan of Clan MacColuim of Castle Tàileach. Their families had been fighting each other for over one hundred years, so long that no one could even remember what they were fighting about, but that mattered little to the two families, and so Isla and Gavan were forbidden from seeing each other.*

*The two young lovers, however, were not easily dissuaded. They would meet at the glen, exactly halfway between the two lands, and spend long hours speaking of a future they would share.*

*Times were hard and very dangerous. Seasons of bad crops and tides of illness swept across the country. Raids between the two neighbouring kingdoms were taking their toll and food was becoming scarce. The girl's father, the Laird of Stormeil, was unsure how he was going to provide for his tenants over the* coming winter, and then one day, he was approached by a Baron, seeking the hand of Isla in marriage.

The Baron was ruthless and had an army of men. He vowed to protect the Laird's tenants and bring in food, and promised to join Stormeil in fighting the MacColuim of Tàileach. All the Laird had to do was give his daughter's hand in marriage.

The Laird despised the Baron, but he knew that without the Baron's help, many of his tenants would die through the winter, and he was already unable to pay the King the taxes he owed. He would lose his castle and his land, and his family would be cast out to fend for themselves. So, the Laird reluctantly agreed to the wedding.

Isla and Gavan continued to meet as often as they could, but it was growing increasingly dangerous. In tears, Isla told Gavan of her father's plan to marry her off to the Baron. But she was followed by some of her father's men and their romance was discovered. Isla bargained with her father's men to release Gavan, promising she would return with them, and pleaded with Gavan to leave. Then Isla was taken back to the castle and locked in her room until the wedding.

Gavan told his father the Laird of Stormeil's plan. It was quickly decided that Gavan must wed Isla and end the planned union of the Baron and the MacCoinnichs, lest all at Castle Tàileach face being destroyed by the Baron when he joined forces with Isla's father.

The night before the wedding, a lavish feast was held in Castle Stormeil. The girl, grief-stricken over her upcoming marriage to the brutal Baron, asked to be excused when she could take no *more, and her mother, feeling sorry for her, urged her father to allow her to leave.*

*Returning to her bedchamber, she discovered a message from Gavan. He told her he had men waiting to rescue her, and with the help of her trusted maid she managed to slip through the castle once everyone had fallen asleep.*

*Reunited, the lovers rode to a nearby church to be married.*

*The next morning the Baron's army, upon discovering Isla was gone, headed off towards Tàileach. Along the way they met up with the newlyweds. The Baron demanded the girl be handed over, but he was met by the minister, who announced he had already wed the two. The Baron, fuming at having been tricked, sent his men immediately into battle, during which both Isla and Gavan were killed.*

*The horror of losing their children united the warring clans and they immediately joined forces, and fought the Baron and his army, killing them all.*

*From that moment on, the two clans, united by marriage and bonded by grief, eventually became one.*

*The graves of Gavan and Isla were put on the border of the two lands and a monument was built in their honour, where it stood for hundreds of years as a sign of reconciliation and friendship between the two families for generations that followed.*

*But legend says, if you stand beneath the arch under a blanket of stars on a clear night, you may see Gavan and Isla, reunited once again, sharing in death the wedding dance they were never able to have in life.*

# Four

An annoyingly persistent sound echoed from somewhere in the distance, slowly dragging Elle from sleep. As she emerged from a foggy slumber, she eventually identified it as her ringtone and pulled her pillow over her head, trying to ignore the noise. But after a brief silence, the phone rang again, and Elle reluctantly rolled over to answer it.

'Good morning, darling. Are you available today? I just received a phone call from Terry Bartholomew. He'd like to do Gran's will reading.'

Elle opened her eyes and immediately winced. She had forgotten to shut her blinds the night before and bright sunshine streamed in through her bedroom window, reminding her just how much wine she had drunk last night.

'Elspeth?' Her mother's brisk tone brought her back to the matter at hand.

'Yes. I'm here.' Did she *have* to yell?

'Are you able to make it today?'

'To what?'

She heard her mother's tongue click in impatience. 'Terry Bartholomew's office, for the reading of your gran's will. Are you all right?'

'I'm fine. I overslept.' And seemed to be suffering from a slight hangover. 'I thought the will thing wasn't until next week?'

'It wasn't. Terry wanted to move it forward because he's going away. So, we'll see you at ten?'

Elle put a hand to her head as she forced her brain to re-engage. What day was it? She had work, but she was on late shift today. Damn it, she had no excuse.

'Elspeth, are you sure you're all right? There's a bug going around.'

'I'm fine. I'll be there.' She ended the call before her mother had a chance to really start the third degree. Elle felt punished enough as she gingerly massaged her throbbing forehead, before heading into the bathroom to shower.

※

Walking into the office of Bartholomew and Bartholomew was like stepping back in time, and not in a particularly good way—more into a chaotic, pre-computer-age time. In Mr Bartholomew's defence, the firm *did* have a computer, it was just that the filing system seemed to have exploded from the filing cabinet and now resided on every conceivable flat surface in the office.

Elle could almost feel her mother's eye twitch at the sight of the mess, but she didn't say anything as she leaned down to kiss her cheek, before giving her dad's arm a gentle squeeze. She was so caught up in her own grief over losing Gran that she sometimes forgot that her dad had also lost his mum. 'How you doing, Dad?'

He patted her hand and smiled in a way that didn't quite crinkle his eyes the way it usually did, and they shared an understanding glance before Elle took a seat beside her youngest brother, Malcolm.

'It's a shame your brother and sister couldn't stay until today,' her mother said, tucking her skirt tightly around her legs as she eyed the outdated, lino-covered floor. 'So we were all here.'

Elle kind of wished she didn't have to be here either. She had other things on her mind—like, if it was sound . . .

Thankfully, there had been no further incidents, and in the harsh light of day it was a lot easier to put things in perspective. She'd been under a great deal of stress yesterday, that was all. Elle tipped her head back to rest against the wall behind her and closed her eyes.

'Big night, sis?' Mal asked, eyeing her smugly.

'No. Why?'

'You're wearing your sunnies inside.'

Damn it. She quickly slid them onto the top of her head and fought against cringing at the bright fluorescent lights overhead.

'Whoa, yeah, maybe you should put them back on,' Mal suggested.

'I just didn't get much sleep last night,' she muttered

defensively. 'Anyway, what are you still doing home? Don't you have to get back to dissect something in a lab?'

'I got an extension. I'm currently ahead in everything anyway.' He shrugged.

Of course he was. 'Wouldn't have anything to do with a certain Becky Sloan, would it?' she asked casually, but she saw her brother's eyes widen slightly.

'What?'

'So, it's *true?*' she said, smirking. Her parents stopped their conversation and turned towards them.

'Keep your voice down,' Mal whispered.

'You and Becky?'

'How the hell did you find out?'

She looked at her brother sympathetically. 'I think you've been away too long. Nothing happens around here without everyone knowing about it. Besides, I work in gossip central.'

Elle only just refrained from laughing at Malcolm's worried expression. 'I'm kidding . . . it's not all over town. Lilly said she saw you two having a drink the other night . . . I was just pulling your chain.' But now she realised maybe it had been something after all. 'Is it serious?'

'No,' he said, a little too quickly. 'We've just been catching up while I was in town.' Becky Sloan had been in her brother's year at school and the two had been an item for a short time before he moved away to university. Her parents hadn't been thrilled about the union. Becky had a bit of a reputation for going through boyfriends, and in a small town, that was usually enough to start a rumour or two. But Elle always thought she was nice enough. Maybe a little rough around the edges in a small-town kind of way, but she seemed happy and friendly whenever Elle ran into her.

Elle never did understand how the two of them had ended up together, though. They seemed complete opposites. Her brother had always been a science nerd, while Becky seemed to gravitate to the sportier guys—the footy players and cricketers. Yet they'd been crazy about each other for those few months, before Mal had left town.

'I thought she was engaged to some guy who worked for the mines up north?' she said quietly.

'What? Oh. Yeah, I don't know. We just caught up for a drink . . . as mates.'

She narrowed her eyes a little at that but was cut off from interrogating him further when Mr Bartholomew came to the door and waved them into his office.

'Thank you all for coming. My sincere condolences for your loss,' he said, eyeing them with a solemn look before clearing his throat and shuffling the papers he picked up from his desk. 'Shall we get started?' he asked, looking up and over his glasses at her parents briefly before continuing. 'This is the last will and testament of Iona Kinnaird, revised on the first of August this year,' he read, and Elle felt the familiar heaviness descend on her once more. She hated when the finality of it all hit her in the face like this. Her mind flickered briefly to the previous evening, but she pushed the thought away firmly as the solicitor read her gran's words.

*'My belongings are to be divided among the family as they see fit, with exception of the special items that have been marked with individual's names.'*

They had already been informed of the labelled items—Gran had made no secret of the fact she'd already decided who got what, and over the years it had been a family joke about having your label swapped if you misbehaved. The special things had already been claimed—the china and crystal and the jewellery, none of which Elle had particularly wanted, save one necklace with a crystal dragonfly pendant that she had always loved.

'*The house is to be sold immediately*,' Mr Bartholomew continued, looking over the top of his glasses once more. 'This was a strict stipulation. Mrs Kinnaird was adamant that the house be put on the market as soon as this will had been read,' he went on, before glancing back down. '*And my estate left to my son, Alister Kinnaird.*'

Elle frowned as his words caught her attention. The house? She'd known of course that it would be sold eventually, but she assumed that her parents would delay this for a while since she was still living there. What was the hurry?

'*I bequeath a sum of ten thousand dollars to each of my grandchildren, Lachlan, Lauren, Elspeth and Malcolm to use in any way they see fit. It is my wish that my ashes be taken by my granddaughter, Elspeth, to Scotland, where I have always wanted to return. I have set aside money to cover this request in Elspeth's name, and my title, Lady of Glencoe, is also to be passed on to her.*' The solicitor leaned across the desk. 'Lady Elspeth,' he said and handed Elle an envelope as everyone swapped bemused, if not slightly amused, glances at the mention of her new title.

Elle sat back in her chair, the words from last night echoing in her mind as she stared at the envelope in her hand. *It will all be explained tomorrow.* If this had all been in Elle's head, how had Gran known about the will being read today?

'Elle.'

She flinched as her brother called her name. 'You coming?' Mal asked, now standing beside her chair. She looked around and realised everyone else was already walking towards the door.

'You really don't look good,' Mal told her, shaking his head.

'I don't actually feel that good,' she said, biting her lip anxiously as she considered asking her brother if maybe he had also been hearing voices lately, then dismissing the idea immediately. If anyone would look at her as though she were crazy, it would be Malcolm. He would tell her that scientifically there would be some logical explanation for it all, and then probably tease her about it forever more. That was the problem with her academic family—they were always so . . . logical.

'Can you tell Mum and Dad I had to go?' She didn't wait around for his answer, slipping out the front door while her parents were in discussion with the solicitor. She wasn't up to conversation right now. Her hands shook as she inserted her key into the ignition and drove home to get ready for work. She wished she'd called in sick earlier, but there hadn't been time.

Maybe she wasn't losing her mind after all. That would be a relief . . .

*I hope you're heading for the travel agent*, Gran said, and Elle swerved, swearing loudly as she quickly corrected the car.

*Language, dear.*

'Gran! I could have killed us!' Elle yelled.

*Well, technically, I'm already dead, so don't worry about me.*

'That is not *at all* comforting,' she managed, once she was driving straight, on the correct side of the road again.

*The ticket?* Gran prompted impatiently.

'Gran, I told you, this is ridiculous. I can't just up and go to Scotland right now,' she snapped, checking her rear-view mirror conspicuously for any sign of someone in the back of her car and finding it empty.

*Yes, you can. You have the money. You don't have to work. There's nothing stopping you.*

'I *do* have to work . . . I still have three weeks, and then I need to find another job.'

*Not straightaway. You have ten thousand dollars,* Gran reminded her cheerfully.

This was absurd. She was arguing with a ghost. A ghost that actually had a point. No. That was silly. She was supposed to be proving to her parents she was responsible. Using her gran's inheritance to fly off to the other side of the world was the opposite of responsible.

*Technically, dear, you're not using your inheritance. That money in the envelope is to reimburse you for following through on the promise you made.*

'What, you can read my mind too?' she asked nervously. This was going to get very awkward.

*I don't have to. I know you too well.*

Well, that was a relief. 'Hang on, does that mean you can't or that you just didn't *need* to?' Elle asked suspiciously.

*Look, there's a carpark, right in front of the travel agent. How lucky is that? I think it's definitely a sign.* Gran pointed excitedly. *Pull in.*

'Did you do that?' Elle asked as she found herself parking. 'Magically make a park appear?'

*I'm a ghost, not a magician, dear,* she said drolly.

'Of course. Silly me,' Elle muttered.

*Well? What are you waiting for? Let's go in.*

'Gran, would you stop. Geez. You were never this pushy before.'

*Well, I should have been. If I'd pushed harder maybe we would have gone on that trip together while I was still here,* she said.

Guilt immediately overwhelmed Elle as she heard the sadness in her gran's voice. Of all the things Iona could have said to her, nothing hit home harder than that. Gran was right. Elle should have tried harder to make it happen. She'd kept putting it off, and all the while Gran got frailer by the day, until her accident made it impossible to go. 'I'm sorry, Gran. It was my fault you never got to go home.'

She heard a long sigh. *No, it wasn't your fault. I could have gone at any time over the years. But I do want to go now. It's time.*

What could she say to that? Seriously? There was no argument that would hold up, and she wasn't sure she wanted to find one. When she heard that Gran had put aside the money for this trip, she'd felt a flicker of excitement stir. A trip to Scotland. It had been their dream—hers and Gran's—for so long and now she was in a position to actually do something about it. Could she? Should she? Take a leap and be this spontaneous? There were a whole raft of reasons why this was a really, really bad idea right now. But then again . . .

Opening the car door, Elle stepped outside and headed into the travel agency with a defeated sigh and the beginnings of a smile.

# Five

'You've lost your job?'

Elle watched her mother's face morph from confusion to surprise to outright disappointment. She had waited until a couple of days after the will reading to work up the courage to mention the subject, and this was exactly why.

'It wasn't my fault. I was put off because I cost them too much money.'

Her mother took a deep breath and sat across from Elle on the lounge. 'Well, now might be the perfect time to look into those courses we've been talking about.'

*You've* been talking about, Elle thought silently. Elle had been looking into some local art courses and was tempted to put her name down for a couple, but that wasn't the kind of thing her mother meant. Her mum had been hinting very strongly that Elle should go back to university to study something serious—something career-worthy.

'Maybe it's a sign,' Caroline said pointedly.

'Actually, speaking of signs,' Elle started nervously, 'there was something else I had to tell you.' She paused, deciding not to mention the fact that Gran's ghost had been visiting her. 'I've decided I *will* take Gran's ashes to Scotland after all. I'm leaving on the sixteenth.'

'What? The sixteenth of when?' Her mother's professionally-shaped eyebrows rose in alarm.

'This month . . . in three weeks.'

'You're not serious.'

'You heard what Mr Bartholomew said. Gran made me promise.'

Caroline shook her head and waved a dismissive hand. 'Don't be ridiculous, you can't possibly fly off to Scotland now, not after you've just been fired.'

'*Not* fired . . . put off,' Elle corrected.

'It's out of the question.'

'I've already bought the ticket.'

Her mother stared at her again.

Elle suddenly wished she had waited until her dad was home before breaking the news. At least when he was there they had a referee to step in. 'Mum, I promised her. It's what she wanted. You were there at the reading.'

'It's not something that has to be done *right now*.'

'It kinda is,' she said dryly. 'It's what Gran wants . . . I mean, wanted.'

'So, you're going to fly off to Scotland, with no job and no way to support yourself?' her mother said, still staring at her as though she'd just announced she was going on *Married at*

*First Sight* to pretend-TV-marry a complete stranger on national television. 'The money your gran left you isn't supposed to be thrown away on some . . . holiday. Malcolm has invested his, and I seriously recommend you do the same, before it's all gone.'

Of course he had. 'I don't plan on touching that money. I've got some savings, and Gran's envelope paid for the ticket and accommodation. It's all taken care of.'

'You know, you were actually beginning to act responsibly, but I see that didn't last very long,' her mother said, leaning back and crossing her arms. Her blonde shoulder-length hair was cut in a no-nonsense bob that swung elegantly around her face, somehow managing to convey her disappointment and irritation in one graceful movement.

'Seriously?' Elle said, staring at her mother. 'I was *beginning* to act responsibly?' Usually she could wear her mother's criticisms, but this hurt. 'Since when did you *ever* think I was acting responsibly? And if so, why the hell haven't I heard you say that? I mean, you're so quick to point out where I'm doing everything wrong, why is this the first time that I've heard you say I might have been doing something right for a change?'

'That's not what I meant,' her mother said stiffly.

'I know I'm a disappointment to you and Dad. I've tried to be what you want, and it made me miserable. I'm sorry I'm not academic like everyone else in this family, but I can't help that.'

'You didn't give it a chance.'

'I gave it two years, Mum.'

'No,' she pointed out firmly, 'you *gave up* after two years. You don't see things through. You start everything and then give up if it's too hard. You have to learn to push yourself.'

'It *was* too hard. I didn't understand it. I only applied for university to keep you happy.'

Her mother's lips clamped together in a thin, firm line. 'Blaming others is not going to solve anything, Elspeth,' she snapped.

Elle took a breath and fought to keep her temper under control. 'I'm not blaming anyone. I'm happy with my life. I had a job, I pay taxes. It's what most people do.'

'You're settling.'

'I'm happy.'

'Really? You don't go out. You don't have a boyfriend. You work in a job that's not challenging you at all, and you may pay taxes but you don't pay rent.'

Okay, there was no argument there, she had it easy where paying rent was concerned. That was how she'd managed to save so much money, but it had been at Gran's insistence. She *did* pay for groceries and electricity, though, and all her other living expenses.

'And need I remind you,' her mother cut into Elle's thoughts, 'that your grandmother's house is going on the market, so what plans do you have for your living arrangements?'

Yes, Gran had stitched her up nicely there. She was pretty sure the stipulation to put the house on the market *immediately* had been in order to force Elle's decision to head overseas.

'I just don't see how this trip is practical at this point in time.' Her mother shrugged.

*Tell her I insisted*, Gran spoke up, giving Elle a start. *Tell her.*

*Yes, because telling her that you haunted me until I gave in is going to salvage the situation.* Elle couldn't quite believe she was having a conversation in her head with her dead grandmother while her mother sat in front of her, oblivious.

*I'm not sure I like that sassy tone*, Gran said with a huff.

'Elspeth!' her mother barked, frowning at her. 'Are you listening to me?'

Crap. 'Look, I'm sorry you don't agree with my decision, Mum, but I'm old enough to make my own choices, and this is something I need to do.' She leaned over and kissed her mum's cheek, before standing up. 'I have dinner plans,' she said without elaborating. It was dinner with her best friend and a five-year-old, but that was beside the point.

She hated fighting with her mother. She was always left feeling deflated. Usually she didn't argue, it was easier to just let her mum say what she needed to say and let it go, but today it really hurt. Maybe she was just overly sensitive because of everything that was going on—losing her job, losing her gran, the funeral, Gran returning from the dead—just the usual, normal, everyday things. Elle gave a frustrated sigh. She knew what to expect when she'd brought up the subject of going to Scotland—there was always going to be vocal disagreement—but it was done now, so she could only hope that things would settle down.

She just wished it could be easier. Maybe it would be if she were more like her brothers and sister. They never seemed to cause their parents any headaches, or her mother to rub her temples as often as she did around Elle. She knew of course they *had* given her parents their fair share of grief, but they'd never locked horns over anything major like school or their career paths. They all somehow knew what they wanted to do and got the grades to get there.

Elle, on the other hand, had known she was a problem the first time she saw her mother have a shot of whisky before they left the house for parent–teacher night, just to brace herself.

Phrases like, 'Elle needs to apply herself', and 'With a little more concentration . . .', were the usual conversation starters, before teachers would go on to ask about her siblings and how they were doing. The only bright part of the evenings came when they sat down with Elle's art teacher and the phrases were more like, 'Elle has a creative flare', and 'Elle's work has been exceptional', but by then her parents had already started to silently question where they'd gone so wrong with kid number three, and 'Only getting good grades in art isn't going to get you into university . . .' would be the start of the lecture she would hear on the drive home.

With an irritated sigh, she pushed away her frustration. What she needed was a night with her best friend and some Rose time to put things back in perspective. She just had the rest of the day to get through first.

※

She kept the list in the top drawer of the buffet in the lounge room. It was in a gorgeous fabric-covered notebook Gran had given Elle one Christmas as a child, and they had begun to record all the things they wanted to do together. Elle hadn't looked at it in a long while.

Elle smiled as she flipped through the pages then hesitated, her smile slipping slightly as she read a new entry that hadn't been there the last time she'd looked through the book. It was written in her gran's beautifully slanted handwriting.

*Find Stormeil Castle. My final resting place.*

When Gran had asked Elle to take her ashes back to Scotland, Elle had assumed she wanted to be placed with her family, in Portsoy, the little fishing village where Gran had grown up.

'Why would you want to be left there?' she wondered aloud.

*Because that was my ancestral home.*

'But it's a ruin,' Elle said, no longer surprised to hear her gran's voice. 'We don't even know exactly where it is.'

*My father took me there once, when I was just a little girl,* Gran said softly. *He asked me what I'd like for my birthday and I told him all I wanted was to visit Stormeil Castle. I thought he'd forgotten, until my birthday came around and we went on a trip. It was just him and me. My mother had passed the year before and I suspect he needed to get away from things for a while. So, we went in search of his family's castle.*

Elle sat still, intrigued by this story she had never heard and wondering why now, all of a sudden, Gran was telling it.

*I remember we walked for what seemed like miles. Until we reached the spot. The whole way, my father kept telling me, 'Now, Iona, remember, the castle is a ruin now. It's been gone a very long time.' I didn't care, I just knew I had to go there—be in the space where it once stood. When we came over the rise ... I saw it. I saw the castle standing as proud and beautiful as it once stood—for just a fleeting moment it was there, the imposing stone walls of the fortress towers either side of the gatehouse and its huge drawbridge ...*

*I don't know how I knew what it looked like, I'd only ever heard stories and it wasn't until years later I found an old sketch in a library book, and realised it was exactly the same as what I saw that day. I felt as though I'd been there before. I know how that probably sounds—like I'm some silly old goat losing her marbles.* She chuckled, and Elle swallowed hard. *I can't explain it and I don't expect you to understand, all I know is I want to go back there now. Just as desperately as I wanted to go there as a small child that day with my father.*

Elle sat for a long while in silence. 'Okay, Gran,' she finally said. 'If that's where you want to go, that's where I'll take you.' Back to Stormeil Castle.

*Thank you, dear,* Gran said quietly. *But before that, we need to get through the rest of the list,* she said, her voice brightening.

Ah, the list. Elle flipped back to the first page and smiled as she traced her finger over the drawings she'd done years earlier.

*You were always more interested in doodling than in the list itself,* Gran said, and Elle could perfectly picture her tolerant smile.

There were pages and pages of Elle's artwork. She stopped at one picture where clearly she had been attempting to teach herself to draw a unicorn to scale. She smiled with reluctant admiration for the attempt. Not bad for a thirteen-year-old.

Turning the page, Elle came to the list. It was set out with a title page and elegant scroll writing.

1. *Edinburgh Castle*
2. *The Old Town*
3. *Palace of Holyroodhouse*
4. *Eilean Donan Castle*
5. *Clava Cairns*
6. *The Kelpies*
7. *The National Museum of Scotland*
8. *Loch Ness*
9. *Inverness*
10. *Culloden battlefield*
11. *Isle of Skye*
12. *Drive through the Highlands*
13. *Find Nessie*
14. *Eat haggis (*Gran*. Not Elle!)*
15. *Find a unicorn*
16. *Stay in a castle*

In later years they had added places of interest from *Outlander* that they wanted to visit:

17. *Find Jamie's Lallybroch*
18. *Doune Castle*
19. *Find a Scotsman in a kilt*

Elle smiled wistfully as she remembered sitting beside Gran out in the garden compiling their list. Now it was really happening. Despite all the reasons why this was not a good time to go, there was no denying the excitement she felt building at the thought. She was going to Scotland.

※

'Elle, love, are you home?'

Elle looked up from her computer when she heard the front door open.

'Hi, Dad,' she said as he came into the kitchen and put a cloth grocery bag on the bench. 'I guess you've been speaking to Mum.'

'Yes,' he replied, dropping a kiss on her head. 'She told me about your job . . . and the trip.' He raised an eyebrow as he pulled out a chair across from her and sat down.

'Dad . . .' she started with a drawn-out sigh.

'I know what your gran said in her will,' he cut her off quickly. 'But there wasn't any timeframe put on it. You don't have to do it right now.'

'I just feel as though this is the right time, Dad. Gran's money, losing my job . . . it seems like it's all happening for a reason.' The reason being that, as crazy as it seemed, it was important enough for Gran to be hanging around to make sure it happened.

'Look, you don't have to be the one to do this. Your mother and I can take the . . . well, we can do what Mum wanted. Actually, I'm not even sure that's what we *should* do, to be honest. I mean, I don't think she thought that part out very well.'

'Scattering her ashes?' Elle asked hesitantly. Alister Kinnaird was never flustered, but he was tinkering on the cusp of it at the moment as he straightened his shoulders and shuffled in his seat a little.

When he finally looked at her, he gave a quick shake of his head. 'What are we supposed to do? If she wants to be returned to Scotland, where do we go to . . . be near her?'

Elle hadn't thought about that, but clearly it was upsetting her dad. She hesitated, wondering if she should mention Gran's recent reappearance. But something held her back. Although Alister had loved his mum, he had never put much stock in her stories of fairies and superstitions, so he probably wouldn't believe that Gran had taken to talking to her now from the afterlife. So instead she reassured him. 'I don't think we need to have her ashes to be near her. I still feel Gran all around me and I don't think that will change just because her ashes aren't here anymore.'

'With your pa, we have a grave, somewhere to go to,' Alister said quietly. 'I just don't understand why she didn't want to be buried next to him.'

Elle sat by her dad and covered his hand with her own, and all the while she felt more than heard Gran's heart breaking. 'I think Gran just really missed Scotland, and this was her way of finally going home. It's what she wanted.'

'But is it? Really?' her dad asked, looking up from the table covered in Gran's favourite tablecloth, the one painted with bright sunflowers. 'It doesn't make any sense she should be laid to rest on the other side of the world.'

'It's what she wanted. More than anything,' Elle said gently. 'She made me promise, the last time I saw her in hospital. I think it's really important to her.'

Alister gave a tired sigh and rested his head in his hands. After a few moments he looked up again with a weary kind of acceptance. 'Okay. If you think this trip is that important, then I'm not going to try to talk you out of it.' He stood up and brought over the bag from the counter, placing it carefully on the table before her.

Elle stood up and looked inside. It contained nothing but a plastic box, shaped much like a house brick.

'Your gran's ashes,' he explained when she glanced up at him. 'You'll be needing them, I guess.'

Elle wasn't sure what she'd been expecting; she'd never seen someone's ashes before. In the movies they were always in an urn or some fancy vase with a lid.

*Well, that's a wee bit depressing*, Gran said, as though looking over her shoulder. *And he brought me over in a shopping bag?* She gave a little harrumph of disapproval.

*I'm sure we can find something a little more suitable, later*, Elle reassured her.

'I'd better get back to work, I've got a full schedule this afternoon,' Alister said, kissing her cheek before waving goodbye.

'Dad's got a point, Gran,' Elle said, after she heard the front door close. 'Your family *is* here.'

*Yes, that's true, but I also have family in Scotland. Ancestors. It's where I was born and where every generation of my family before me was born as far back as time remembers.*

Elle got that. It really was something special to be able to trace your family line back so far, but she could also see where her father was coming from. Gran was his mother and he wanted to have a place to be able to visit her.

'You know, I saw this story about a woman who lost her son a while back. He had a bucket list of places he wanted to go but never had the chance to do it, so she set up a Facebook page and people from all over the world were sent a small packet with some of his ashes in it to scatter, so that he could go there. Maybe we could do something like that. Leave some of . . . well, leave some here for us.'

*You want to divide me up and shove me into little plastic bags?* Gran sounded horrified by the thought.

Elle frowned. 'I just thought maybe leaving some of . . .'

*Me? You mean leaving some of me here?* Gran supplied pointedly.

'Okay, sorry I mentioned it,' Elle said, shaking her head and putting her hands up in surrender.

*No, Elspeth, I don't think I'd like being divided up . . . I mean, what if I need to be in one piece . . . so to speak.*

'Need to be in one piece for what?' Elle asked cautiously.

*Well . . . for whatever comes next.*

'How does it all work?' Elle asked, suddenly unsure of almost everything. 'Is this like the first stage or something?'

*I don't know,* Gran said, sounding slightly bemused. *It's not like anyone gave me a handbook.*

'Do you remember . . . dying?' Elle asked curiously.

*Not really . . . I mean, I remember being in the hospital and I could hear everything. That reminds me, darling, you must tell your brothers and sisters that I was very touched that they all made the trip home to say goodbye to me. That was really special. I was a very lucky old woman to have been loved so well by such beautiful grandchildren.* Elle felt her throat clog up once more with tears. *And you must remind your father, often, how much I loved him. He was the best son I could ever have wished for. I know he doesn't understand—bless his heart, he was always such a serious child.*

That made her think. 'Gran, how come the others can't hear you?'

Elle almost heard the soft smile in her gran's voice. *They aren't listening.*

'What do you mean?'

*It doesn't matter now,* Gran replied simply. *What matters is I'd rather not be divvied up into zip-lock bags,* she finished dryly.

Elle gave a silent sigh of exasperation. Was she really having this conversation? 'Okay, we won't leave any of you behind.'

*Good,* Gran said, in a tone that dismissed any further discussion on the subject.

Maybe there was still time to book in a quick session with a psychologist before she flew out. But what if they found out she was, in fact, unstable? Would they let her leave the country? On second thoughts, maybe it was best not to.

# Six

'So, let me get this straight,' Lilly said. 'You've booked a ticket to fly to Scotland, just like that. Out of the blue?'

'Technically it's not out of the blue. You know I've been planning this for ages.'

'Ah, yeah,' Lilly replied doubtfully, 'but you haven't ever done more than talk about it. I just figured you never would.'

'Well, now I am.'

'Hey, don't get me wrong, I'm all for it. I think it's awesome, I just don't understand what finally made you do it.'

'I told you, Gran left the money and I promised her I would.'

'Yeah, but I was talking to you the day before yesterday and you didn't say that you were about even thinking about it.'

Elle shrugged offhandedly. 'Things changed.'

'What things?' Lilly asked, watching Elle closely.

'Why is everyone suddenly so invested in my life choices?' Elle snapped, and then was instantly sorry when she saw the surprised hurt on her friend's face. 'Sorry. I'm still recovering from this afternoon's *discussion*,' she said.

'You know that's just how your mum is,' Lilly said calmly. 'She loves you, and I think this is just her way of trying to point you in what she thinks is the right direction.'

'Yeah, I know.' Lilly didn't have to elaborate. Her own mother had been a messed-up piece of work—too drunk to care for a child properly, and Lilly had pretty much raised herself. Her mum had kicked her out of home after a huge fight and then left town only two weeks after Lilly had Rose. She hadn't even bothered to see her grandchild and hadn't spoken to Lilly since. Gran had taken Lilly in after she'd left home, and helped her to find a place of her own after the baby was born, and for that, Lilly had adored Gran almost as much as Elle had.

Elle knew how lucky she was to have parents who genuinely cared for her, even if they did come with frequent lectures and the feeling that she was always being compared to her siblings and found wanting. And in their defence, her brothers and sister had never purposely made her feel that way. It wasn't their fault they were all born smart. She knew that if she ever needed them—any of them—they'd be there for her in a heartbeat. They were all just a bit caught up in their own lives lately.

'I know there's more to this,' Lilly said, killing any hope Elle may have had of changing the subject.

'You wouldn't believe me if I told you,' she said wearily.

'I've known you your whole life. Why wouldn't I believe you?'

Elle eyed her best friend carefully. She trusted Lilly implicitly, but this was too weird. And yet, she desperately wanted to talk to someone about it. Should she risk sounding like a freak? Who else could she confide in? She couldn't imagine telling any of her family—they would just use it as another chance to diagnose her with something, to tell her she was too naive, too ready to believe Gran's stories about fairies and spirits, and simply incapable of accepting that Gran was dead.

'I'm going because Gran asked me to go,' she blurted before she could change her mind.

'Yes, I know.'

Elle took a breath before continuing. 'No, like, she *came to me*.'

'Came to you? Like in a dream?' Lilly asked.

'Not exactly. More like in the toilets at work.'

'What?' Lilly was watching her curiously.

Okay, that probably wasn't the best way to start. 'I was freaking out because Michael had just sacked me and . . . she was there.'

There was an awkward silence as the two women stared at each other.

'She was there? You saw her?' Lilly asked slowly.

'Well, no, I don't see her. I just hear her, like she's just . . . *there*.'

Lilly poured a glass of wine and handed it over. 'Okay.'

'That's it?'

'What do you want me to say?'

'Honestly? I was expecting, "You're crazy," or something similar.' Elle took a generous sip of the wine.

'It's not unusual to still feel people you love when they die,' Lilly said, tilting her head thoughtfully. 'I believe they *do* hang around for a while.'

'You do?'

'Sometimes I seriously wonder about you, Elle,' she said, rolling her eyes. '*Hello?* I've been doing tarot readings since high school, remember? And maybe if you'd let me do a card reading on you, you'd realise this isn't such a big deal.'

Elle had to admit that Lilly was right. She wasn't sure why she had always been reluctant to let Lilly do a tarot reading for her, only that in the back of her mind were Gran's stories about the 'gifts' people sometimes had. Gran believed in things like that—a lot of her stories were about women and healers and ancient rituals, and they had scared Elle a little. 'So, you think hearing Gran is . . . normal?'

Lilly shrugged. 'If that's what's happening, then who am I to argue? If she's telling you to go to Scotland, you should listen.'

*She always was a sensible young thing*, Gran said warmly.

'Look, Elle, I'm not going to tell you you're crazy,' Lilly said, reaching over to top up their wine glasses. 'In fact, you're one of the most down-to-earth, honest people I know, so if you tell me you're hearing your gran, then I believe you are.'

'But isn't that . . . *strange?*' Elle rushed to ask.

Lilly lifted her glass and pointed towards her bookshelf. 'I have an entire library of new-age books covering everything from aromatherapy to Buddhism . . . I'm probably not the best person to ask to define strange.' She chuckled. 'Elle, your gran was a very special lady. She took me in when my mum turned her back on me, and I will never forget that kindness. She had strong ties to her homeland, and if anyone was determined enough to come through and make her wishes known—then it would be Iona.'

*See?* Gran piped up, sounding somewhat smug.

'Yes, but it's more than that,' Elle said, ignoring Gran. 'She bakes biscuits.'

Lilly lifted an eyebrow.

*You should have left it at hearing the voices, dear*, Gran said. *I think we've lost her.*

'Never mind,' Elle said quickly. 'The thing is, she wants me to take her to Stormeil. The castle. We don't even know where it is—not exactly. And that's where she wants to be scattered.'

Lilly looked at her thoughtfully. 'Elle, you know I spent time with your gran when you were away at uni. She was there for me during one of the scariest times of my life. I'm not saying we shared the same relationship that you did, but I will say we found we had a lot in common. You've listened to her stories your whole life. You know how important they were to her. If she's still here, there's clearly a reason, and I think you're doing the right thing by listening to her.'

Elle smiled, her heart a little lighter. Lilly was right, again—she had grown up on Gran's stories, and she did remember believing in them wholeheartedly when she was a child. But she also remembered being teased by her older brother and sister, and at some point she'd stopped talking about the stories with anyone other than Gran. Elle liked to think she had a relatively open mind about things, which was probably from Gran's influence, but the wary side of her—the side that cautioned her to keep quiet—undoubtedly came from the rest of her family, who were far more analytical. 'Well, whatever it is,' Elle said to Lilly, 'she's certainly being very persistent, so we're off on an adventure.'

'Embrace it, I say.' Lilly smiled. 'You never know where it might lead you.' She held her glass up in a toast. 'I miss you, Iona. But have fun on your adventure.'

Elle felt Gran's warm smile filling the room with light and love. She hoped Lilly could feel it too.

'Now,' Lilly continued as she set about preparing dinner, 'tell me everything you have planned so far. *Everything*. Ooh, maybe you'll find Jamie Fraser,' she gushed with a dreamy smile.

*Outlander* had been one of Elle's favourite book series growing up. Gran had given her the first book when she was a teenager, and she'd been hooked. The epic love story of a World War Two combat nurse travelling back in time to eighteenth-century Scotland had pretty much ruined her for teenage love—no high-school boy could possibly compete with Highlands warrior James Alexander Malcolm MacKenzie Fraser.

'That would solve quite a few of my problems right now,' Elle agreed. Visiting some standing stones so she could fall through time sounded like just what she needed.

※

Spring was definitely in the air and the days were getting warmer. Usually Elle would feel a little sad about saying goodbye to her winter clothes and boots, ready to pack them away until autumn came around again . . . but not this year. This year she got an extension. It would be the start of autumn in Scotland and she would enjoy the cooler weather for a few extra weeks. She had already started to throw clothes into her suitcase in anticipation, and she'd made a list of art supplies she wanted to take along on her trip. Elle could already feel her pencil gliding across the paper as she captured the places she visited.

As she walked out of The Pottery and Craft Bar with a bag filled with pristine new pencils and sketchpads, as well as an art book she'd been eyeing off for a few weeks, her phone rang. Her sister's name flashed across the screen.

'Hey,' Elle answered.

'Hi,' Lauren said, sounding slightly distracted.

'What's up?'

'Nothing, I just thought I'd call and say hello.'

Immediately Elle became suspicious. Usually when the two sisters called each other, it was to sort out parental gifts and birthday parties. Lauren was older than Elle, had a career as a solicitor and was married with a toddler. Lately it seemed the two sisters had nothing in common except for their parents and siblings, and their conversations had been getting fewer and farther in between.

'How have you been?' Lauren asked.

'Fine,' Elle answered. Lauren was never one to waste time on small talk.

'I hear you're going overseas?'

Ah, so that's what this was about. 'I take it Mum called you? Did she ask you to try to talk some sense into me or something?'

'We both know that's never going to happen,' she said blithely. 'You've never listened to any of my advice before—why would now be any different?'

Blunt yet honest. That was her sister all right.

'Yes, I'm going to Scotland. No, you can't talk me out of it. Yes, I know what I'm doing.'

'Right. So we've got that sorted, then,' Lauren said dryly before giving a small huff. 'Look, Elle, I get it. I know Mum can push a little hard sometimes and I do feel sorry for you—I know you and Mum have always clashed and I get that you think she's just trying to make your life difficult, but she's not.'

'Lauren, I—'

'I know what you're going to say. You didn't like university. I know, okay? I saw how you were when you were down here. And I feel a little bad, actually. I was so caught up in my work, and Anthony and I had only just got married . . . I should have made more time for you, to help you settle in more. I'm sorry I wasn't really there for you.'

Elle hesitated before answering. This wasn't their usual line of conversation. Things never got particularly deep between them. 'You have nothing to be sorry about. It wasn't about not settling in. I just didn't want to be an accountant. I didn't know *what* I wanted to be.'

'Then it's probably time you figured it out, Elle.'

Why did everyone think it was so damn easy? If it were just a matter of sitting down and coming up with an answer for what she wanted to do with her life, wouldn't she have come up with something by now?

'That's what I plan on doing,' she said, 'as soon as I get back from Scotland.'

'Are you doing okay?' Lauren said, again surprising Elle when her voice dropped gently. 'You and Gran were always close. I imagine you're feeling a bit lost without her.'

Elle swallowed painfully as sudden emotion squeezed tightly. 'Yeah, I really miss her.' She cleared her throat to get herself back under control. 'How's Lucy? It was really good to see you guys again,' she said, genuinely meaning it but also needing to change the subject. As sad as the occasion had been, having all her siblings and their families under the one roof had been nice.

'Lucy's great. She's been to toddler gymnastics this morning and we're heading out to her swimming lesson after lunch. I think she's really missing having her aunty and cousins to play with, though.'

Lauren was her big sister and Elle loved her, but they were so different that it was often hard to find anything other than Lucy to talk about. 'Maybe when I get back I could come down and visit for a few days,' Elle said tentatively.

'I'd really like that, Elle. Maybe while you're here we can sort out what you want to do?' she added, her rapid change in tone spoiling what could have been a hallmark moment. 'Melbourne has some great universities.'

Elle's blood began to boil at the comment. 'Sure. Maybe. Well, I have to get going. Thanks for calling,' Elle said, unlocking her car and throwing her art purchases on the back seat.

She slammed the door shut behind her with a little extra force, and sat in the driver's seat feeling a mixture of hurt and annoyance. Maybe she really *had* been switched at birth. Did everyone have a bossy big sister who always thought she knew so much more about everything? When was her family ever going to accept that she had her life and they just needed to worry about their own?

The trip couldn't come around soon enough.

☙

The next three weeks flew past. The *For Sale* sign went up, and Elle knew she had to go through the painful process of packing up Gran's house.

The majority of Elle's belongings could be stored in a half-dozen boxes and kept in her parents' shed, but going through Gran's things had been a lot harder. She knew that her father in particular was finding it difficult to pack away the remaining remnants of his mum's life, despite him not being the overtly sentimental type.

'There's something confronting about realising you're officially an orphan, Elle, no matter how old you are,' he'd said only the night before when the two of them were alone at Gran's, carefully boxing up photo albums and going through the mundane bits and pieces of paperwork and personal correspondence in Gran's writing desk.

Most of what was left held only sentimental value, which in Elle's eyes was more important than any of the assets that had already been distributed among the family. It was hard to look at pretty much anything in the house and not feel an overwhelming urge to put a 'Keep' sticker on it.

'Elle, you can't keep it all,' her mother said wearily, as they started a second day of clearing.

'We can't just toss everything either,' Elle said, clutching the green glass vase to her chest.

*Darling, your mother's right. It's just clutter,* Gran said gently.

'It's not clutter,' Elle snapped defensively, causing her mother to raise an eyebrow. Maybe it was just an ugly green glass vase, but it was part of Elle's childhood memories and so it had meaning.

*Pauline gave me that vase for Christmas one year,* Gran told her dryly. Pauline, Gran's sister-in-law, had the uncanny knack of rubbing everyone she came into contact with—especially Gran—the wrong way. *Toss it, dear,* Gran said firmly.

Reluctantly, Elle placed it into the box marked 'Donations' and gave a small sigh.

'No, not that!' Elle called in alarm as her father lifted the square yellow footrest to carry it out to the trailer for the tip. 'Drop the pouffe, Dad,' she said, blocking his path to the front door.

'You cannot possibly want to keep that,' her mother said with barely disguised disgust.

'I do.'

The heavy, old-fashioned footrest had been part of her grandparents' lounge-room decor forever. The faded baby-poo-yellow vinyl was not an especially attractive piece of furniture, but Elle had used it as a table for her snacks as a child and even now, just the sight of it gave her warm fuzzy feelings.

*I remember buying that*, Gran said with a sigh. *Horace Lambert sold that to your grandfather and me when we were first married. We bought all new furniture. That was when they made things to last. You don't get that kind of quality now*, she added with a note of disapproval.

The Lamberts had once owned a furniture store in the main street, but it had been closed since well before Elle had even been born. It was still referred to by locals as Lamberts', though, despite the fact it had become various different businesses over the years and was currently a newsagent.

'I'll keep the lounge suite and dining table too.'

'We don't have enough room to keep all the furniture, love,' her father said, shaking his head.

'Why would you need it, anyway?' her mother asked.

'For my own place.'

'And when will this be happening?' Caroline asked, a marked change in her tone.

'When I get back from Scotland, I suppose.'

'Have you given any thought to what you'll be doing?'

'I've got feelers out,' Elle said, more confidently than she felt. 'I'm sure I'll be able to find another job as soon as I get back.' The fact she hadn't had any feedback yet was a little disappointing, but there was no need to tell her mother that yet. Nor that because she'd discovered if she applied for a UK passport, being eligible through her grandmother, she could work as a resident *if* she chose to stay on a bit longer and find a job to support herself as she travelled.

'I think you need to give returning to study serious consideration while you're away. Things aren't going to be the way they were here, now that Gran's gone.'

'What's that supposed to mean?'

'Come on, Elle,' her mother said in that condescending tone Elle hated. 'You never really had to face up to things while Gran was alive. You came home and moved in here. You had a place to live, which was how you managed to live comfortably on that meagre wage you've been making at Brown's all this time. You'll have to live in the real world once you get home, Elle. Gran's not here to prop you up anymore. It's time to grow up.'

*Now, darling*, Gran cut in anxiously, *remember, she's just trying to help.* But it was too late. As usual, her mother's aim had been a direct hit.

'Grow up? Because that's how you see me, isn't it? As a kid, still. Just because I haven't got some degree after my name like the others, it somehow makes me immature in your eyes.'

'You have the ability to do more with your life than waste it away here.'

'I don't, Mum,' Elle said, her voice straining. 'That's what I've been telling you my entire life, but you won't listen because you can't accept the fact that one of your children is less than perfect.'

She saw her mother shake her head in exasperation as she usually did during this conversation and her father tried to jump in and change the subject, but Elle refused to let it go.

'I don't have the ability to do what you want me to do. I just don't. I know it. I've accepted it. Some people just aren't academic. There's no shame in that,' she added pointedly. 'I'm okay with not being book smart. I'm okay being average. *You're* the one who has a problem with it. Heaven forbid Caroline Kinnaird has a child who doesn't become successful in some important career.'

'This has nothing to do with that,' her mother countered. 'This is about you and your future.'

'This is about *you*. Please don't insult what intelligence I *do* have by pretending it's anything other than that.'

'That is completely ridiculous,' her mother snapped.

'It's hurtful actually,' Elle said, quietly now. 'I just wish you could be happy with who I am.'

Her mother opened her mouth, but Elle shook her head and turned away to pick up her car keys. 'I'll come back later and finish packing. I have to get to work.'

She walked down the front path hoping she didn't trip over due to the blur of tears that had filled her eyes.

Why couldn't her mother see her the way Gran had? Her mum was right about one thing, though: life for Elle was going to be different around here now she didn't have Gran to turn to, and the thought scared her more than she cared to admit.

*She loves you, darling. She really does. She doesn't mean to come across so bluntly. She's just worried about you*, Gran said.

'Which is ironic, considering I'm living right on their doorstep where they can see everything that's happening, and not hundreds of kilometres away going to uni and doing God knows what, like the others.'

*You mother's always been a worrier. She likes security. You know how her parents were,* Gran said gently.

Caroline's family were very different to the Kinnairds. Indeed, Elle's other set of grandparents were about as opposite to Gran and Pa as it was possible to get. Granddad Ashcroft had never been able to hold down a job while Caroline was growing up, leaving Granny Ashcroft to be creatively thrifty stretching the little income they had to keep her four children fed and clothed in their government-subsidised house.

Elle knew that her mum had always felt like a square peg in a round hole in her family—which was ironic considering she couldn't seem to understand Elle's predicament. All Caroline had wanted to do was go to university and make something of her life, and she'd done it by working hard and getting a student loan to put herself through her studies. Elle was extremely proud but a little daunted by her mother's drive.

Elle didn't need a Bachelor of Psychology to see the issues that had come from her mother's upbringing, and how they influenced the way she saw the world. In her mother's eyes, the success of her children was a guarantee they would be able to provide for their own families the way she had provided for hers, so their Christmases wouldn't be filled with second-hand toys or randomly picked gifts from charity organisations.

It always amazed Elle that for a smart woman, her mother could be very obtuse when it came to understanding people. It didn't make it any less hurtful, though, when she continued to wield that sword of righteousness over Elle's head.

'She's an education snob, Gran,' Elle said. 'She may have her reasons for being like that, but it's time to stop using it as an excuse. Granny and Granddad weren't bad people just because they didn't have a degree and fancy careers. Mum might have hated growing up like that, but she has no right to try to force everyone else into how she thinks we should all live.'

*She'll come around*, Gran said quietly. *I think this time apart will do wonders for both of you.*

# Seven

The next morning, as she sat at the table after being summoned for breakfast at her parents' place, her father cleared his throat and made an announcement. 'I've been in touch with my cousin, Alice, in Scotland. She's sent her address and a phone number for you to organise a time to visit once you get over there.' He slid a piece of paper across to Elle.

Caroline, busying herself with buttering her toast, didn't look up.

Portsoy, Elle knew from Gran's stories, was located on the Moray Firth Coast of northeast Scotland, in Aberdeenshire. On the map it looked somewhat isolated, almost in a straight line north from Edinburgh, as far as you could go before you ran out of land.

'I can't believe we've never met any of Gran's relatives after all this time.'

Her father shrugged. 'Your gran and pa didn't have a lot of money when they were first married. Flights weren't as cheap as they are now.'

'Do you think they'll be okay with some stranger dropping in?'

'They seemed excited.'

Elle wasn't sure she liked the idea of being foisted onto complete strangers simply because they were related, but she was looking forward to meeting them, nonetheless. Pa's family were close and she and her siblings had grown up knowing all their cousins, aunts and uncles from the Kinnaird side, but Gran had left her family behind in Scotland at fifteen years old, and seemingly never looked back.

'Your father's been in contact with a few of his cousins over the years,' her mother reminded her.

'But we've never actually *met* them,' Elle pointed out.

'Well, I've already told them you'll be coming over, so make sure you give them a call once you're there to let them know when you'll be arriving.'

Gran was conspicuously quiet on the whole matter, which made Elle somewhat curious considering she sensed an unsettled kind of feeling surrounding her. But with so much to do before she left, Elle was too busy to ask about it now. She would sort out the prodigal-rellie visit later, once she got there. It would all be a moot point if she missed her flight because she hadn't finished packing.

'Damn it!'

Elle stood with her hands on her hips as she stared down at her suitcase on the bed. This was the third time she'd repacked it, taking more things out—and the stupid thing still wouldn't close.

Sixteen days' worth of winter clothes was turning out to be quite heavy. Whoever decided on the baggage weight limit had obviously never had to travel overseas in autumn, Elle decided.

*Do you really need all those boots?* Gran asked.

'Yes. They're all my favourites. I can't go without my boots,' Elle griped.

*Then take out some of those jeans. How many pairs do you have in there?*

'Seven.'

*Seven! Good grief, child. Who needs seven pairs of jeans?*

'They're not all the same kind. There's skinny jeans, those ones are a dark wash, I need a pair of good jeans for going out, and a couple that are stretchy for travelling . . . And anyway, I need some decent clothes if we're going to meet the family.' She paused, glad of the chance to bring up the topic. 'Why were you so quiet when Dad was talking about them?' she asked gently. 'How do you feel about me visiting?'

*I think it's wonderful that you'll get to meet them. From what I gather, Alice and Peter are very nice people.*

'So, Alice is your sister's daughter?'

*One of them, yes. The youngest, I believe. She came around quite a long time after the others were born.*

'Why didn't you ever talk much about your sister?' Elle asked carefully, and waited through a few moments of silence before Gran replied.

*I left Scotland when I was only a child. She was a lot older than me. We've been apart far longer than we were ever together.*

It was so unlike the Gran she knew. The Gran who wouldn't go more than a few days before checking in on her son and grandchildren, even when they all lived in the same town. It really didn't make sense. Elle realised she had never given it more than a fleeting thought when Gran was alive. Too wrapped up in her own life, she supposed, to bother asking many questions about her grandmother's life before she became Gran. It hit Elle then—she now had the second chance most people never got to ask all the things that had never occurred to her before.

'So, why *did* your father decide to leave Scotland?'

*I don't think he really wanted to, but he had no choice,* Gran said with the slightest hint of bitterness. *Times had grown hard and my parents were forced to sell the farm. Then my mother died and my father struggled to find work. An opportunity to move to Australia came up and so he took it.*

'But why didn't your siblings go too?'

*By then, my brothers were all married and had their own land, and my sister had her family. I was the youngest. I didn't have a choice.*

Something in Gran's tone caught Elle's attention. 'You didn't want to move?'

*No. But I couldn't stay with my sister at the time, and I couldn't let my father move to a new country all by himself.*

Another pause, and then Gran continued, her tone now lightly dismissive. *It was a long time ago. None of it is important now.*

'What about your dad's side of the family? The ones who'd once owned Stormeil Castle? Could none of them have taken you in?'

*The castle had long since gone from the MacKenzies by the time my father was born*, she said wistfully. *His father, my grandfather, had a falling-out with his family and we didn't know any of them.*

'So, why do you want Stormeil to be where you're . . . placed? Why not Portsoy, where you grew up?'

*It's hard to explain, darling. My father always spoke about Stormeil as if it were a magical kingdom, like the tales of King Arthur. The story of Isla always resonated with me, even as a small child. It's not something I can really explain—it's like I've always been drawn to it.*

'But you never lived there . . .'

*No*, Gran said simply, *but my ancestors did, and even though they've been dead and gone for centuries, I feel connected to them. I know it mustn't make sense . . . I only ever went there the once.*

And with that, Elle was left in silence. Clearly Gran had shared as much as she was prepared to for now. Elle knew she shouldn't pry, but something bothered her about Gran's reaction to visiting the Scottish family. There was more to the story, Elle knew it, but for now she would have to tuck her curiosity away. She wasn't going to give up, though. Right now she had to focus on getting them to Scotland, but once they were there she *would* get to the bottom of it.

Elle sat down on the hard chair and let out a long breath. She'd made it through security, repacked her backpack, pulled her shoes back on, and located her departure gate—now all she had to do was wait. And people watch. Airports were great for that.

It was something of a shock to arrive in Sydney International Airport from sleepy old Jessup's Creek. There were *so* many people. They flowed along the wide walkways between gates like a river of people of every colour, culture and age. Groups of kids on school or sports trips, followed by harried-looking teachers and parents. Families with small children, pushing prams and dragging ladybug and dragon roller bags. Couples still on a wedding high and about to head off on a honeymoon. The list went on and Elle found herself filling in the time trying to work out where everyone was heading off to.

This was the first time Elle had travelled outside the country and she was battling a mixture of excitement and anxiety. So far she had completed leg one of her trip, flying from Armidale to Sydney, and now leg number two was approaching: Sydney to Dubai. After a brief stop there, she would board her final leg to fly to Edinburgh.

She had already killed some time browsing through the duty-free shops and purchasing gifts for her Scottish relatives. It was hard enough to choose for relatives she had known all her life, much less for people she had never even met. In the end, she figured she couldn't really go wrong with a couple of pens, a few key rings, a set of decorative shot glasses with Australian animals on them and some stuffed native animals.

Gran had been quiet so far, and Elle had no idea what that might mean. Part of her was relieved; looking like a weirdo, talking to herself, would have been guaranteed to draw attention to herself and have airport security detain her—not an ideal way to start her trip. Perhaps it had something to do with being relegated to carry-on luggage. It had been surprisingly easy to transport cremated ashes. She had documentation from the funeral home stating what the box contained, and after placing them on the conveyor belt along with her backpack, shoes and jacket, it was a simple matter of screening and then collecting at the other end. Now, with the ashes safely packed back inside her backpack, there was nothing left to do but wait for the flight to be called.

When boarding finally commenced, Elle found her seat, smiled at the older couple sitting beside her and pulled out the book she had been saving for the flight. She decided the best way to handle the long trip ahead was to completely block it out of her mind. So, she did. After all, how bad could it be?

When would this nightmare end?

Elle shifted in her seat, again, trying to find a comfortable spot and giving up, again. The couple beside her, lovely as they were, had got up every hour, on the hour, to go to the toilet since the moment the first seatbelt sign had gone off after leaving Sydney. Elle had tried hard to remind herself that long-distance travel was difficult for everyone, but it was getting past a joke. She had thought she would be able to sleep for most of the trip, but that had proven impossible when she was constantly being woken up to allow her travel companions to get out of their seats.

When the third and final leg arrived, she breathed a sigh of relief and smiled farewell to her companions, who went in the opposite direction once they landed at Dubai. In just another seven hours this would all be over, she reminded herself, determined to hold onto what little remaining excitement for the trip she had. The next flight was on a smaller aircraft but it was still full, and Elle's dreams of ending up with a spare seat beside her ended abruptly when a large man stuffed his carry-on suitcase in the locker above and wedged himself into the seat beside her, promptly taking both armrests, leaving Elle to scrunch up against the window.

*Fantastic*, she muttered silently.

*Come on, darling, only a few hours to go. You can do this.*

*Oh, now you show up*, Elle replied, gritting her teeth as her neighbour squirmed beside her, his elbow making contact with her arm, without apology. *You better not have been floating up around first class.*

*It's very nice up there*, Gran said, a smile in her voice. *I should have suggested you spend a little more on an upgrade.*

*A little more? Try the cost of a small car, and then some. It's criminal the amount they charge for a few more inches of leg room.*

*Oh, they have lots of leg room. And champagne . . . and seats that convert to beds.*

*That's not helpful right now, Gran.*

*Sorry. Never mind, not long now until we get there. Close your eyes and get some rest.*

Within minutes of taking off, that's exactly what the man beside her did, and Elle spent the remainder of the trip pushing his head off her shoulder and turning the volume up on the TV show she was trying to watch to drown out the accompanying snores.

This was surely what hell was like.

# Eight

'Bit of a dreich day.'

The heavy Scottish accent threw her as she took a moment to decipher the taxi driver's words.

'I'm sorry?' she asked, finally giving up.

He ducked his head and pointed up at the sky out the front windscreen. 'Dreich. Y'know—wet, windy, horrible weather.'

'Oh.' Elle brightened immediately, understanding. It *was* a rather overcast, dull-looking day, but she was so happy to finally arrive that she hadn't really noticed.

'Where'd you fly in from?'

'Australia,' Elle said. 'I can't remember what day it was when I left,' she added dryly.

'Long way,' he agreed.

A bloody long way. Elle sat back in her seat and tried to soak up as much of her new surroundings as possible as they drove through the streets of Edinburgh. The driver happily chatted away as he deftly manoeuvred his cab along roads no wider than a narrow residential street back home, which here had to fit massive tour buses and other vehicles side by side through the ancient city.

They made their way from the relatively open spaces of the airport and through house-lined streets, until eventually the roads became cobbled and the buildings grew decidedly older. Brightly painted fronts sat alongside restaurants, cafes and tourist shops, as well as instantly recognisable chain stores, all flashing past in a rainbow of colours. Tourists carrying maps and backpacks stood in the middle of the rocky roads taking photos, while locals moved briskly around them, going about their usual Wednesday. Cyclists rode in and out of traffic, swerving effortlessly as pedestrians and cars pulled out around them.

Cathedrals and statues, churches and fenced graveyards sat between fashion stores and gift shops. The buildings, most made from stone blocks, ranged in shades of sand and brown and light grey, to darker greys that reminded Elle of the wet rocks down in the creek they swam in back home.

Maybe it was the dreich day—she smiled a little at the new word she'd learned—that made the city look so morbid and dark, but she suspected that even in bright sunshine these old buildings would look eerie, like something out of medieval storybook. This was in stark contrast to the atmosphere, though—it was anything but bleak. There was so much *life* here.

Cars merged and cut in front of them and Elle held her breath, expecting a loud curse or the blast of a horn, but none came from her driver or from any of the vehicles around them.

'Everyone's so polite on the roads over here,' she ventured after another car decided it was in the wrong lane and swiftly cut across a bus in front of them.

'There's no point getting upset,' her driver said, catching her eye in the rear-view mirror with a lopsided smile. 'It doesn't get you where you're going any faster to blow the horn,' he added with a shrug.

The taxi dropped her off in front of a row of elegant townhouses in the new part of Edinburgh. Elle chuckled a little. Even the *new* part of Edinburgh was older than most buildings in Australia.

She pushed open the large front door of the guesthouse and looked around the hallway, taking in the pretty chandelier hanging high above the winding wooden staircase. The stairs were covered in a deep maroon carpet leading to a first-floor landing with a white door. Elle put her suitcase down and breathed in a musty scent—not altogether unpleasant, but something she assumed these old buildings would all have in common.

'Welcome!'

Elle jumped slightly as a tall, thin man swept into the hallway and clasped both her hands in a hearty handshake. 'You must be Elspeth?' he said, and she detected a slight Italian accent, which she hadn't been expecting in Scotland. 'My name is Enzo. Welcome to the Balmore. I see you've had a long flight, you look tired,' he said sympathetically, peering into her face. 'Let's get you settled in your room,' he added, barely pausing for breath as he took hold of her suitcase and headed for the staircase. 'It's a very steep climb. I'm used to this, you can see from my very athletic body,' he said with a chuckle, and Elle was left staring dumbfoundedly after him. He had reached the first landing before she'd managed to make any sense of what was happening and hurried after him.

'Breakfast is between seven-thirty and nine-thirty, and you just come down to the dining room whenever you're ready,' he was saying from up above her.

Elle's legs were beginning to burn by the second floor. She looked up and saw the man still climbing, barely out of breath as he chattered on. She heard a key jiggle in a lock as she reached the third floor and held onto the bannister as she tried to catch her breath. Dear God. She had no idea how out of shape she was.

'Okay, there you go. All set.' He smiled at her brightly. 'Anything you need, you just come down and find me, *kay?*'

She managed a quick nod and smile as he moved past her and disappeared down the stairs with a friendly wave. Elle shook off the daze she found herself in after the whirlwind check-in and stepped into the room.

The roof sloped down over the double bed, which Elle was tempted to collapse on after her exhausting travel experience. Instead she moved towards the window at the other end of the room and looked out over the small back garden at a sea of chimneys and brick buildings that spread out behind her townhouse.

She was here. Finally.

She placed her backpack on the wing-back chair beneath the window and carefully took out the box from inside, unwrapping it from its plastic-bag cover and sitting it on the windowsill.

'There you go, Gran. Welcome to Edinburgh.'

There was no reply, but she felt somehow that her gran was hovering about somewhere close by. This whole afterlife business was still a mystery. Elle had been tempted to ask Gran where she went when she wasn't here with her, but she had held back, uncertain if she *really* wanted to know.

Elle had always vaguely believed that you went to heaven once you died, but her family wasn't terribly religious—even Gran had never been one to discuss religion. Instead of stories from the Bible, Elle had grown up on Scottish legends full of fairies, ghosts, magic and mystical encounters. Maybe heaven was where fairies and goblins lived when they weren't getting up to mischief down here? After all, Christianity adapted pagan rituals and celebrations into modern-day events such as Christmas, Easter and Halloween, and certain traditions overlapped with druid and Celtic history, so to Elle it wasn't a huge stretch to think that religion was all really one and the same story, just told by different storytellers.

Elle turned away from the window and eyed the bed, moving towards it like a long-lost friend. She let out a low groan as her tired body finally stretched out flat for the first time in thirty-five hours.

Elle opened her eyes and stared at the white ceiling above her, momentarily disorientated.

*Morning sleepyhead*, Gran said.

Elle reached for her phone and checked the time. Eight-thirty? She'd fallen asleep fully dressed yesterday afternoon, and slept right through.

*There's no time to sleep in. We need to get started on our bucket list.*

Elle muttered under her breath as she sat up and yawned widely, struggling to dislodge the fog of sleep that clung to her. 'I'm having a shower and then I'll do the talking thing,' she said, climbing from her bed.

The website had described the bathrooms as 'compact', but to Elle, 'miniscule' would be more accurate. However, she couldn't care less about the ridiculously cramped amenities in her room; all she cared about was the blessed hot water washing away the long-haul flight and reviving her humanity.

As she dressed, feeling halfway human again now that she had washed her hair, Elle could finally exhale an excited breath of relief. All she needed now was a coffee and she would be ready to take on this adventure.

The small room off the main entrance contained the dining room, and she hovered uncertainly at the doorway for a moment, wondering what to do.

'Take a seat. Any table,' a tiny German-accented woman said as she walked into the room from behind Elle. 'You ordered breakfast?'

'Ah, no. I don't think so.'

'You order breakfast the day before. You no order. Coffee?'

God yes. 'Yes, please.'

'You want toast?'

'Um, sure. Yes, please,' Elle said quickly. She felt she was somehow already on the woman's bad side and didn't want to further alienate her.

'Sit. I bring.'

'Okay then.'

Across from Elle, two women were eating their breakfast. One looked over and offered a smile. 'She's all bark, that one,' the woman said in a heavy American accent. 'Just fill out the form on the front table before you leave this morning. There's cereal and juice in the room next door.'

'Thank you,' Elle said, grateful for a heads-up on how things worked.

Within minutes the German woman was back, setting down a rack of toast cut into triangles along with butter and an assortment of condiments on a small plate, before pouring mercifully strong, fragrant coffee into a cup. Elle took a deep breath, filling her lungs with the heavenly aroma—and instantly all felt right once more in the world.

*Come on, come on*, Gran muttered impatiently.

*Gran, I'm starving. Just give me a minute.*

*You could take the toast with you. What is it you kids are always saying? Multitask!*

*Gran, right now I'm talking to a ghost, eating and trying to combat jetlag—that's about all the multitasking I'm capable of.*

Elle refrained, just, from rolling her eyes at the small huff she heard in response.

After breakfast, she headed back upstairs to her room to decide what to do on her first full day in Edinburgh.

*The list, quick, get the list,* Gran said, then practically squealed with girlish glee as Elle pulled the notebook from her suitcase pocket.

*The Castle,* Gran said before Elle could read the list aloud. *The Old Town. Holyroodhouse—oh, I wonder if the Queen might be visiting? It's her summer house, you know,* Gran added notably.

'So I read,' Elle agreed, 'but I don't think we should get our hopes up that you'll bump into her, Gran.'

*You never know . . . Come on, let's go, we're burning daylight.*

'Burning daylight,' Elle muttered, shaking her head as she grabbed her backpack and coat and locked the door behind her. 'Seriously, Gran, where do you come up with this stuff?' The Gran she'd known had always had a sense of humour, but Gran like this . . . she seemed younger, more carefree.

*It's not much fun growing old, you know,* Gran said, picking up once more on Elle's thoughts. *You forget the last time you were able to run, or to jump up out of a chair or bed. I suddenly feel so much more . . . free. Like a young girl again, almost,* she finished wistfully.

Elle's mind went back to Gran's last few months, and how swiftly she had gone downhill after her fall. It had been so sad to watch her deteriorate right before their eyes. Elle shook off the memories. Happy Gran was here with her now, and that was what mattered.

The footpath was wet as though it had rained overnight and the air was crisp, but not as cold as Elle had anticipated for mid-September. As she followed the map towards the Old Town, the fresh air cleared the remaining jetlag fog from her mind. Buses rushed past on extremely narrow roads, and cyclists zoomed to and fro, dodging cars and traffic, but hardly any horns blared.

Elle took in everything around her, and as much as she disliked cities in general, the atmosphere of this one was like nothing she had experienced before. As she merged onto the Royal Mile, she found herself absorbed into the current of tourists flowing in an endless stream towards the same destination—the huge grey fortress of Edinburgh Castle ahead.

Everywhere Elle looked, buildings of stone towered around her, and cobbled streets and footpaths curved their way through townhouses and buildings. It soon became clear that if she were going to see even a fraction of this amazing city in the few days she had planned, she was going to need a faster way to get around. Spotting the bright red bus, she made her way towards a ticket seller and purchased a pass to travel the city highlights. It was about the most touristy thing you could do, but she didn't care as she slipped in her ear phones and listened to the recorded tour guide tell her about the places they passed and things she could do.

She spent the day happily roaming the streets, overwhelmed by the city's age and beauty. Everywhere she turned was something that made her mouth gape even wider. Like the Witches' Well near the Castle Esplanade, a seemingly innocent and unremarkable spot but for the history surrounding it, filled with terrible tales of terror and torture. According to the tour guide, as many as three hundred people, mostly women, were burned at the stake for witchcraft right here at Edinburgh Castle. Or the fact that Edinburgh used to be called Auld Reekie, due to its unsanitary state. Like most places before indoor plumbing became the norm, the streets were literally filled with human and animal waste. The poor lived in tenement buildings that could be as tall as fourteen storeys, and they all tipped their waste out the windows onto the streets below. It was so hard to imagine, looking at the beautiful clean streets now. Something told her if she'd gone through standing stones and been hurtled back in time like Claire from *Outlander*, she would not have coped very well at all. Elle didn't even like camping—the thought of walking down the street dodging human excrement and having the contents of a chamber pot tipped on her head would have probably done her in.

But it didn't stop her loving history. She took a tour of the Palace of Holyroodhouse and got chills just thinking about the centuries of lives who had lived in the place.

'And this is the Royal dining room, which Her Majesty and members of the Royal Family use when they are in residence at the Palace,' the tour guide informed them as they entered the room. Within pale olive walls a long, surprisingly simple-looking dining table ran almost the entire length of the room.

*Did you hear that?* Gran said in an awe-struck stage whisper. *The Queen eats her dinner in here!*

Elle could just imagine Gran's face. She had always been a die-hard Royal fan. But it was further on in the tour, upstairs in what their guide called the Mary, Queen of Scots' Chambers, that Elle really found herself intrigued. They climbed a narrow, steep and winding staircase into the oldest section of the palace, built almost five hundred years ago, to find Mary's bedroom.

This was the actual bedroom of Mary, Queen of Scots, Elle reminded herself, trying to absorb the enormity of where she was. She had always been fascinated by the past, and to find herself standing in the very same spot as such a monumental historical figure was seriously blowing her mind.

'Just off the bedchamber,' their guide announced, 'is the tiny supper room where Mary was dining on the ninth of March in 1566 when she witnessed the murder of her private secretary, David Rizzio, who was killed by her jealous husband, Lord Darnley, and a group of powerful Scottish lords. If you look closely you can still see the bloodstains from Rizzio's body in the outer chamber where he was left for all to see.' Goosebumps broke out along Elle's arms as she looked around and tried to imagine the terror that had unfolded in this room, more than four centuries ago. If these walls could talk.

*It's not the walls you need to worry about*, Gran said in a rather deadpan tone.

'What?' Elle glanced about nervously, half expecting to see a ghostly apparition manifest itself before realising how ridiculous that was, considering she was travelling with her very own member of the dearly departed.

'Gran, how come I can't see you?'

*You can't?*

'No.' Elle suddenly felt a little concerned. 'Should I be able to?'

*Huh,* Gran said. *Well, I guess that explains why you've nearly sat on me a few times now and you keep walking through me.*

'So, why can't I see you?'

*I don't know, darling, I'm new to all this too, you know. But I guess that's also why you didn't find the gentleman in a tunic, wearing a rather long sword, a little odd back in the hallway.*

'The what?'

*Never mind, dear. Quick, hurry up, we're being left behind.*

Elle glanced around and realised the rest of the party had left and headed back downstairs. As fascinating as she found Mary's rooms, she didn't have any great desire to find herself alone in them. Certainly not after Gran's little announcement. God knows who or what might be lingering about the place.

Elle could have stayed all day and not had her fill of the beautiful palace, but there was still so much left to tick off the list and time was getting away.

Back outside on the Royal Mile, Elle was surprised by the number of tourists here in September. She'd never seen so many—even on her rare trips to Sydney there hadn't been this many people swarming the streets. It made her itch to get to someplace quieter.

Everywhere she looked was another souvenir shop, or a kilt maker. Tartan appeared in almost every shop window in some form or other, and the tourists flocked like seagulls on a chip.

She wandered up and down the hilly streets, stumbling upon Instagram-famous places such as Circus Lane and the beautiful Victoria Street with its brightly coloured shopfronts. As she followed the crowds, heading back towards the newer part of Edinburgh where she was staying, a sign caught her eye.

*Look. An* Outlander *tour!* Gran gasped. *Remember when you showed these to me on the computer? We were going to go on one. Go inside.*

'Haggis Tours,' Elle said, reading the name of the tour company on the front window. 'You want to go on a tour named after a dish wrapped in sheep intestines?'

*It's authentic*, Gran insisted.

Elle pushed open the glass door and stepped in. 'They're a bit pricey,' she murmured, taking the leaflet from the desk.

'Oh, they're well worth it,' a woman behind her said, unexpectedly. 'Have you read the books?'

Elle saw the light of excitement in the older American woman's eyes and smiled as she nodded.

'Oh, then you have to do one of these tours. It was the best thing I've ever done. I've been here twice and I've done three different ones,' she gushed. 'I loved this one, it went for six days, but it was the best.'

Elle eyed the brochure the woman plucked out and pushed into her hands. 'I don't really have the time to do a six-day one,' she said, ignoring Gran's disappointed protest.

'Then that one is a must,' the woman nodded at the original brochure Elle had picked up. 'It's only a day trip but it'll be enough to whet your appetite. I promise you, it won't be your last tour.'

*What are you waiting for*, Gran prodded impatiently. *Book us some tickets.*

'Oh, for goodness sake,' Elle muttered, pulling her wallet from her bag as she moved across to the front desk.

*This is going to be so much fun*, Gran said, sounding like a kid at Christmas as Elle walked out with a ticket for tomorrow in her hand.

The late-afternoon shadows thrown by the old buildings blocked the last feeble rays of sun as Elle made her way back to the guesthouse. There was a distinct chill in the air and the temperature had dropped noticeably. People rushed past on their way home from work, and the sounds of bus air-brakes hissing as they pulled into bus stops and out again lent a chaotic soundtrack to her walk. There was a different feel to the city in the late afternoon than in the morning. Maybe most of the tourists had headed home earlier than she had, and now she was experiencing a different Edinburgh.

As she walked past a pub with bright flowers in a window box, the smell of sizzling meat snagged her attention. She was starving. With a quick glance at her watch Elle decided she may as well have an early dinner. She approached the service desk and a young woman with a ponytail came over and smiled. 'Are you looking for a table?'

'Yes, please.'

'For how many?'

'Just one,' Elle said and hoped it didn't sound as pathetic as she imagined.

'I might put you over here, if that's all right?' the waitress asked, leading Elle towards a long timber bench where a number of high stools were placed. Maybe this was the losers' corner where all the loners were placed.

'What would you like to drink?'

'Just a white wine thanks,' Elle smiled, accepting the menu the woman whipped out from her apron and handed over.

'I'll be back in a jiffy,' she promised before walking away, her ponytail swinging jauntily behind her.

Elle picked up the menu and read through the mouth-watering offerings, surprised to find so many Americanised dishes before deciding she really *did* fancy a big juicy hamburger and chips.

'What can I get you?' her waitress asked, returning with her drink and a notepad in hand.

'I'll have the Ultimate Burger, thanks.'

'The . . . Ultimate Burger?' the woman repeated, lifting her eyes from the notepad to look at Elle intently.

'Yes, please,' Elle said, a little unsure about having her choice of meal questioned.

'It's a very big burger.'

'That's okay. I'm starving,' Elle said with more conviction. She really *was* hungry.

'Okay then, but I hope you wore your stretchy pants,' the waitress added doubtfully, before taking the menu and walking away.

Elle sipped her wine as she waited for her food to arrive. Eating alone wasn't exactly the worst thing in the world. It gave her more time to observe her surroundings. The pub was cosy, with low ceilings and timber furniture. Apart from the modern Celtic-sounding music playing over the loudspeakers, the general sound of voices raised to speak over the top of it could have made this any pub in the world, even Jessup's

Creek. There were still a few empty tables, but it was busy, people in business suits and work attire making up a large portion of the clientele.

She smiled as she listened to the conversations going on around her. At the table behind her two men were conducting a job interview, while two tables across a group of women were laughing and getting rowdier by the minute. Her ears picked up on the distinctive rhythm of the Scottish brogue—the male version deep and rolling while the female accent was a little higher pitched but just as melodic.

'Here you go,' her waitress announced, depositing a plate with the biggest burger Elle had ever seen. 'Enjoy.'

*Oh, that does look good*, Gran said with a wistful sigh. *I'm going to miss food.*

Elle hesitated, momentarily losing her appetite. It was sometimes easy to forget the facts: Gran was dead.

*Elspeth Jane Kinnaird, you stop that.*

Elle knew Gran really wasn't happy if she used her full name.

*We're here to have fun. Now, hurry up and eat that burger before it gets cold.*

Almost on cue, a tantalising waft of barbecued beef filled her nose and her stomach grumbled impatiently. Elle eyed the burger and tried to work out a plan of attack, but she was too hungry to worry about how much of a mess she was about to get into, and decided to just dive straight in.

As she finished the last bite and was wiping her fingers on her third paper napkin, she looked up when a glass of wine was placed on the bench in front of her.

'Oh, I didn't order another one,' Elle said apologetically.

The waitress nodded towards the bar, where three men sat looking over at her. 'It's from them. You've got yourself some admirers.'

*Admirers? What the hell?* Elle glanced awkwardly from the wine glass to the men, and then to her horror saw one of them walking across the crowded bar towards her. He was dressed a little more casually than some of the other office workers—he'd ditched his jacket on the back of his chair and his sleeves were rolled up—but he clearly had headed to the pub after work. 'I hope you don't mind, but we thought you deserved a drink after that effort. We've never seen a girl eat a burger like that before,' he said.

Elle felt her face begin to redden. *Oh. Dear. God.* She'd had an audience the entire time she'd been stuffing her face. This was beyond embarrassing.

'I was really hungry,' Elle said trying for a blasé tone, but instead it came out sounding more like an apology.

'It was impressive. Not many contenders manage to finish the Ultimate Challenge.'

'The what?' Elle asked nervously.

'Here you go, congratulations.' The waitress returned, holding out a T-shirt, and then called out to the entire bar, 'Ladies and gentlemen, a big hand for the latest Ultimate Burger Challenge winner.'

The *what?*

*Well done, darling,* Gran cheered.

Elle found herself accepting the T-shirt the woman held out—white, with the cafe's name stamped across the front alongside a cute cartoon burger high-fiving a bowl of chips—as the neighbouring tables applauded. 'Thanks,' she managed weakly.

*Oh, darling, how fun!* Gran enthused.

*Kill. Me. Now.*

'Are you ready for the bill, or would you like dessert?'

At the mention of dessert, Elle felt an uncomfortable wave of nausea threaten, and she quickly shook her head, letting out a slow breath and waiting for it to pass before she stood up.

'Come and join us at the bar,' the man who'd bought her a drink offered, turning his gaze back towards his mates. Elle managed a feeble smile and a tiny wave at the men who saluted her with their glasses of beer and looked to be settled in for a long night.

'Thanks, but I've got an early start in the morning and need to get home. Thank you for the drink though.' Good manners and a healthy dose of awkwardness made her reach for the glass on her table and toss it down in pretty much one large gulp, before instantly regretting her decision—the wine only added to how full she felt. She turned away from her fan club and headed for the front counter.

'You only pay for your drink tonight,' her waitress told her at the cash register with a cheery smile. 'Now, hold your T-shirt up and smile,' she added and held up her phone. Elle had barely lifted the T-shirt when a blinding flash went off, sending a curtain of white dots cascading across her vision. 'Check our Facebook page later this evening. Enjoy the rest of your night.'

Outside, Elle welcomed the cold blast of air against her flushed face.

'Oh God, I'm so full,' Elle moaned silently. 'I wish I hadn't eaten that damn burger. What was I thinking?'

*You polished it off like a seasoned pro. I'm so proud of you,* Gran chuckled. *Who would have thought—an Ultimate Burger-eating champion in the family.*

'I'm pretty sure that's not something to skite about, Gran.'

*Of course it is! And you have a T-shirt to prove it*, she added. *You should wear it tomorrow.*

'I am *not* wearing a T-shirt with a cartoon burger on the front, Gran.'

*I don't know why not. That was quite an achievement.*

Elle reached down and undid the button of her jeans and let out a sigh of relief before an unexpected, very unladylike burp erupted from her. 'Excuse me,' she said, looking around and hoping no one had been close enough to hear. It was time to find a taxi and get home before she managed to further humiliate herself.

*Check the face book*, Gran insisted much later, once Elle had pulled on her stretchy, comfy pyjama pants.

'It's just Facebook, Gran, not *the face book*,' she explained again. She'd lost count of the number of times they'd had this discussion in the past.

*Well, whatever it is, check it.*

Reluctantly, Elle typed in the pub's name and clicked on the page, then groaned out loud as a photo of a wild-haired, startled-looking tourist with tomato sauce smeared in the corner of her lip stared back at her. *Congratulations!* was written across the bottom of the photo, and Elle died a little inside. For the first time ever, she was grateful for the time difference back home.

'No one must ever know of this, Gran,' she said, clicking off her phone, mortified.

*I'll take it to my grave*, Gran vowed solemnly, and Elle thought she detected muffled laughter, which she pointedly ignored.

As Elle approached the tour office early the next day, she saw a group of people—mainly older women—milling around a man holding a clipboard. Elle noted with amusement the handful of men who had clearly been dragged along by their wives and looked anything but thrilled.

'Maybe we'll find Jamie,' one woman whispered excitedly to her friend as they waited to board the bright yellow bus.

'Oh, the things I'd do if *I* found him,' her friend sighed, and Elle hid her smile at the thought of these two rather round older women showing the fictional male lead of the *Outlander* series a thing or two in the romance department.

*Silly women*, Gran tsked.

*Oh come on, Gran, you thought Jamie was a bit of all right too when we read the books, if I recall.*

*Yes, well, at least I have the good sense to remember he's fictional*, she sniffed.

Gran hadn't watched the TV series, preferring, she told Elle, to keep her own image of the characters in her head. Elle, on the other hand, had loved seeing her favourite books re-created on the screen, and was now more than a little excited to be heading out to visit the locations used to bring Claire and Jamie Fraser's story to life.

The driver, a redheaded Scottish woman named Gillian, made Elle smile as she gave a running commentary of Edinburgh's history as they drove through the streets and out of the city. The tour, though touted as an *Outlander* day trip, also covered a lot of Scottish history, which seemed to interest the men a lot more as the day wore on.

Their first stop was Doune Castle, used as Castle Leoch and also the place where *Monty Python and the Holy Grail* was filmed. The village of Doune was a quaint, pretty place standing in the shadow of the great fort. As the big bus squeezed its way through some narrow streets and crossed a little bridge, Elle caught her first sight of the castle and her excitement grew as they prepared to visit their first *Outlander* location.

Stepping inside the cold stone walls, armed with her headphones for the recorded guided tour, Elle found herself momentarily disappointed that there was nothing *Outlander*-like about the place. The courtyard looked much smaller than in the TV series and was empty of the carts and horses and blacksmiths she had somehow expected. Elle suddenly had a new appreciation for all the smoke and mirrors of moviemaking that managed to create a TV set out of the bare bones of the original castle. However, her disappointment was soon forgotten as she followed the tour and began to learn about the real-life history of the castle—which had more highs and lows than any fictional show could hope to dream up. All the while Gran was chirping in her ear, talking over the recorded voice on her audio guide, sounding like an excited school kid on an excursion.

On the bus Elle found herself chatting to a fellow tourist, a woman named Bridget from Texas, who proved very entertaining with her low drawl and love of telling a good story. Bridget was in Scotland alone, doing an *Outlander* tour while her fiancé was away on a boys' fishing trip in Alaska.

*Well, that seems like a marriage doomed to failure,* Gran whispered.

The next few stops were a lot more *Outlander*-looking, as they stopped at Culross and Falkland—both villages used in the series, and both looking exactly like they did on the screen—then on to Midhope Castle. Of all the places they ventured during their tour, Midhope was the one Elle had most wanted to see. Used as the fictional Lallybroch, it looked exactly like it did in the show and as she had imagined it while reading the books years before. But more than the *Outlander* connection to these places they visited, Elle loved the real history attached to them. The castles were all ruins now, but they were each home to a long, prestigious and fascinating history.

Gillian proved an absolute delight with her droll commentary and the extra bits and pieces of information she dropped into conversation.

'Linlithgow Palace was the birth place of both King James V of Scotland and Mary, Queen of Scots,' Gillian stated in her rolling Scottish accent as she wheeled the bright yellow bus into an impossibly narrow street and parked to let them explore the ruins of the once-magnificent royal castle.

Elle ran her fingers along the rough, cold stone of the old castle walls and tried to imagine the events these old buildings must have seen. Some of the castles had stood for more than eight hundred years, their foundations sometimes dating back even further to the Romans, and earlier. It was so hard—and yet exhilarating—for Elle to try to wrap her mind around the sheer enormity of just how old the history of this country was.

There was *so much* to try to take in and she was often overcome by unexpected emotion. Elle wasn't sure what it was exactly—awe mostly that she could be in the presence of something so incredibly old and beautiful. But it was also wonder. If only she really could step back in time for a while, she thought. How amazing that would be. Maybe that was the real draw of the books she loved and the popularity of these tours based around it. Being here and feeling the energy that hung around these old buildings made her yearn to go back to catch a glimpse of life as it had been all those centuries ago.

The tour was nowhere near long enough for Elle to have made use of her sketchpad, but the countless photos she had taken would serve as inspiration to draw to her heart's content once she was back in her room, and she couldn't wait.

When the bus pulled to a stop in front of the busy shopfront back in Edinburgh later that afternoon, Elle felt happily drained. It had been an incredible day full of experiences she would never forget.

*I told you it was a good idea,* Gran said, clearly chuffed with herself.

'Yes, Gran, you were right. It was a great idea.'

She climbed the winding staircase back at the guesthouse and groaned as she took the last step onto the landing outside her room.

She was going to have buns of steel after this trip if the number of steps and hills she'd so far climbed were any indication of the rest of her time in Scotland.

As Elle sat cross-legged on the end of her bed that night, the map spread before her, she traced the route they would take the next day.

'I booked tomorrow's accommodation before I knew Dad had gone and set up a meet-and-greet with the family,' Elle mused, frowning at the enormous map that covered most of her bed. There was a lot to be said for a good, detailed map, but did they *have* to make it almost to scale? There was no easy way to read it without needing to fold the bloody thing into segments.

'Oh, Elspeth, we've been so looking forward to your call,' her dad's cousin Alice had said when Elle dialled the number Alister had given her, and the excitement and genuine warmth in the woman's tone made Elle feel slightly guilty about thinking of ways to get out of the visit. 'When can you get here?'

'Um, well, that's what I was calling to work out,' Elle had stammered, put on the spot. 'I'm still in Edinburgh at the moment but I'm picking up the hire car tomorrow. I thought maybe I'd make my way up there over the next few days.'

'And you'll be staying with us?' Alice asked, more as a statement than a question.

'Actually, I've already booked a room. A treat to myself, really,' Elle said quickly, hoping she hadn't caused offence. And it wasn't entirely a lie: she hadn't just booked *any* room in *any* place, it was a real life, honest-to-God manor house.

On her bucket list of Scotland, she had wanted more than anything to stay in a castle. Just for one night. Just to say she had. The idea had seen her excitedly scrolling through online booking places in search of castles to stay in, only to discover that her bank account and her dreams were working on two *very* different wavelengths.

Until she discovered Durn House. It took her breath away the moment she spotted the photo of the beautiful manor house lit up in all its elegant, eighteenth-century country-mansion glory.

Much to her relief, Alice hadn't argued and seemed thrilled when Elle told her where she had booked. 'Oh, it's lovely. I've been there often. They do a bonnie high tea.'

So, now, with accommodation booked prior to discovering she had to travel in a completely different direction to where she had intended, she had figure out how best to zigzag her way across the countryside.

*I think we should go and see our plot of land*, Gran piped up.

Elle sighed. This *had* been something Gran had talked about ever since Elle had given her the gift, so it was only fair she make the effort. 'I guess it's as good a place to start as any.'

Their plot was part of a nature reserve located in Appin, which according to Google was a drive of an hour and forty-four minutes. Elle typed in the details of the trip and felt a ripple of excitement run through her.

Tomorrow would be the real start of the adventure. She and Gran had a car and a map, and with only a few exceptions, no timetable. She couldn't wait to get started.

# Nine

Elle came to a stop in front of the compact two-door Fiat and double-checked the number the guy had given her. Sending a doubtful glance at her suitcase, she trudged back to the office.

'Excuse me,' she started, waiting for the bored attendant to glance up from his computer screen. 'I think I have the wrong number. I was supposed to get a Ford Focus, a *four-door* car,' she added pointedly.

'Or similar,' he told her.

'Excuse me?'

'When you booked your car, it says on the contract, *or similar*. We don't know what vehicles we'll have on hand when you get here.'

'But it's tiny.'

'You booked a small vehicle.'

'Yes. But not *that* small.'

The young guy gave a weary sigh and hit a few keys on his computer. 'I can get you a Focus, but it won't be here until tomorrow.'

She sighed. 'No, don't worry about it. I guess I'll have to make do.' Dragging her suitcase back to the car, she walked to the rear of the vehicle and opened the boot. After a few moments of consideration, she wrestled her luggage into the back and winced as she leaned her body weight against it, praying it had shut without breaking anything.

She placed her backpack on the passenger seat before settling into the driver's side, familiarising herself with the instruments before starting the car.

*Seatbelt?* Gran reminded her.

'I have,' Elle said, glancing down at her chest.

*I'd feel safer if I had one on, not that I doubt your driving abilities, darling, but we* are *in a different country.*

Elle glanced at the backpack before leaning across to secure the belt across it.

'Right,' she said, studying the car's navigation system. 'Let's set this baby.'

*Oh, I can't wait to see my plot of land,* Gran enthused. *Which is now your plot of land,* she corrected.

As much as Elle loved the joy her title gift had given Gran, she was now having serious regrets about the purchase. The gift allowed the purchaser to use the title of Lady or Laird with an official certificate and registered plot of land, which could be legally passed down to family members. With a catch in her throat, Elle remembered the day in the solicitor's office where he announced it was now hers.

*Lady Elspeth of Glencoe*, Gran said. *That has a lovely ring to it.*

'Okay, Lady Iona, keep your shirt on. You do remember that we're only talking one square foot of land here, don't you?' Elle warned.

*It's not the size of the land one owns*, Gran replied pompously.

'Okay,' Elle said, with a resigned air. 'Let's go and find this plot.'

The GPS kept her on track with a calm, efficient voice, and once she was out of the city and had the initial few miles under her belt, Elle felt herself relax. She recognised some of the road they had travelled during the bus tour, before the wide freeway eventually changed to a two-way highway as she headed for Appin, just out of Glencoe.

The road wound its way through small villages and roundabouts, through rural areas with sheep and freshly harvested hay bales scattered across the landscape like huge marshmallows. Eventually the farmland gave way to winding lochs and wide-open marshes. The change in scenery was subtle at first, and then all of a sudden, mountains rose from the flat lands—huge, barren-looking mountains that dominated the skyline as far as Elle could see.

Cars were parked along the various narrow pull-off areas, as their owners, scattered across the moorlands, went off to climb and wander around the wild-looking countryside. The scenery was breathtaking. Green valleys ran between massive mountain ranges, and small streams branched out like narrow veins until they merged into wide rivers and then spilled out into large, still lochs. The ground was a patchwork of lush, too-green-to-be-true grass and heather in varying shades of mauve, brown and orange, changing as the cooler weather began to set in.

Elle pulled off to the side of the road whenever she found a safe place to do so, in order to take photos and soak in the majestic views. It was too hard to take it all in as she drove, dodging large coaches and tour-group buses and trying not to run up the back of other rental cars as their drivers veered to unexpected stops to take photos.

*Beautiful, isn't it?* Gran said wistfully.

'It's stunning,' Elle murmured, though there seemed no words powerful enough to truly describe the beauty. 'Is this how you remember it?'

*Oh, aye*, Gran said on a sigh. *It's still the most bonnie sight I've ever seen.*

Elle found it hard to leave the mountains behind—though it seemed one never truly did in Scotland; they seemed to rise up all around the highlands—but as she drove closer to their destination, the road seemed to follow the water. Eventually they arrived at the reserve, and Elle climbed out of the car, grateful to stretch her legs.

'Well, here we are, Gran.'

*Hmm. Somehow I expected it to be . . . bigger.*

'I'm sure it's bigger once you start walking around.'

Elle took her phone out and went to the app that would take them to the coordinates of their plot. They followed a walking trail up a steep incline and along a row of densely planted pine trees. The air was cool and crisp and quiet.

*This is a nice place to own land*, Gran said as they came to a stop on the trail and Elle shuffled around until the compass on her phone was pointing in the right direction.

'We need to go up in there,' Elle said, eyeing the dark forest of trees ahead of them. When they had started out she had passed a few people walking back to the reception office, but she hadn't seen anyone for a while. She was pretty sure there was nothing to be afraid of—it wasn't as though they were going to be attacked by a wolf or a wild bear ... she wasn't actually sure if Scotland even *had* wolves or bears now she came to think of it—but the dark forest ahead of her definitely conjured up images of Little Red Riding Hood, and Elle recalled how *that* story hadn't ended particularly well—especially for the grandmother.

'Ah, actually,' Elle said, turning sideways and taking one step forward into the first row of huge trees just off the track, 'it's saying *this* is your plot. Right here.'

*Here?* Gran said, sounding doubtful.

'Yep. These are the coordinates all right. Right, here,' she said, stepping up to the nearest tree and patting its trunk affectionately. 'One square metre of prime Highlands property with a massive tree on it.'

*Are you sure?*

'Come on, Gran, seriously? Does it matter? It all looks *exactly* the same. There's a whopping big tree planted smack-bang on every inch of this area.' Elle pulled out the little castle figurine she'd bought in an Edinburgh gift shop the day before, and placed it at the foot of the tree. Straightening, she snapped a photo. 'There you go, Lady Iona: your castle,' she said triumphantly, with a flourish of her hand towards the miniature castle nestled in the moss at the foot of the massive pine. It kind of looked like an aerial view of an estate, she thought—if you squinted a little and tilted your head slightly, and used your imagination.

*Thank you, darling. It's perfect*, Gran said, and Elle smiled sadly. She'd never dreamed she would one day be standing here, back when she'd clicked that *buy* button on the title website last Christmas. Yet here she was. Although these titles and land plots were intended as a promotional gimmick, to raise money for conservation of the land, it meant something to both of them. And it was certainly an ingenious way to get people to donate money to a cause.

Elle took a deep breath of the cool, clean air and closed her eyes as she savoured the moment. It was nice to soak up the tranquillity of the forest around her. This time last week she was still in Jessup's Creek. She felt a ripple of the strange mix of disappointment and guilt she had carried the last few days before her departure. Part of her was angry that her parents thought of her trip as unnecessary and wasteful, which made her doubt her decision and also feel a little guilty. It had dampened her excitement in the lead-up to leaving. But damn it, she had a right to make her own choices even if no one else thought they were the right ones. The phone call to tell them she had arrived safely, though, had gone smoothly enough. She'd kept it short, and they had ended the call with,

'Have fun,' so she supposed they had finally come around to accepting her need to fulfil Gran's wishes.

Elle pushed away the seed of doubt that had tried to return. She was here. She was excited and she was going to enjoy this trip no matter what.

⁂

Dunkeld looked like it had jumped out of the pages of a fairy tale. As Elle drove across the narrow stone bridge that led into the main street of the town, she sighed with delight at the white-painted stone buildings and shops lining the road, and the overflowing baskets of brightly coloured flowers hanging from window frames and walls.

The pub she'd booked was just as she'd imagined a Scottish pub would look. The blurb on the booking app said that the Royal Dunkeld was built in 1810 and had once been a coach inn. The grand staircase—another bloody staircase—took her to her room, which looked out onto the main street, where the box of flowers outside the window brightened up the overcast sky.

The late-afternoon air chilled Elle's face as she headed out to explore the village. She reached the end of the main street and came to the beautiful old stone bridge that connected one side of the town to the other across the fast-flowing River Tay. As she headed back she looked for a place to have dinner, and settled on the Atholl Arms Hotel, a pretty, whitewashed building that overlooked the river.

In just about every place she'd eaten so far she had noticed the same dish featured on the menu and had never been game to ask about it, but tonight as her waiter came to take her order, she decided to get adventurous. 'Cullen Skink,' she said, looking up at the young man. 'What *is* it?'

'It's a thick, creamy soup,' he replied in a New Zealand accent. It was so strange to hear an accent that almost felt like home—well, close enough to home—that she felt an instant kinship. 'Made with smoked haddock, potatoes and chives. It's pretty good.'

'Oh, so it's fish,' she said, relieved.

*What did you think it was?* Gran asked, sounding confused.

*I don't know . . . lizard?*

Gran made a startled choking kind of sound and Elle jumped, causing her Kiwi waiter to give her an odd glance.

'It does sound really good, actually. I'll have that, thanks,' she told him quickly, handing back the menu.

*I can't believe you thought the Scots were mad enough to eat lizard*, Gran hooted.

As it turned out, the soup *was* delicious and she walked back to the Royal later that night feeling tired, but happy that she'd survived her first day driving in Scotland.

According to the map, it was only a four-hour drive to Kilmuir, the area of Skye where Stormeil Castle was supposedly located. It still amazed Elle how everything was so close in Scotland. Back home pretty much nowhere was only four hours away. She had once driven to the Sunshine Coast to pick up her sister, doing a thirteen-hour drive in a day.

*We're not heading to Skye yet, are we? We've still got so much more to explore,* Gran piped up.

'I've only booked the stay for sixteen days, Gran. I'm just checking to make sure we're still on track with our time.'

*You can change your flight if you need to. It's not set in stone, is it?*

'Well, it kind of is. I'm not sure changing flights is that easy.'

*We've got plenty of time,* Gran dismissed her.

'I wasn't planning on going to Skye tomorrow, just looking at options.' Elle wasn't in any hurry to get to Skye; the sooner they reached Skye, the sooner they would be at the castle and Gran's trip would come to an end. It was a sobering thought. Would fulfilling Gran's final wish be the end of their time together? There were so many unknowns about this crazy situation. Elle still wasn't entirely sure whether or not she was hallucinating, and she couldn't just ask someone. Perhaps, if this did turn out to be some delusional refusal to let go of her grief, then maybe it was better to just let it all play out and see what happened when it came time to scatter Gran's ashes. Immediately she pushed the thought away. There was a lot to see between now and then, and they still had the visit with the family before they prepared for the final leg of the journey.

'It'll be nice to finally catch up with your family,' Elle said as she got ready for bed, then frowned when there was no reply. 'Gran?'

It wasn't just her imagination—every time something came up about her family, Gran went quiet. 'What's wrong?' Elle tried again, but there was no answer.

She tried to picture what it might have been like for Gran to now return to her family after a lifetime apart. Elle knew there was something in the past that had caused a rift between Gran and her sister—there had to be, because Elle knew how important family was to her grandmother. Growing up, Gran and Pa had been a huge part of her life. They lived only a few streets away, and Elle and her siblings saw their grandparents pretty much every day. Which is why this whole thing with her Scottish family didn't make sense. Gran clearly didn't want to talk about it, but that didn't stop Elle's determination to get to the heart of it.

The next morning, Elle negotiated the narrow winding roads with relative ease, stopping at a few small villages along the way, happily taking photos and poking about in the quaint shops. Pitlochry was nothing short of enchanting with its medieval buildings lining the streets. Elle stopped at a tea house that extended to an art gallery as part of a renovated barn. The owners were an English couple, and Elle talked with them for over an hour about different styles of art and techniques. She purchased a beautiful seascape that she could imagine hanging on her parents' wall and organised to have it shipped home as a gift. She ignored the pricey conversion from pounds to Australian dollars—and the fact that she would most likely make it home before the painting did—and instead felt happy that she had been able to support a local artist.

As she headed back towards the coast, she caught glimpses of ocean before she passed through miles of farmland once again. The ruralness of Scotland, the abundance of agriculture, had surprised her. It almost felt like being back home—except for the accents and the haggis . . . and the bagpipes. She smiled as she mentally ticked off another list item: *Find a Scotsman in a kilt*. She'd passed one earlier in the day, standing on a street corner playing the bagpipes.

She was headed towards Stonehaven and the famous Dunnottar Castle. Set out on a lonely headland, it had featured in just about every Scotland tourist brochure in the lead-up to her trip. As Elle arrived she saw what was becoming a familiar sight at the bigger tourist places—groups of people being herded on and off buses by harried tour guides, barely having any time to wander—and she was again thankful that she had no strict schedule. How much of this beautiful place would she have missed if she only had a few minutes to look around? She had to admit that Gran's insistence about this trip had been a good thing after all.

Parking well away from the tourist coaches, Elle set off on the long winding walk that would take her to the imposing-looking castle in the distance.

The ruins held an atmosphere she couldn't quite describe; history seeped through the cracks in the stone—she could almost feel the castle watching her, daring her to stop and ask it to tell her all the stories it held within its walls. And there would have been many.

High inside some of the dank towers, thick green moss covered the walls. There was nothing of the grandeur this place would once have held. Indeed, as Elle read the tourist plaques describing how the rooms would have looked in their heyday, she found it hard to imagine the timber panelling and plaster that had once covered these rough stone walls, now eroded by time, weather and war.

The views from the remaining windows, however, were breathtaking. Elle stood looking down on craggy cliff faces that dropped away into the ocean below, and out over the sweeping coastline and hills surrounding the headland. Further below the castle were caverns where signs warned of ghostly encounters from past occupants, but all Elle could do was smile. Surely ghosts would be a little too daunted by the number of tourists wandering through the halls of the castle to bother making an appearance nowadays, and she wondered about how Gran was coping.

*I'm having a wonderful time. I've been busy chatting*, Gran piped up on cue.

Elle gave a small, resigned sigh.

*Don't you want to know to whom?* Gran asked and Elle could picture the twinkle in her eye.

'Not really,' Elle said calmly.

*You really aren't much fun, you know*, Gran said with a small huff.

'Gran, I'm still coming to terms with the fact I'm talking to *you*,' she said pointedly.

*Well, I just met a lovely Earl and a very sweet kitchen maid. Did you know that our Mary also visited here?*

Elle laughed. 'It's almost as if we're following in *our Mary's* footsteps. That Queen of Scots sure got around.'

When she headed back to the car, Elle took out her sketchpad and found a place to sit with a view of the castle in the background and fields dotted with huge bales of hay in the foreground. Storm clouds were brewing in the distance behind the castle, and Elle found herself lost in the moment as she captured the scene on paper, her hand skimming across the page in quick movements, her mind oblivious to how much time had passed. When she'd finished, the first drops of rain had begun to fall, forcing her back to the car—the only one remaining in the carpark. She found a small pub room for the night and went to sleep dreaming of windswept castles and the sound of crashing waves below.

# Ten

'So, this was where you grew up?' Elle asked the next day as they drew closer to the small coastal village. It was very beautiful, with miles of farming land overlooking the ocean.

*Yes,* Gran gave a happy sigh. *I had a wonderful childhood here.* Elle heard the smile in her gran's voice and could picture her faraway gaze in those vivid blue eyes.

*Take this next exit,* Gran said as they passed the Portsoy sign, and Elle turned onto a road that took them down a steep hill to a cemetery near the water.

Elle climbed out of the car and looked around, breathing in the salty air. 'Who are we here to see?' she asked, sliding her sunglasses on top of her head to read the names on the closest gravestones. 'Gran?'

Elle let out a frustrated breath, deciding she would just have to wander around until Gran did whatever she wanted to come here to do.

It was a lovely graveyard, as far as graveyards went. Elle walked along a few rows before she stopped in front of a familiar name. MacKenzie. There were in fact quite a few, which wasn't surprising, but seeing a Lachlan and a Malcolm just a few graves over, Elle stepped over to take a closer look. Both men had died before she was born—in the late sixties and early seventies, which fitted the times that Gran's brothers had passed away. She took a deep breath as she realised that these must be Gran's older brothers, the men Elle's two brothers had been named in honour of.

She searched the rest of the names, and when she found Gran's mother she instantly felt a sinking sensation in her stomach. She had never met this woman, buried here for such a long time, and yet Elle felt an instant connection to her. These people were her family. Long gone now, but still connected. After a while, it was clear to Elle that Gran wasn't in a talkative mood, and she headed back to the car, leaving Gran alone to whatever business she wanted to attend to here.

On the walk back Elle frowned as she spotted something familiar sitting on top of a tombstone: a pair of sunglasses that looked just like hers ... Absently, she put her hand to the top of her head and felt nothing. She hadn't realised she'd lost them, and had no idea why they were sitting folded neatly on top of a headstone she wasn't even sure she'd walked past earlier. She glanced around, thinking maybe someone had picked them up and left them in plain sight for her, but there didn't appear to be any other visitors.

'Gran, this is freaking me out,' she murmured, snatching the glasses up and shoving them in her pocket, then glancing down at the gravestone. *Duncan Campbell*, the inscription read. *Dearly loved and missed by his wife, Adelle, and their seven daughters.*

*Seven children he had*, Gran said, sounding sideswiped.

Elle frowned at the name, trying to place it, but came up blank. 'Who was Duncan, Gran? Is he a relative?'

*No. Just someone I once knew.*

The wind picked up and blew across the water, making Elle shiver. 'I'm heading back to the car now, Gran. Alice will be expecting us . . . well, *me*.' Gran didn't reply, and Elle's hands were getting cold. She'd had enough of cemetery exploring for now. What she needed was a loo stop and a hot coffee.

'You have arrived at your destination,' Elle's GPS informed her as she slowed to a stop outside a gorgeous granite house. The whole street was made up of the beautiful stone buildings. Some were grand three-storey masterpieces, others were smaller but still elegant. This one was a quaint two-storey home with bay windows set on either end of the ground floor and what appeared to be loft rooms on the top storey.

'This is it,' Elle said, feeling a sudden attack of nerves. She was about to walk into a house full of complete strangers.

*They're not strangers, darling. They're your family*, Gran said, and Elle heard the slight wobble in her voice.

'I wish you'd been able to come and visit them, Gran.' Elle felt the familiar weight of guilt settle in her stomach once more. 'I'm so sorry I kept putting it off.'

*Enough of that,* Gran said briskly. *I could have come back here whenever I wanted, and I chose not to. We're here now.*

*But too late.* The thought slipped out before Elle could stop it.

*Not for you,* Gran said gently.

Elle climbed out of the car and walked through a small gate into a stunning garden and lawn, along a simple gravel path that took her to the front entrance. Before she was halfway up the path, the front door opened and a woman about her mother's age came out, smiling with her arms wide. Her short grey hair was cut to frame her cheerful face and shaped to taper in at the base of her neck. She was dressed in a cardigan and jeans and wore a pair of fluffy slippers.

'You must be Elspeth,' the woman said in a thick Scottish brogue.

'Yes, I am, but please call me Elle,' she said, smiling, before a gasp of surprise squeaked from her as she was pulled into a tight hug.

'Ah, it's so good to finally meet you. I'm Alice, your, well . . . let's see, your granny was my mum's sister, so your father's my cousin and you'd be my second cousin?'

'Or something like that,' Elle chuckled.

The woman shook her head as she looked at Elle. 'You look so much like the photos of your gran when she was younger, bless her soul. We were so sad to hear of her passing. It hit my mother something fierce.'

Elle kept smiling but was instantly worried for her gran. There were sure to be more than a few painful memories shared, and she wasn't sure if Gran was prepared to hear them.

'Oh, now look at me, standing here yabbering on! Let's get you inside, you must be tired from your long trip.'

Elle didn't get time to reply before she was whisked inside and into a front parlour where a small group were seated on lounge chairs scattered around the room.

'Elspeth, these are my daughters, Grace and Aila. My husband, Peter, and my mother, Moira.' Elle smiled as she moved into the room and was greeted by the welcome party.

Alice's daughters seemed to be around the same age as Elle, both quite tall, with auburn hair. Elle found herself staring; it was like looking in a slightly blurred mirror. Their hair was darker, a reddish brown, as opposed to Elle's distinctive copper colour, but they had the same long, curly locks and the freckles she had always cursed. Grace had an understated elegance about her, while her sister, Aila, seemed more outgoing, dressed in a long skirt, long-sleeved roll-neck top and some awesome chunky Doc Martin boots.

Grace, the elder of the two, had a small child on her lap and as she moved the little girl to her other knee, Elle noticed a large baby bump. The child peered shyly up at Elle with big dark eyes. 'This is Maisie,' Grace said.

'Hello,' Elle said, smiling at the little girl, who snuggled in closer to her mother.

'You're not shy,' Aila, the younger of her new cousins, teased her niece, reaching over to poke her playfully in the ribs. 'You just want your awesome Aunty Aila,' she said, putting out her hands to Maisie. 'Come on, give your ma a break.'

Elle smiled at the exchange and felt a pang of homesickness at the thought of Rose and her own nieces and nephews back home. She loved playing the fun, cool aunt too. Though, she couldn't quite imagine being a mum yet. She was struggling to get her own life together, let alone trying to raise a child as well.

'I love your boots,' Aila said, dragging Elle away from her contemplative thoughts.

'Thanks.' Elle grinned, glancing down to admire her deep-red ankle boots appliqued with flowers and buttons. 'They're new. I have a bit of a boot addiction, actually. I really like yours too,' she added.

'You look so much like Iona,' the older woman said suddenly, her lap covered by a pretty crocheted blanket, drawing Elle's gaze towards her. She seemed a lot older than Gran had been, and Elle saw a walking frame beside the chair. Moira's light grey, almost white, hair was pulled back into a neat bun, and despite her frail appearance her eyes seemed bright and alert.

'That's what I said too, Ma,' Alice said.

'It seems like just yesterday when she waved goodbye at the train station,' the old woman said wistfully.

Elle was distracted as she listened. *Gran? Are you here?*

'I always hoped that she'd come back one day. We left so much unsaid.' Moira's voice faded away before she shook her head sadly. 'And now it's too late.'

'Come on now, love,' Alice said, sitting on the corner of her mother's armchair and wrapping an arm around her. 'Elspeth's come all this way to visit us. We don't want to sit around being all glum now, do we?'

It was hard to know how to reply. On one hand, Elle felt just as sad about Gran not getting back here while she was alive, but on the other, her curiosity was more than a little piqued. Why hadn't Moira ever come to visit Gran? Had there been more to the story? She understood that Gran and Pa had issues with travel and they hadn't always had a great deal of money, but even on their worst days, Elle couldn't imagine *never* seeing any of her siblings again.

Elle half expected Gran to butt in and tell her to stop making a mountain out of a molehill, but there was only silence, which convinced her more than ever that there was something else going on here.

'Will you have a cup of tea?' Alice asked, standing up and heading towards the door.

'That would be great,' Elle said, moving to follow her.

'No, you stay here, take a seat, the girls will give me a hand,' Alice said, waving her over to a chair near Moira.

The room went rather quiet once Alice and the other two left, and Elle smiled a little nervously across at Peter, Alice's husband, who until now had sat quietly in the corner of the room.

'How'd you find the trip?' he asked.

'Oh, great. I followed the coast for most of it, then went inland. We . . . *I* wanted to see as much as I could.'

'Aye, it's a bonnie drive up the coast,' he nodded. 'Finding it all right to drive over here?' he asked.

'I am. Thank goodness.' She smiled. 'It helps that we both drive on the same side of the road.'

'Not like those Americans,' Peter said with a slight grumble.

'It would certainly be tricky remembering which side of the road to use,' she said, more for conversation than the sake of argument.

'It's good to see you again, Iona,' Moira's soft voice floated across the room and Elle looked up swiftly, before realising the woman was talking to *her*.

She swapped a quick glance with Peter, who gave a small smile and slight shake of his head.

'I've missed you,' the older woman continued. 'After all these years . . .' Her voiced faded away momentarily. 'I regret that I didn't stand up to Hamish and Father. I should have let you stay, sister,' she said, so softly that Elle only barely made out the words. Before she could reply Alice bustled back into the room and the moment was gone with a clink of crockery and rattle of bone-china tea cups.

'So, what do you do back home?' Aila asked as Elle took her cup and helped herself to a biscuit.

'I work in a supermarket.' Elle shrugged. 'At least I did until I recently got put off,' she added, before realising she probably shouldn't have started the conversation with the fact she was unemployed. 'What about you?'

'Grace and I have a shop in town. Giftware and the like,' Aila said before taking a bite of her biscuit.

'Oh wow,' Elle enthused. 'That's impressive.' She couldn't imagine being in business with her sister. They would have killed each other by morning tea on the first day. 'How long have you had the shop?'

'Going on two years now,' Grace answered, handing her daughter a treat before reaching for the cup her mother had prepared for her. 'You must pop in and visit when you're in town. We're on the main street—you can't miss us.'

'I'd love to,' Elle replied, then nodded towards Grace's round belly. 'You look like you're going to have your hands full.'

Grace rolled her eyes and grinned. 'Tell me about it. It's been a godsend being my own boss during this pregnancy, though, I can tell you.'

'Your dad mentioned you have siblings?' Alice said when there was a short lull in the conversation.

'Yes, there're four of us. I'm third in line. I have two brothers and a sister.'

'Your dad certainly made up for being an only sibling, then,' Alice said with a chuckle. 'It's a shame Iona only had your father. This family has a habit of breeding like rabbits.'

'Gran loved babies,' Elle agreed. 'I think she'd have had a houseful if she and Pa had been able to.' It had been something she'd heard Gran tell her mother once, after her third great-grandchild was born. *Babes are the most precious gift of all. I often wish I'd been able to have a houseful.*

'Ah well, sometimes it's just not meant to be. Do any of your brothers and sisters have children of their own?' Alice asked.

'My eldest brother and my sister both have kids. Lachlan has two boys, and Lauren has a daughter.' She took out her phone and shared some photos.

'Oh, what bonnie wee cherubs they are,' Alice crooned, before passing the phone around to the others.

The afternoon flew by as they happily chatted, and Elle couldn't believe it when she glanced at her phone and saw the time.

'I guess I'd better get checked into my room before it gets too late,' she finally said when there was a break in conversation.

'Will you come back for dinner? We can't have you sitting up there in that big old place all alone on your first night in town,' Alice said, though it was clear that she wasn't exactly asking; it was more of a statement.

Elle liked Alice's bossy mothering. It reminded her of Gran. It was so different to her own mother. Caroline simply wasn't the mother-earth type. Elle frowned at the thought. She wasn't exactly a snow queen either—she melted when her grandkids were around, and Elle remembered cuddles and goodnight kisses when she was growing up. It was just that lately there didn't seem to be anything more than disappointment and frustration between them. She missed the way they used to be.

Elle tried to hide her sudden sadness behind a smile. 'That would be lovely, thank you.'

# Eleven

Elle caught her breath as she drove slowly through the gates of Durn House. It was at the end of the road, within walking distance of Alice's house, and it looked every bit the fairy-tale manor in reality as it did in the website photos.

As she walked through the large timber door, she found herself in a lounge area. Artwork hung on the walls and soft lamp lighting gave the place a warm, homely glow. Elle stopped and soaked in her surroundings. She could almost feel the house breathing—there was an energy about it. Old houses had a special quality that she hadn't felt in their younger cousins back home. Maybe they absorbed all that history, and that was the reason they just *felt* alive. A young man dressed in a suit appeared from another room, and smiled as he greeted her.

'Welcome to Durn House.'

'Hello, I've got a booking for a couple of nights. It's under Kinnaird,' Elle said, returning his smile.

'I'm Kurt. Here, let me take your luggage,' he said, effortlessly lifting her suitcase. 'Come with me and I'll get you checked in.'

She waited while Kurt took a key from a wall behind the bar and then she followed him to a beautiful wide staircase that swept upwards. When they reached the top floor, he opened a door that led through a narrow hallway to the end room, and unlocked the door. The Dunbar Room, the plaque on the door read as she walked into the suite.

'Oh, it's beautiful,' she gasped.

Kurt put her suitcase down and smiled benevolently. 'This is my favourite room too.'

After he left, Elle put her handbag on the bedside table and then crossed the room to open a set of French doors, gasping in surprise at the huge bathroom revealed behind them. In one corner was a massive high-sided claw-foot antique bathtub, and in the other, in stark contrast, was a modern shower stall. The mix of old and new gave the room a subtle kind of luxury that had Elle shaking her head in disbelief. It was all so . . . fancy. She had never stayed anywhere like this before—an authentic manor house in the Scottish Highlands.

Closing the door, she turned and gazed at the huge queen-size bed in the centre of the room with its imposing timber bedhead. High up in the slanted attic-style roof was a tall window that allowed the last rays of afternoon sunshine to filter into the room. She kicked her shoes off and sighed in relief as her feet touched the soft carpet.

*Now, this is the kind of place fit for a Lady*, Gran said.

'Where have you been?' Elle asked as she lay down on the bed and closed her eyes.

*I always loved this old place. Of course, when I was a girl, it didn't look like this. It was a private home back then and quite rundown.*

Elle let silence settle between them for a few moments before she asked, 'Gran, what happened between you and Moira?'

*The past is the past. No point getting into all that now.*

'I thought the past was exactly why we were here,' Elle countered, her eyes still closed. 'You want to go back to Stormeil, and it hasn't existed for hundreds of years.'

*That's different.*

'Maybe I can help make it right.' She waited, but there was no reply. Gran's ability to come and go as she pleased was proving quite annoying, to say the least. Opening her eyes, Elle glanced at the clock and realised she had to get moving. The family mystery would have to wait for now, but she wasn't going to let it go without a fight.

There was a distinct nip in the air as Elle walked the few minutes down the road for dinner with her family. She breathed deeply and filled her lungs with the clean autumn scents around her and felt a strangely peaceful sensation settle within her. She couldn't wait to explore the seaside town tomorrow.

Alice welcomed her as profusely as the first time they met, and Elle felt instantly at home as she was again ushered into the sitting room.

'Ma was a bit tired from today's excitement, so I gave her dinner early and put her to bed,' Alice said, before introducing Elle to some new faces. There was Grace's husband, Tyler, who was tall and lean and quiet, and another of her father's cousins, Eunice, and her husband, Ted, who had travelled from nearby Cullen. Peter and Ted had both been fishermen before they retired and had similar burly builds and friendly, outgoing natures. Tyler, on the other hand, seemed more reserved, and Elle learned that he was a professor at the University of Aberdeen.

Elle nervously handed over the souvenir gifts she had brought from Sydney and was relieved when no one seemed overly offended by anything; though she wished she'd found somewhere to buy a bottle of wine to share. No one seemed at all worried that she hadn't contributed to the dinner, though, and as they squeezed in extra chairs around the dining table, Elle's eyes widened at the amount of food being brought out. Glasses were filled and Peter made a toast welcoming Elle to the family.

'*Slàinte mhath*,' he said, raising his glass, and memories of hearing Gran say *slan-ge-var* at Christmas filled her with a bittersweet warmth.

'This looks amazing,' Elle said, eyeing the dishes. Only some of them looked familiar, but whatever they were, they smelled divine.

'This is smoked haddock kedgeree,' Alice said, seeing Elle hesitate as she tried to decide what to put on her plate. It looked like a risotto and had a very strong smell of smoked fish. 'That's black pudding, and there's Balmoral chicken, which is chicken breast stuffed with haggis and has a Glayva sauce. And those are haggis bon bons.' She pointed to another plate with little round deep-fried breadcrumbed croquettes, which Elle piled onto her plate and then, taking advice from Alice, added a dollop of creamy sauce that had a strong scent of whisky.

The meal was a happily chaotic affair, and even though Elle struggled at times to understand so many beautifully lilting Scottish accents, she felt completely at ease, as though she'd been part of the family all her life.

'That was amazing, Alice. Thank you so much,' she said, sitting back in her chair with an empty plate in front of her.

'I hope you left some room because there's dessert to come yet.'

Elle bit back a groan as a large trifle dish came out. Cranachan, she was told, was made with toasted oats, thick cream and raspberries—and it was absolutely delicious. The clootie dumpling, though, was very familiar.

'Gran used to make this,' Elle said, surprised when she spotted it.

'And probably used the same recipe,' Alice said with a fond smile. 'This came from my great-grandmother.'

*My grandmother*, Gran said softly. The mention of someone familiar and obviously very important was enough to bring Gran back.

Elle had spent countless hours in Gran's kitchen watching her mix the flour, cinnamon, spices, grated apple, suet and sugar before wrapping it all in a cloth and boiling it in a huge pot, like a dumpling.

As Elle took a spoonful, she savoured the familiar taste, closing her eyes briefly as a flood of childhood memories washed over her. It tasted just like Gran's. Elle found it hard to swallow as her throat tightened at the thought that she would never have another of Gran's clootie dumplings again.

*You have the recipe—you know how to make it*, Gran said gently.

*It won't be the same.*

*It will be, over time. I always thought of my grandmother every time I cooked it for you, just as she would have thought of her grandmother*, she said. *That's why we pass things down, our stories and our recipes; it's how we keep those we love close to us.*

'Are you all right, Elle?' Aila asked quietly from beside her.

Elle opened her eyes and cleared her throat quickly. 'Sorry ... I was just thinking about Gran,' she said, blinking quickly before summoning a bright smile.

Aila put a hand on her arm and gave a reassuring squeeze, and Elle was grateful the moment seemed to have gone unnoticed by everyone else. Later, despite the protests of others not to worry about helping, Elle escaped to the kitchen, carrying a stack of plates and putting them on the counter near the sink next to Alice.

'Oh, I'm sorry about all that. It must be a wee bit overwhelming for you, but once my sister Eunice heard you were coming for dinner, there was no stopping her. She had an appointment earlier when you arrived, so she's a bit annoyed that I got to meet you first,' Alice chuckled.

'That's all right. I'm used to big family dinners.' Only, they weren't usually quite that noisy. Things were more reserved around the Kinnaird table, with more discussion about current news topics and politics, and less simple jovial conversation.

'We're just so excited to have you here,' Alice said, wrapping an arm around Elle's shoulder as she walked past.

Something warm and fuzzy unfolded inside Elle's chest at the spontaneous words, and she cleared her throat again. 'I'm excited to be here too.'

Aila came into the kitchen carrying more plates and together they started to pack the dishwasher, working in an amiable silence.

'You and your gran were close, I take it?' Alice asked after a while.

Elle nodded. 'I lived with her when I came back from Sydney.'

'You were flatmates? With your gran?' Aila said with a surprised chuckle.

Elle grinned. 'We had a great time.'

'I can't imagine living with Granny,' Aila said, eyeing Elle doubtfully.

'Elspeth's gran was a bit younger than yours.' Alice shrugged.

'What did you do if you wanted to bring a fella home or something?' Aila asked, wiggling her eyebrows.

'Aila!' her mother scolded.

'What? I'm only asking.'

Elle laughed and shook her head. 'Sadly that never really came up. Let's just say there's a bit of an eligible-bachelor drought in Jessup's Creek.'

'Oh, I hear you. We've got the same problem around here.'

'Go on with you,' Alice tutted. 'There're plenty of nice boys in town.'

'What good's a *nice* boy, Ma?' Aila said drolly and winked at Elle.

'Aila Fitzgibbon, you are not too old to get a skelp, young lady.'

'How long are you staying, then?' Aila asked, wisely changing the subject.

'I'm not sure. I thought I'd play it by ear for a while and see how I go. I can always find a job if I decide to stay longer than I was expecting and run out of money.' She grinned.

'That's smart.' Aila nodded.

'I didn't mention that to my mum, though. She thinks sixteen days is plenty of time here.'

Aila smiled. 'That's smart too, I'd say.'

'Alice, can I ask you something about Moira? Earlier she said something—she thought I was Gran, and she was talking about something in their past.'

She saw Alice's cheery smile falter slightly, and her eyes lost their crinkle. 'She's been diagnosed with Alzheimer's. She has her good days, though—like today. This is the best I've seen her in a long while. She's been looking forward to meeting you. But there're other days when she's confused, mostly when she gets tired, and relives the old days.'

'Do you know what happened between the two of them?' Elle asked, deciding to risk it.

Alice looked at her quickly before starting to wipe down the bench. 'Not really . . . Occasionally she comes out with strange things—bits and pieces—and I'm fairly sure she's talking about Iona, but she doesn't talk about their past whenever I've tried to bring it up on a good day.'

'It's sad that they never had a chance to fix things between them.'

'Yes, it is,' Alice agreed with a brief, cheerless smile. 'Still. Here we are, a new generation, and I for one am very glad that I've had a chance to meet one of our Australian cousins.'

'Me too.' Elle smiled back. Their meeting had been so much better than she'd anticipated. She hadn't expected to fit in with a bunch of strangers so easily—and that's exactly what had happened. She felt comfortable around them, like she'd known them a lot longer than a few hours.

But now more than ever, Elle knew that whatever had driven the two older sisters apart all those years ago needed to be resolved. She wasn't sure for whose benefit exactly. Maybe Gran needed some closure. Maybe that was the whole reason behind her lingering around and her insistence to be brought back here. Or maybe it was for Moira. Or maybe it was just because Elle hated an unsolved mystery and couldn't let it go. Who knew, but one thing was certain, she needed to get to the bottom of it.

The following morning was crisp as Elle stepped outside the hotel after breakfast. The air smelled clean and fresh. She spent some time taking photos of the stone bridge just outside the gates of Durn House, along with the pretty stream, and though she was itching to sit and draw, she knew it was time to call home.

Glancing at her watch, she dug out her phone. Both her parents should be home from work by now.

'Hi, Dad,' she said when he answered, and felt a little tug of homesickness at the familiar voice.

'Carol!' her father called out after barely greeting his daughter. 'It's Elle on the phone.'

She waited until she heard the rustle of movement and could picture her parents huddled over the phone as they searched for the button to put her on speaker.

'Are you there?' her father asked.

'I'm here, Dad.' Elle smiled. She really did miss them. 'Hi, Mum.'

'Hello, how are you?'

'Fine. It's going great. I met Alice and Peter and their family last night.'

'How was it?' her mother asked.

'It was . . . really nice.' She thought back to the warm welcome she'd been given. 'They said to say hello to you both.'

'That's nice,' her mother said, before launching into a debrief of her earlier conversation with Lauren about what Lucy had been up to. Her older sister and mother had always had a lot in common, and their daily phone calls were the highlight of her mother's day.

'So, what are your plans for today?' her father asked once her mother paused.

'I've just finished breakfast and I'm about to go poke about around Portsoy. It's absolutely beautiful here,' she said, staring up at the manor house before her.

'Seems like you're enjoying yourself.'

'I'm having the best time, Dad.'

'It certainly sounds like it.'

'Actually, there was something I wanted to ask,' she said, feeling a little as though she were going behind Gran's back. 'Do you remember Gran ever mentioning if anything happened between her and the rest of the family over here? Something that upset her?'

'Why's that? Did someone say something?' her mother asked, and Elle knew from her voice she was most likely frowning.

'No,' Elle said hastily. 'It's just a feeling I have, that there was something keeping Gran from coming back. Her older sister Moira lives with Alice and Peter, she thought I was Gran for a minute, but she's not well . . . I just get the feeling that something happened.'

'I can't recall Mum ever saying anything,' her dad said. 'Although, she didn't really talk much about family.'

'Don't you find that a bit strange?' Elle had never asked Gran much about her childhood either, because, well . . . she was her gran and Elle had never really stopped to think much about what her life might have been like. To Elle, she was simply *Gran*.

'As a kid, I remember Dad saying Mum would get upset if she talked about Scotland because she missed her family,' Alister said. 'I guess I never really pressed her on the past because of that. But she never mentioned any falling-out with anyone or anything like that.'

'Having met them, I just don't understand the distance thing between Gran and her sister.'

'Darling, not all families are close. It was a long time ago. She had a new life in Australia and had obviously drifted apart from her older siblings. Besides, she was a teenager when she left Scotland. They'd probably become strangers to her,' Caroline said matter-of-factly.

'I guess so,' Elle eventually said, although somehow it just felt . . . wrong.

'I hope you're keeping track of your spending,' her mother cautioned. 'It's easy to get carried away.'

Elle bit back a familiar flare of irritation and forced herself to answer calmly. 'I'm being careful, Mum. I better go. Just wanted to check in and let you know that I met the cousins.'

'It was good to hear from you, love,' her father said.

'Be careful,' her mother added firmly.

'I will. Love you,' she said before ending the call and letting out an unsatisfied breath. Maybe her parents didn't think there was anything strange about Gran and her family, but Elle was still sure there was more to the story.

# Twelve

Elle decided to leave the car behind and walk into town. The morning was cool but not too cold, and the village was barely ten minutes by foot. She enjoyed exploring all the twisting laneways as Gran chatted about the people who had once lived in the stone cottages that led to the seventeenth-century harbour.

Old stone warehouses surrounded the walled harbour, and the water was so beautifully clear that she could see the sandy bottom. Elle snapped photos of the whole scene, focusing especially on a little red-and-white fishing boat moored there, then walked around to the small headland. She sat on a bench overlooking the sea on the other side of the harbour and took out her sketchpad, then quickly lost herself in capturing the view before her.

A large wire sculpture of a dolphin had been erected on the point, and beside it stood the remains of what was generally deemed to be an old salt house, though its exact origins were still debated by the locals. The old stone wall with a glassless window stood defiantly on the headland, refusing to give up its perfect position overlooking the ocean before it, and Elle vowed to come back at sunset when she knew the sinking sun would look spectacular caught through the framed window.

Packing her sketchpad away in her oversized handbag, Elle headed up the hill towards the main street and her cousins' shop, passing quaint stone cottages with low rock walls and pretty gardens full of bright flowers, then past an old pub that had *Established in 1825* written on a sign above the doorway.

Walking along the main street, Elle was almost surprised to see traffic once more. As she left the postcard-perfect harbour, which felt as though it had been left standing in the seventeenth century, it was strange to step back into the present day once more. She found the shop, Made With Love, and smiled as she walked inside. Everything about it made her happy, from the deep-teal-painted front and the double glass window with a beautiful display of artwork and draped throw rugs, to the delicate scent of candles wafting through the air as she opened the front door.

Aila broke out into a wide smile as she looked up from the counter and spotted Elle. 'What are you doing out and about so early?' she said.

Elle smiled. 'I thought I'd come down and say hello. What a beautiful shop,' she said, her gaze wandering about the room. On one wall was a framed sketch of a lighthouse, and Elle moved closer to look. 'Is this a local artist?' she asked, inspecting the artwork. 'Look at the detail,' she almost whispered.

'Well, yes, actually—Grace drew it.'

'Grace?' Elle snapped her head around to look at Aila. '*Our* Grace?'

Aila smiled. 'Yes, our Grace. Before she got married she had a lot of her work in art galleries in London and a couple over in Paris.'

Another piece of the puzzle fell into place. Elle had obviously been kidnapped from the Scottish side of the family and taken away to live in Australia! 'What happened?'

'I came home for Christmas one year and fell in love with my high-school sweetheart,' Grace said, coming out from the back of the store to stop in front of the framed drawing on the wall. 'I left London and moved back home to get married.' She shrugged.

Elle stared at her older cousin for a few shocked moments before turning back to the lighthouse. 'It's beautiful.'

'Thank you,' Grace said, her smile widening. Elle saw her gaze drop to the handbag on Elle's shoulder. 'Do you sketch too?'

Elle blinked. 'Oh. No, not really. I mean, I don't do it professionally or anything . . . just for fun.'

'Can I see?' Grace held one long, elegant hand out and Elle felt a blush begin to creep up her neck. That was the other thing she'd always hated about her complexion—the slightest hint of embarrassment managed to light her face up like Rudolph's nose.

At Grace's expectant look, Elle reluctantly withdrew her sketchpad and handed it over. 'They're nowhere as good as yours,' she stammered. Oh dear God, a woman who'd had her art hung in famous galleries around the world was about to look at Elle's untrained attempt at drawing. This was beyond mortifying.

As Grace silently flipped through the pages, Aila stuck her head over her older sister's shoulder to inspect them as well.

'What art school did you go to?' Grace asked after a few moments.

'Art school?' Elle practically squeaked. 'Oh, I didn't do art school . . . I've just done a few classes at the craft centre back home. Like I said, I just fiddle around with it.'

'You've never been classically trained?' Grace asked, lifting one perfectly sculpted eyebrow.

'No,' Elle said uncertainly, feeling as though she were back in maths class in high school giving the wrong answer to a question.

The sisters swapped a telling look before returning to flip through the rest of the pages.

'These are really good,' Grace said, observing Elle with the kind of intensity a scientist might scrutinise some foreign species they had never come across before.

'They're *really* good,' Aila added enthusiastically.

'For someone who has never studied art, you have a remarkable perception and natural eye for capturing the subject matter.'

'That means she's really jealous that she had to study art for years and you can pick up a pencil and just do it,' Aila added with a wink.

'Oh no, I don't think you've got anything to be jealous about. Seriously, I just love drawing.'

'My sister is an annoying brat, don't listen to her. I *am* actually a bit jealous, though,' Grace said with a grin.

'Have you sold any of your sketches?' Aila asked, heading back to the counter.

'Sold?' Elle stammered. 'Ah, no. I've done a couple for gifts for friends and stuff,' she said hesitantly, picturing the mural she'd painted on Rose's bedroom wall for Lilly a few years ago, and the brightly coloured butterflies and fairies she'd had framed for her niece's birthdays. 'But I don't actually do anything with my drawings.'

'Would you be interested in putting a couple of these up in here? We can put them on commission. This piece is the last one we've got for sale, and I always have people coming in to look for new art.'

'Really?' Elle asked, eyeing the woman doubtfully. This had to be a joke.

'We can give it a go,' Grace said with a shrug.

'Sure . . . I guess so.' This was crazy. People were going to be looking at her drawings on display?

'Brilliant,' Grace said, turning away to head out the back of the shop with Elle's sketchpad. 'Come and pick the ones you'd like to use.'

For the next half-hour the women went through Elle's sketches, carefully making their selections.

'I really like this one,' Aila said, holding up a drawing of two children skipping along a path—Elle had sketched it while sitting in Princes Street Gardens in Edinburgh. Elle had loved the way she'd managed to capture the laughter on their little faces and the carefree joy of kids just being kids.

'And I like these two,' Grace said, pointing to one of a streetscape along the Royal Mile with the cobbled streets and shop windows, and one Elle had drawn of the harbour just this morning.

'Good,' Grace said with a definitive nod. 'If it's okay with you, I can get these framed by a framer I use a few doors down and we'll add the cost into the price we'll sell it for. Then we can work on a commission basis.'

'Um . . . I guess so,' Elle stammered, still shocked that they were actually discussing the possibility of selling her artwork. 'Whatever you think works best.'

'Let's see how they go and we can re-evaluate if need be later.'

The phone rang and Aila went to answer it, then stuck her head around the corner to say it was her mum and that Elle was invited to dinner tonight.

'Oh, I don't want to intrude,' Elle said.

'I'm sorry, did you think it was a question?' She grinned. 'There's no point arguing, Mum's expecting you.'

'Okay,' Elle laughed. 'Then I'd love to.'

Elle left the shop a little later, wondering what on earth had just happened.

※

'Can you believe it, Gran? My sketches are for sale.'

Elle's pencil skimmed across the page in light strokes, outlining the stone bridge in front of her and the little creek that ran underneath it. The ferns and trees and undergrowth that grew along the banks made it look like a scene from a storybook, and she could almost picture being lost in the deep, dark forest beyond.

*So they should be*, Gran said with a note of pride. *They deserve to be up where everyone can see them.*

Elle studied the page before her critically, feeling like something was missing, before smiling as she sketched in a tiny fairy fluttering around the ferns and another at the top of the page, closer and in more detail.

*They're in your blood*, Gran said with a wistfulness Elle had only ever heard when she told Elle stories of Scotland. *You see them too.*

'See them? No,' Elle said. 'But I feel like this is exactly the kind of place you would find them if they were around.'

*Look harder*, Gran urged, and Elle frowned as she looked up from her picture and into the forest grove below.

Surely she wasn't seriously looking for fairies?

*Wheesht*, Gran hushed. *Stop thinking and just look.*

Elle's gaze roamed from the ferns to the water, watching as it bubbled and trickled its way beneath the bridge, making rapids over the rocks that rose in the shallow bits, while on the edges it seemed to almost stop and sit still. A flitter caught her eye in the trees, and she searched for something moving, unable to spot what it was. Another flutter, and a splash drew her attention, her gaze passing over butterflies bobbing in the ferns and grass as she wondered what the hell she was supposed to be looking for. Her eyes went back to the butterflies briefly, before noting that they were darting rather than fluttering, and the closer she looked the more the shape of their wings seemed to change. Elle stared as the blue—now almost translucent—wings made a graceful dive into a flower, before soaring high up into the foliage above. She gasped. This was no butterfly. This was . . . She wasn't sure *what* it was, but it definitely *wasn't* a butterfly.

*See?* Gran said smugly. *You just have to stop thinking so much, and look at what's around you.*

Elle glanced back down at her drawing and felt her heart race. What she'd just seen was eerily similar to what she'd been drawing. She wasn't sure what to make of that, so she did what any rational person in the situation would do—she packed up her belongings and scampered, without a backwards glance, to her room to get ready for dinner.

---

'So, what are your plans for the next few days?' Aila asked that night over dinner with her parents and Elle.

'I really want to go to the Culloden battlefield and Loch Ness,' Elle said, mentally ticking off two more items from the list.

'Aye, Culloden is a grand place,' Peter said, nodding. 'Lots of history there. But Loch Ness . . .' He gave an unimpressed growl that Elle had learned was a typical Scots thing. 'It's just a tourist gimmick.'

'Well, it's not like I believe Nessie's really there, but I guess I can't really come all the way to Scotland and *not* visit Loch Ness.' Elle grinned.

'I never said she wasn't there,' he corrected, keeping a straight face. 'I'm just saying, they've managed to commercialise it for the tourists.'

'Do you want some company?' Aila asked, reaching for her glass of wine.

'You want to come along?' Elle asked, surprised by the offer.

'Sure. I haven't been to Culloden since high school. It'll be like a mini road trip,' she said brightly.

'Are you sure you won't mind going to all the touristy places?'

'Nah, it'll be fun,' she assured Elle.

'Okay, then.' Elle beamed, and renewed excitement began to bubble inside her at the idea.

'I'll pick you up tomorrow morning,' Aila said. 'That's settled.'

Elle smiled all the way back to her room at Durn House. It would be fun to spend some time with her cousin and have someone to talk to—other than Gran. The past few days Gran had been a lot quieter than usual, and Elle knew it had to be something about being back in her hometown that kept Gran away; she only wished she knew what it was. Elle felt a lingering sadness whenever she thought about her gran's reticence, but she wasn't sure how to fix it, or even if she could.

Time flew by the next day as the two girls chatted and laughed and drove. Elle felt a kinship with her cousin she had never experienced with her sister. Elle and Aila shared a lot of things: their sense of humour, the way they liked to dress, their complexion, and more importantly, they were both living in the shadow of an over-achieving older sister who seemed to have her life completely together.

'I love Grace,' Aila said, between licks of her ice-cream cone as they strolled along the picturesque banks of the canal in Fort Augustus, watching the boats wait patiently to progress through the sequence of locks. 'Really, I do, but there are times when I just want to scream: "I'm not you! I have my own life!"' she said, and Elle heard the frustration beneath the light-hearted remark. 'I get it,' she went on. 'She worked hard and she had this big career. She was a somebody in the art world, she followed her dream and made it, but I'm not like her. I don't crave something more than what I have. Owning my own business was *my* dream, but it's like, if it's not going to become some global chain store, then how are you happy enough to just be a gift store in Portsoy?'

Elle found herself momentarily surprised by her cousin's remarks. They were so *familiar*. 'I understand exactly,' she finally said. 'It's the same thing with my family.'

'I mean, what's so bad with running a gift store in Portsoy?' Aila asked, widening her eyes and shaking her head at the stupidity of the question.

'Nothing at all,' Elle smiled.

'Right?'

Elle finished her ice cream quickly so she could take some photos of the town, with its giant tank-like water steps rising in tiers through the centre of town. 'You really wouldn't want to be in a hurry,' Elle murmured as they watched the yacht stranded behind the gates of the lock as it waited for the one in front to fill with water so it could make its painfully slow progress towards the open water ahead, and then continue its journey along the river.

The canals had been created to connect the east and west coasts of Scotland and to save ships the long and dangerous trip around the top of the country to get from one side to the other. As interesting as the locks were, Elle was more captivated by the town itself. It was just so pretty.

Later, when they reached the battlefield at Culloden, a totally different mood descended. Walking out onto the moors, where such a horrific battle had once taken place—a battle that changed the Highlands way of life forever after—had a very sobering effect on Elle.

Culloden had played a significant part in the *Outlander* series, and Elle had been drawn to its history through the characters' eyes, but standing here now, and looking across the huge expanse of open ground, it suddenly became far more personal. They stopped to read details of the battle from the information boards scattered about the walk, and viewed a 360-degree battle-immersion film where the sights and sounds of battle blasted around the small auditorium.

This was more than a gimmicky *Outlander* tourist site. Much, much more.

'The battle lasted barely an hour and within that time, thirteen hundred men were killed,' the recorded voice in the visitor centre had informed them gravely. Right here on this open moor, Elle thought with an unexpected rush of emotion. It seemed impossible to comprehend that such an atrocity had taken place in what was now such a tranquil spot. There was a stillness about the place. Not silence, but sound felt muted somehow. She gave a shiver as she thought of the bloodshed and terror she would have been looking upon from this very spot, had she stood here more than two hundred and seventy years before.

*I should have liked to have visited before, when I was alive.* Gran's voice appeared as a sad whisper in her ear. *There's only sadness here. So many lost, sad souls trapped within this place. This is not a place for me now.*

*Gran?* Elle asked, but Gran had already gone.

They left Culloden, Gran's words still ringing in Elle's ears, and continued on. Elle fell in love with the little village of Drumnadrochit and visited a Loch Ness Monster exhibition—Aila insisted they take the obligatory photo with a statue of Nessie, which allowed Elle to tick off number thirteen on the bucket list—before they stopped and explored Urquhart Castle on their way home.

As they stood at the top of the main tower, overlooking the beauty of Loch Ness below, Elle briefly closed her eyes. She felt the rough stone of the castle beneath her hands, her imagination trying to capture how it must have all looked in its prime, and piecing together the history they had heard about in the auditorium before they reached the castle itself. Elle still struggled to imagine the brutality that seemed to go hand in hand with the history of these places—the wars, the raids, the slaughter. Strangely, though, other than at the battlefield earlier, she hadn't felt any real prickling of anything sinister. It all felt so calm and peaceful. Maybe bad vibes washed away after a while; after all, they were only a fraction of time in a very long history. Maybe that old saying, 'Time heals all wounds' was true—even for castles.

'What do you think happened between our grandmothers?' Elle asked Aila after a while.

'I dunno,' Aila replied with a small shrug, dragging her attention away from a pair of Italian backpackers, who were snapping photos nearby. 'For a long time I dinna ken we even had any relations in Australia. She never talked about your gran.'

'It doesn't make any sense. Both sides of the family seem big on the whole "family is everything" vibe,' Elle said, using her fingers to punctuate. 'What would cause two sisters to have such a huge falling-out?'

'Did your granny not give you any clue?'

'She won't say a word,' Elle said with a frustrated shake of her head.

'You mean, *didn't* say a word?' Aila said, giving her an odd look.

Elle's gaze flittered away uncomfortably. 'Yes, of course that's what I meant,' she said quickly with a little laugh.

'There are times when Granny goes off in her own little world,' Aila said after a few minutes. 'It does no good to try to correct her when she calls me by other people's names or starts talking to me about people she knew from the old days, so I just let her go. Sometimes you can piece together things. There was this one time, though, that she got talking about my granddad. She was really worked up about it. I have no idea who she thought I was, but it must have been someone she was very close to.'

'What was she worked up about?'

'She kept saying she was sorry and started crying something terrible, before she said something about "the poor wee bairn".'

'What do you think she was talking about?'

'No idea.' Aila shrugged. 'I tried to ask her about it but she wouldn't say. Sometimes she just kind of slips in and out of the moment. I don't think she realises she does it.' They stood in silence for a while before Aila eventually said, 'So, you're really going to go looking for this ruined castle, then?' She leaned back against the stone wall to look at her cousin thoughtfully.

'Among other things,' Elle hedged. 'But yeah, it was important to Gran to find Stormeil. The story's been a big part of my life—Gran always talked about it.'

'Granny read me *Hansel and Gretel* as a bairn too, but I don't particularly feel a need to go traipsing about the woods looking for a witch's house.'

Elle grinned. 'It was just our thing, I guess.'

'Well, I think you're crazy, but full points for dedication.' Aila smiled before turning her attention back to the two backpackers, both handsome men, who were now looking over at them. 'I don't know about you, but I've suddenly got a hankering for a bit of Italian,' she murmured.

Before Elle could reply, Aila was striking up a conversation with the men, and then just minutes later all four of them were seated inside the castle's cafe drinking coffee.

Lorenzo and Andrea were far too good-looking for their own good, and Elle suspected the pair had left a string of broken hearts across the United Kingdom. They'd been backpacking for the past three months, and Elle found their stories fascinating.

'So, you just walk . . . everywhere?' Elle asked.

'*Sì*,' the dark-headed, sleepy-eyed Lorenzo replied, smiling. 'We walk. People offer us rides too,' he added, 'sometimes.'

'But what if you don't get a lift? You just have to walk? Along these narrow busy roads?'

'We get lots of rides,' Andrea answered simply with a shrug and a sexy lopsided grin that made Elle feel like a flustered thirteen-year-old.

'If you're heading north, we can give you a lift?' Aila said. She sent Elle a quick glance that practically screamed, *We. Are. So. In*, before her optimistic smile faltered.

'Unfortunately, we are heading south, and we have a ride. But thank you. We're just waiting for them to finish looking at the castle . . . Ah, here they come now,' Andrea said, waving a hand above his head.

Aila and Elle watched as two equally attractive men approached the table, both dressed in tight jeans and wearing T-shirts with *EDINBURGH* stamped across the front.

Elle bit back a small giggle as she saw their two Italian studs send the two newcomers the same sexy grin that had mesmerised her and Aila earlier.

'Are you ready to go?' one asked in what Elle thought might be a Ukrainian accent, as the four men swapped lingering glances.

After they waved off their coffee mates, the two women burst into fits of giggles.

'I must be getting rusty or something. I swear my radar is usually spot-on with guys,' Aila said, shaking her head. 'Boy, did I read that wrong.'

'Oh well, it's probably for the best.' Elle grinned. 'I try not to date men who are prettier than me.' Which sent them both into hysterical laughter once more.

'But how hot were they?' Aila said, almost wistfully as the cousins walked arm in arm back to the car.

Never in a million years would Elle have approached a pair of strangers like that. But Aila was a force to be reckoned with. She was so outgoing and confident, and why wouldn't she be? She was beautiful. Her bubbly, outgoing personality was infectious, drawing people to her like a moth to light and Elle had simply tagged along for the ride. But oh, what a ride. She couldn't remember when she'd last had this much fun.

Later that evening, tucked up in bed, Elle's thoughts once again turned to her gran.

'Gran?' she said into the darkness. 'Are you okay? What happened at Culloden today?'

*I'm okay, dear. I'm sorry, I didn't mean to make you worry.*

'Is that what you are, Gran? Trapped here?' The thought had been playing on her mind.

*No, I don't think so. At least not in the same way the men I saw today were. That was different. They were so bereft . . . so sorrowful. It was truly awful, Elspeth. But that's not how I feel. I'm here because I want to be. There is something that is holding me here, though, but I'm not quite sure what it is.*

'Is it me? Am I holding you here?' What if her grief was somehow causing Gran to stay? What if Gran ended up like those lost souls she spoke about at Culloden? Elle couldn't bear to think of Gran wandering around miserable and lonely forever.

*No, my darling, it's not you. I'm glad you're enjoying your time with Aila—she's a feisty one, that girl. I like her. She'll be good for you.*

'Gran, please tell me what happened with Moira,' Elle said, feeling suddenly frustrated by the lingering feeling that persisted. 'Maybe that's got something to do with why you're here?'

Her question was greeted only with silence.

Elle let out a frustrated growl and stamped her foot like a two-year-old throwing a tantrum. 'This disappearing-whenever-you-don't-want-to-talk thing is getting really old, Gran,' she said to the roof. Then hoped no one was passing outside the door who might wonder who she was yelling at.

Why would Gran not have wanted to be part of these people's lives? They were her family. It just didn't make any sense.

# Thirteen

The next day, Aila had to work, but Alice and Peter happily offered to take Elle for a drive to do some more sightseeing.

She hadn't imagined having local tour guides when she'd arrived in Portsoy. It was supposed to be a quick visit—more like an ambassador for the Australian branch of the family, before heading off to tick off the remaining items on the list—but instead Elle was thoroughly enjoying herself and had extended her stay. So, for now, the rest of the list had been put on hold.

'I'm sorry we couldn't take the whole day to show you more of the countryside,' Alice said as they arrived back at her house after a morning spent visiting the picture-perfect village of Fordyce, as well as the nearby settlements of Sandend and Portknockie. 'But I didn't like to ask my neighbour to sit with Mum for too long,' she apologised.

'No, that's fine. I really appreciate you taking the time to show me around. I had a lovely morning.'

'Oh, that's good. We wanted to do some touristy things with you while you were here, but we're a bit limited with Mum. She can't travel very long in a car anymore.'

'It must be hard,' Elle sympathised.

'Oh, don't get me wrong—I love having her living here with us, I honestly couldn't bear the thought of leaving her in a nursing home, but her care is becoming more full-time nowadays. Poor darling. But Elle, would you mind sitting in here with her, while I get lunch?' Alice asked once they went inside.

'Of course.' Elle smiled as she sat across from the big, comfy recliner where the older woman lay.

Moira smiled as she watched Elle thoughtfully. 'Did you have a good day?' she asked so softly that Elle had to concentrate to untangle her accent.

'I did. There's so many beautiful places around here.'

'Aye, there are,' Moira nodded faintly.

She seemed a lot more focused today than Elle had seen her before, and so, biting the corner of lip for a moment, Elle decided to take the risk and ask the question that was driving her more than a little crazy.

'Moira, I hope you don't mind me asking, but I was wondering if you could tell me a little bit about my gran . . . about Iona?' she asked in a rush.

Moira didn't seem surprised by the question, she simply smiled faintly before asking, 'What would you like to know?'

'Everything,' Elle said, relieved that the older woman seemed happy to talk. 'What was she like as a little girl?'

'Ah,' Moira said with a sigh. 'She was a bonnie wee thing. She was the youngest—a wee surprise for my ma and dad,' she said with a twinkle in her eye. 'She was like a doll, so tiny and with those big blue eyes—just like yours. She was much younger than the rest of us, so she was spoilt rotten by everyone. She managed to twist all the menfolk around her little finger—our father and my brothers, they all adored her. I did too. And then, once Ma passed . . .' Her words seemed to peter out. 'I became more of a mother to her than a sister.'

'What happened, Moira?' Elle asked gently. 'Why did she leave here and never come back?' She wondered if Gran would be upset with her prying.

For a long while Moira didn't speak, and Elle thought maybe she'd drifted off into that confused state once more. She hesitated before bringing up the name—she didn't know how Moira would react, but she was desperate not to lose the story. 'Moira, who was Duncan Campbell?' She wasn't sure, but she suspected he somehow fitted into the story.

Immediately a change came over the older woman's face and she fixed her watery eyes upon Elle firmly. 'You are not to go near that Duncan Campbell, do you hear me, Iona?'

For a brief moment disappointment flared—she'd lost Moira to her memories again, but then she realised, Moira thought Elle was Gran. Elle was in two minds as to whether she should correct her and leave her to rest, or go along with her confusion and see what happened. Before she could make a decision either way, Moira continued.

'You don't need to look so shocked—I know all about him. Lucky for you, Father doesn't, though.' She tsked with a slight shake of her head. 'You're fifteen years old, Iona. He's nineteen—a grown man almost.'

So, Gran had a boyfriend not long before she'd left Scotland. A spark of excitement ignited inside Elle. 'Is that why Iona didn't want to move to Australia? She didn't want to leave Duncan?' Elle tried gently to bring Moira back to the present, but suddenly the woman's expression melted from the stern disapproval of moments before to something that looked almost like heartbreak.

'My poor wee sister,' she said reaching out a hand to touch Elle's face softly. 'So much pain, so much loss.'

*Leave her be.* Gran's voice gave Elle a start.

*Gran, please tell me what happened. What's she talking about?*

'I warned you that Duncan Campbell was no good, didn't I?' Moira said, her voice shaking, cutting into her conversation with Gran. 'He left you to die in that horrible place.'

'What horrible place?' Elle felt herself going rigid and dread began to pool inside her stomach.

'To Inverness,' Moira said, frowning. 'We didn't know where you were. Then Reverend Tulmore came and got Father to take him to the hospital. You'd lost so much blood. They thought you wouldn't make it . . . and the babe . . .' Moira squeezed her eyes shut tightly and shook her head slowly. 'That poor wee soul.'

*Oh my God . . . Gran, what happened to you?*

'Father was so distraught . . .'

Moira's voice wavered, and Elle almost held her breath as she listened to the story being dragged out piece by disjointed piece.

*I never wanted to hurt my family*, Gran said, sounding distressed. *I wanted to keep my baby.*

*Your baby? Dad?* Elle asked, confused. Then she remembered that Moira was talking about Iona when she was only fifteen . . .

*You lost a baby when you were fifteen?* Elle felt a heaviness in her heart as the truth settled sickly inside. *You had an abortion?* She said as it finally dawned on her what Moira was saying. *All on your own?* Elle couldn't even begin to imagine how terrifying the ordeal must have been.

'The whole town was talking,' Moira said. 'Father had no choice but to leave. You have no idea how much I missed him.' She placed a frail hand over her mouth as her lips trembled. 'I lost you both.'

*It wasn't my fault*, Gran protested weakly. *I begged her to let me stay here with her, but she wouldn't.*

'Why wouldn't you let Iona stay?'

Moira continued talking as though she still thought Elle was Iona. 'I wished I'd not spoken so harshly to you before you left. That I'd maybe tried a little harder to convince Hamish to take you in. But it wouldn't have been any use. You wouldn't have had a happy life here if you'd stayed. All that talk . . . everyone knew what had happened. No, it was best that you went somewhere and made a fresh start.'

*She didn't try at all. Reverend Tulmore had scared everyone half to death*, Gran said in a scathing tone that Elle had rarely heard.

*Who was Reverend Tulmore?* Elle asked.

*Our minister. We were devout Christians—our dad, especially so, after our mother's death. The church had a lot more influence back then, and the Reverend was a malicious man. When I was found unconscious, with only a train stub in my pocket from Portsoy, the hospital called the Reverend to see if he could help identify me. He did. He even went on to make an example of me, and gave a sermon about the evils of the flesh as a warning to other young girls.*

Of all the things Elle had imagined the sisters' fight to have been about—this hadn't been one of them. She tried to imagine what her gran, as a fifteen-year-old, would have gone through at the time. Her family, her friends, her whole town looking down on her for having her reputation ruined and no one to turn to.

*Oh Gran*, she said silently, feeling her heart break as it all sank in.

Moira reached out a thin hand and placed it on Elle's arm. 'Tell me you had a good life?' she said, almost pleading. 'I prayed for you every day and wished I'd been able to do something different.'

Elle sighed. Had anyone cared that a young woman had endured the loss of a baby amid God only knew what trauma from some backyard abortionist? Elle felt sick trying to even picture a fifteen-year-old girl going through all that. And then the humiliation of the whole town knowing about it? The local minister using her as a public example? What kind of barbaric society had this been back then? It was a relief that Gran had been taken away from here, Elle thought, fury burning inside her at the treatment her grandmother had suffered at the hands of people who should have cared for her—not shamed her. Suddenly Elle realised that maybe this was the reason Gran had been so protective of Lilly when she'd fallen pregnant and been kicked out of home. Maybe Gran was remembering how it felt to be abandoned by those she loved.

But as she looked at the frail old woman in the recliner opposite her now, some of the fire went out. It was so long ago, and time had all but erased the horrific event from local memory, not to mention from the family. It was obvious this had become a dirty secret everyone had chosen to bury, and yet Elle couldn't help but feel angry.

*I don't want to see her suffering like this*, Gran said sadly. *It all happened far too long ago. Tell her I was happy, Elspeth. Put her out of her misery.*

'I had a wonderful life,' Elle said, holding Moira's pale, watery gaze. 'I found a man who adored me, and I had a family who loved and cherished me every day.' Elle's throat tightened as she fought to hold back her tears. She'd done what Gran had asked, but she refused to let go of her anger completely, adding with a touch of steel to her tone, 'Leaving was the best thing I ever did.'

Moira nodded slowly and leaned her head back against the headrest, closing her eyes.

'Here we are, then,' Alice said, coming back into the room with a tray. 'Oh. Mum's asleep,' she added with a small sigh. 'She must have had a big morning.' Alice smiled at Elle, setting the tray of food on the table. 'Never mind, I'll heat her soup back up when she wakes again, and we'll have ours.' She placed a bowl of soup in front of Elle. Although it smelled delicious, Elle had lost her appetite. Her thoughts were still on the terrible tale Moira had told her. Poor, poor Gran. She forced herself to eat, though, grateful that Alice had gone to the trouble to make her lunch, but she only listened to the conversation with half an ear as she pondered everything she had just learned. Now, finally, things were beginning to make sense.

For one, she knew that Gran had suffered ongoing medical problems and had a hysterectomy shortly after she gave birth to Alister, putting an end to her hopes of having any more children. She knew through snippets of conversation over the years that it had taken a long time for her grandparents to have her father, making them a lot older than most of their generation to bear children, and Gran had a number of miscarriages before finally being able to deliver a healthy baby. To Elle it seemed likely that the abortion in Gran's younger years had caused lasting damage. She wondered if Gran had ever told Pa about it? She suspected she hadn't, considering how hard it had been to get to the truth even now.

Elle was still angry at the woman sleeping so soundly across the room. Maybe it was because she was the only one of that generation left to take her anger out on, and maybe it wasn't fair, but Elle couldn't help how she felt. How could Moira and the rest of the family stand by and allow people to crucify a young girl—their own daughter and sister?

After lunch, Elle pled a headache, which wasn't altogether a lie, and headed back to her hotel room. She thought she had been ready to uncover the truth behind whatever Gran had been keeping from her, but she hadn't been expecting this.

'Gran?' she asked a little tentatively as she lay on her bed. She wasn't sure what all the silence meant, but she knew it wasn't good. There was a heaviness in her heart. 'I'm so sorry you went through all that.' Hot tears dribbled down her cheeks as the enormity of the whole thing came crashing down on her. 'You must have been so frightened.'

*It was all a long time ago. It's forgotten now*, a soft voice floated across to her.

'How did you carry all that around alone for so long?'

*We all live with our sins and secrets, darling.*

'But you were just a child.'

*I was old enough to know what I was doing*, she said a little dryly, before giving a sad sigh. *I thought I was in love. I thought I was going to have a life with him.*

'Did . . . did Duncan *make* you have the abortion?' Elle asked, reluctant to drag up the past but needing to talk about it now that it had been revealed. She had so many questions and desperately wanted to understand it all.

*We were both scared. Both so young. When I discovered I was pregnant, I wasn't terribly worried at first. I was scared of telling my father, of course, but I just assumed that Duncan and I would marry and nothing more would come of it . . . But Duncan didn't want to get married.*

Elle frowned a little at this news.

*Once I realised he didn't love me as much as I thought he had, I panicked. An unwed mother back then came with a huge stigma. I was terrified of telling my father I was pregnant and all alone. When Duncan told me he knew a place that could take care of our situation, I went along with it. I really didn't see that I had much of a choice. But it all went wrong. There were complications. It was horrible.* Gran's voice cracked a little.

After a pause, she seemed to have regathered herself and she sounded a little more in control again. *I think it really scared Duncan—he thought I was going to die. I was still in love with him. I thought he might come to love me as I loved him, but then Father announced that we were leaving. I begged Moira to let me live with her—despite everything, I still loved Duncan very much and I couldn't bear to leave him.*

'And she wouldn't let you stay,' Elle finished, feeling angry again. 'What about your brothers? Wouldn't they have let you stay with them?'

*They had their own wives and families—and enough mouths to feed as it was.* Gran sighed. *I was angry at her for a long time. I took my disappointment out on Moira the most because she'd been more of a mother than a sister to me and I felt as though she'd abandoned me. Then as the years went on, it felt like the past was haunting me, shadowing everything I touched. I held on to my anger because it was easier than giving in to my grief. I thought God was punishing me each time I lost a baby, and I believed that I deserved it. When your father was born, I thought maybe I was finally forgiven for my sins, but he was to be our only child. I stopped being angry at Moira years ago—many, many years ago—but I could never bring myself to face her again. I could never come back here. Too much had been said that could never be taken back, and I guess part of me always felt guilty about that baby.*

'You were just a child yourself back then, Gran.'

*But if I hadn't been so self-obsessed and blinded by love . . . I always regretted giving that baby up so thoughtlessly.*

'Oh Gran,' Elle sighed. She could imagine how difficult it must have been to look back on her past as an adult—older and wiser and regretting the decisions she'd made. It made sense now why she'd been so quiet since returning to Portsoy. Elle would never have come here if she'd realised how many painful memories were attached to this place. But then, if she hadn't come here she would have never met her relatives and found some of her own missing pieces.

She eventually drifted off to sleep and the throb in her head eased, but it wasn't a peaceful sleep. She dreamed of a young girl tearfully watching the shores of her homeland fade from sight as she leaned on the railing of a large ship, longing for a love who had abandoned her and a family she would never live to see again.

# Fourteen

The Portsoy Ice Cream shop had been talked about in the Fitzgibbon household since the day Elle arrived, and she decided that today was the day to see what all the fuss was about. A long counter filled with vibrant colours and more flavours than she could process swarmed before her. Choose a flavour, the woman behind the counter had said. How on earth did anyone actually do that? Fudgey Wudgey, Raspberry and White Chocolate Shortcake, Cotton Candy, Lotus Biscoff, Chocolate Ginger, Ferrero Rocher, the list was endless. She ended up with Fudgey Wudgey because, well, it was kind of intriguing, and she topped it with Lotus Biscoff because she had no idea what that even was—YOLO and all that.

She looked up at a knock on the window across from her and saw Aila waving, moments before she entered the store and sat down at the table. 'So? Was I right? The best ice cream in the world?'

'I have to say, that was a big call to make and I was sceptical,' Elle admitted, spooning the creamy dessert into her mouth. 'However, upon reflection, I think I have to agree with you.'

'Told you.' Aila grinned, before leaving her seat to order a coffee and her own ice cream and returning to the table. 'I'm glad I bumped into you, actually, I was coming to see you later. I'm picking you up tonight.'

'To go where?' Elle asked, lifting an eyebrow.

'Out,' Aila answered firmly. 'It's time you experienced the nightlife in Portsoy.'

Elle smiled at her cousin's dry expression. She could well imagine if Aila were to visit her in Jessup's Creek, a night out on the town would probably be very similar. There were limited places to go—the pub and the other pub and the Ex-Services club, or maybe the Chinese restaurant.

'Can't wait,' Elle said, and she meant it. She really hadn't gone anywhere at night since she'd arrived in Scotland, and with Aila in charge, she knew it would be a night to remember.

※

Elle pulled on her going-out jeans—they had embroidered pockets and had cost almost a fortnight's wages—and teamed them with her blue faux-snakeskin ankle boots and a mustard-coloured high-neck fitted jumper.

The band was loud and the crowd was surprisingly large for a small pub. Elle followed Aila through the old tavern towards a table of four other people, who looked up expectantly as Aila waved hello.

'Elle, this is Joe, Sabrina, Andrew and Steven.'

A chorus of hellos followed as Elle's eyes swept across the faces before her. The three men all had an outdoorsy look about them—possibly farmers, she thought absently, noticing their hands looked tough and cracked and not at all like they belonged in an office. They were dressed in jeans and long-sleeved shirts—not that different to how the men back home dressed when they went out to the pub. The only thing missing was an Akubra hat.

Sabrina had long, straight, shiny black hair and eyelashes so luscious they had to be fake. She was dressed in tight black pants and a loose green jumper that was saved from looking casual by the gold jewellery she wore, adding a very chic touch to the outfit. For a moment, Elle felt a little plain and tried not to squirm. She'd always admired women who could apply make-up with artist-like skill, but even with the help of multiple YouTube tutorials, Elle could never manage to pull off the Kardashian style, no matter how hard she tried.

As they settled with beers in front of them, gradually the awkwardness of introductions warmed into genuine conversation and soon Elle found herself laughing along with the others. The noise of the pub around them meant that Elle had to concentrate extra hard to understand the accents, but she found herself having a lot of fun even when she had to ask Aila to translate for her.

It turned out she had been right in her assumption that the men were farmers, which made her smile. It seemed there was a lot that connected the small community where she'd grown up with this one across the globe.

Throughout the evening Elle tried to unobtrusively work out the group's dynamics. Joe and Sabrina were clearly a couple, but Elle had a feeling there was something under the surface between her cousin and the other two men. Andrew seemed to hang on Aila's every word and was the first one to stand and get her another drink whenever she placed an empty glass on the table before her. He was like a faithful puppy, the way he gazed adoringly at her when she spoke—a tall, lanky, brown-haired puppy. But then there was Steven. He was stocky and muscular with sandy hair and Elle caught him watching Aila across the table with a lazy probing look that every now and again her cousin would catch and hold. They were only fleeting glances, but Elle swore she could almost see sparks.

'So, what do you think of the place, Elle?' Joe asked during a break in the band's set, meaning conversation could be spoken, not shouted.

'I love it. It's a great little town.'

A chorus of scoffs followed her statement, but she knew that Aila at least was only going through the motions. Deep down Elle knew her cousin loved Portsoy, but she got it: your hometown was supposed to be a bit of an embarrassment. Small towns were somewhere young people couldn't wait to leave as soon as possible. Often it wasn't until you left that you realised how much you appreciated the place. Like Elle had.

## Take Me Home

Sydney had been exciting and new for the first few months, there were so many shops and galleries and things to do—so much that it had often taken her all day to decide where to go. There was a lot to be said for limited choice; it was easier to decide what to do with yourself.

'I can't wait to leave,' Sabrina said, reaching for her drink, the clink of her bangles sounding like a fairy chime.

'Some of us don't have the option,' Joe said tersely from beside her.

'Some of us could do whatever they wanted if they could only stand up to their father,' she retorted, and her scathing tone shocked the rest of them into an awkward silence.

'So, you all know each other from school?' Elle asked cheerfully as the couple across from her stared daggers at one another.

'Yep. We go way back. Don't we, Aila,' Steven said.

Interesting, Elle thought as she watched her cousin's gaze flit anywhere but in Steven's direction. 'Sure do,' she said.

'I still remember you with your little pigtails and freckles, arms crossed and staring down the teacher on the first day of kindergarten,' Steven continued.

'A bit of a rebel, huh?' Elle asked, hardly surprised.

'I wasn't ready to get out of the sandpit,' she said defensively, but a smile tugged at her lips as she looked up at Steven.

'I remember you beating up Toby McFlounder for stealing Andrew's hat,' Sabrina added, seemingly recovered from her earlier mood.

Andrew squirmed awkwardly in his chair, and Elle instantly felt sorry for him. 'I had the situation under control.'

'Of course you did,' Sabrina said with a noticeable eye roll.

'He was a bully,' Aila said, and her gaze seemed to soften as she looked across at Andrew and grinned. 'At the time, I was trying to impress you.'

'It worked,' Andrew chuckled.

'Half the class fell in love with you at that moment,' Steven drawled, and Elle saw her cousin's gaze shoot across to his in alarm. 'The other half was too scared to ever talk to you after that.'

'Ha!' Joe scoffed. 'Which half were you in, Steven?'

Steven didn't bother answering, but his slow smile made Elle glance across to Aila, and she found her unflappable cousin blushing.

The night eventually drew to a reluctant close, with everyone other than Elle needing to be up early the next day for work, and they said their goodbyes and parted ways.

It was a lovely clear night as the two girls walked home, and Elle breathed the cold air in deeply.

'So, what's the deal with you and Steven?' Elle asked after a few minutes.

'There's no deal. We're all old school friends.'

'Uh-huh,' Elle said, trying to keep a straight face.

'It's true.'

'If you say so . . . although I have to tell you I didn't feel an "old friends" vibe at all.'

'He's just like that. A big flirt—Christ, he's slept with everything that moves in this town.'

'Oh, so he's the man-whore type?' Elle nodded. 'I know that type well enough, from back home.'

Aila stopped and stared at her for a moment before laughing. 'Man whore,' she repeated, laughing. 'Yep, I think that's *exactly* what he is. Why is it that guys who go and spread their wild oats are treated like some kind of hero, but when women do it, we're just slutty?' Aila said after they'd walked a few moments in silence.

Elle's thoughts strayed momentarily to Duncan Campbell. He had got off scot-free, was able to continue living his life here while Gran was all but chased out of town. Some things, it seemed, never changed.

'I don't know. Maybe they feel a need to keep us in our place otherwise we'll figure out we don't have to put up with a dud root.' Elle shrugged, sending her cousin once more into a fit of giggles.

'Oh my God, where do you come up with this stuff?'

'Well, it's true,' Elle said. 'Look at our grandmothers' generation—they were expected to follow all these society rules, and when they didn't they got punished for it. But what happens to the men involved? They didn't get exported out of the damn country like some kind of criminal.' The words tripped out of her mouth and she wondered if she sounded as tipsy as she felt.

'What are you talking about?' Aila asked, frowning.

'Nothing,' Elle sighed. Clearly Gran's story was still fresh in her mind despite the beers clouding everything else. For a moment she wanted to tell Aila the whole story, but since Gran had basically taken the incident to her grave, it felt wrong. After all, even Elle wasn't supposed to know about it; only, she'd been pushy and uncovered the truth anyway.

'What about you?' Aila asked. 'How many broken-hearted Aussie men did you leave behind to come over here?'

Elle felt a slow smile spread across her face at her cousin's question. 'None,' she said.

'Oh come on—there must be someone?'

'No, not really,' Elle said casually. 'I mean, I dated when I first moved to Sydney—met a few nice guys, but there was no one serious. And then when I moved back home—well, I really wasn't lying when I said there was a man drought. Just about everyone I went to school with moved away years ago and the ones who were left are all married or still single for a reason,' she added pointedly.

'Maybe you've been saving yourself for a sexy Scotsman. A bit of a holiday fling?' Aila said, wiggling her eyebrows comically.

'You never know,' Elle grinned. They continued walking a little longer before Elle said, 'You know Andrew is in love with you, don't you?'

'Yes,' Aila sighed, burying her hands deeper into her jacket pockets as they walked.

'How do you feel about that?' Elle prompted.

'I don't know . . . it's complicated,' Aila said somewhat irritably. Like having a decent guy in love with her, hanging off her every word, was somehow a bad thing.

'I mean, he's great. We've gone out a few times, like, on dates and stuff. He wants us to be more,' she said with a sigh.

'But you don't feel the same way?'

'It's not that I don't think I could come to have feelings for him,' she admitted slowly, 'but it's just . . . I don't know.

Everything was fine until Steven came home,' she finished with a shake of her head.

'Ah,' Elle suddenly understood. 'So, you've always had a thing for Steven, but he left.'

'I guess. I wouldn't call it a thing exactly. We always rubbed each other the wrong way when we were kids, you know? I guess there was this chemistry between us, and as kids we used to fight all the time. It wasn't until our final year at school that I realised we were fighting because there was an attraction neither of us knew what to do with,' she said quietly. 'Then he left town and I thought that was that. But now he's back and I don't know what to think.'

'Has he asked you out . . . since he's been back?'

Aila glanced at her sideways before looking away. 'Not exactly a date. He came around to my place a week or so ago.'

'Oh,' Elle said.

'Yeah. Oh. It was more of a booty-call kind of thing.'

'And?'

'And nothing. That was it. He didn't call, I hadn't seen him since, until tonight. I have no idea what he's thinking. He's still sending me all these sexy vibes that I have no idea how to interpret and he's making me crazy. So, yeah, welcome to my life.'

'Wow. This is so much more interesting than my life at the moment.'

'Shut up,' she said, giving a reluctant smile and lightly pushing Elle with her shoulder as they neared Aila's front door.

'It's true.'

'Yeah, yeah, whatever.'

Aila's cottage was as perfect as anything Elle had ever imagined and she was glad her cousin had talked her into staying the night. Before they went to bed they had a cup of hot chocolate and Elle happily listened to Aila tell stories about her schoolyard antics while steering decidedly clear of the Aila–Steven–Andrew love-triangle dilemma. Still very tipsy, Elle went to bed musing about how everyone had their own issues to deal with, and feeling somewhat better that clearly she wasn't the only one dealing with a complicated and frustrating life at the moment.

She hadn't expected to feel so at home here. She thought she would miss Jessup's Creek more than she did, and it was a surprise to realise that she wasn't homesick . . . at all. Of course, she had only been away a little over a week, so maybe there just hadn't been enough time to *get* homesick, but still, she couldn't deny she felt a kind of kindred connection to the place. When she eventually drifted off to sleep, it was with a soft smile at Aila's gentle snores from down the hall.

Elle had just a few days before she was due to check out of Durn House, and she realised she felt more than a little sad about the prospect. She'd fallen in love with the grand house and would miss it when she left. She had explored more of the area, feeling confident enough to drive herself around finding places to stop and draw.

Today, despite the grey, overcast sky that seemed to alternate between drizzle and heavy showers, she wanted to go in search of the Findlater Castle ruins, just out of town. She thought about putting the trip off in case tomorrow was brighter, but she knew that if she did, something else would come up and she might never get there.

Following the signs, Elle pulled the car to a stop in an open paddock masquerading as a carpark next to a farmhouse. She found it hard not to feel as though she were trespassing when she visited a lot of the touristy places in the area. Most of them were on private property—like this one, where the walking track was between fields of freshly ploughed farmland. The dirt track she followed seemed to go for miles, but with the air smelling fresh after the last shower of rain, and the view so beautiful, she couldn't complain. Eventually she came to a clifftop and an information board about the castle, which seemed to sprout from the sides of a rugged-looking headland below.

She could see a track—which looked better suited to billy goats than humans—that ran around and through the ruins below, but because of the wet grass and the fact the track hugged the edge of a fifty-foot drop down a cliff face, she decided not to tempt fate by heading down there alone. She could picture all too easily a rescue team having to retrieve her body by helicopter from the scene after she plummeted to her death. She was okay with her decision after that, and settled in to sketch the ruins instead.

Elle briefly thought about her sketches in their beautiful new frames on the wall of Made With Love, and felt the familiar flutter of anxiety at the idea of people looking at them. There were times she had allowed herself to imagine how it would feel if she actually sold them, but then she quickly shut the thought down. It was silly to get her hopes up. Why would someone want to pay good money—and she'd actually baulked at the price Grace had put on them—for an artist who had never even gone to art school?

No, it was better to forget they were there and just do what she loved to do—draw.

*We used to come and play around here as children*, Gran said, making Elle jump as she sat looking out at the water and the grey horizon.

'Down there?' Elle asked, shocked as she looked again at the precarious path with no safety rails and the gaping black holes where earth had begun to fall in through the rock structure, causing deep, seemingly bottomless shafts.

*Children have no fear*, Gran answered dryly.

'Oh my God.' There was no way she could imagine children playing in such a dangerous place. The thought made her feel very old suddenly. And like a big chicken. 'I can't believe it's almost time to leave. It's funny—I hadn't been excited at all about this part, and now I don't want to go.'

*Yes, it has a way of stealing your heart.*

'Is there anywhere you'd like to go before we leave?' Elle asked curiously.

*No. I don't need to revisit anything here. But there* is *something I'd like you to do for me, if you can.*

'Of course, anything.'

*I need to make peace with everything, once and for all. I need to forgive my sister.*

'What do you want me to do?' Elle asked.

*Tell her that I forgive her.*

'I'm sure she knows that, Gran.'

*I want you to tell her.*

'Okay,' Elle said, hearing the growing frustration in Gran's voice. 'But Gran. She's not always *here*,' Elle stressed. 'She might not remember we already spoke the other day. It may not do any good.'

*It will. It's something that I need to do.*

When Elle reached the car, she unloaded her bag of supplies into the back and climbed into the driver's seat. She started the engine and put her hands in front of the heater, and once she could feel her fingers again, she headed back into town to Alice's house.

'I was hoping we'd get to catch up with you today,' Alice said, hugging Elle and leading the way inside.

Elle accepted the offer of coffee and was grateful for the fire that had been lit in the front room. Moira sat in her usual spot, tucked beneath her knitted blanket, eyes closed as she tapped her fingers to a song that apparently only she could hear. It wasn't looking promising for a conversation this deep today, Elle mused as she gingerly took a seat beside the older woman, smiling as Moira opened her eyes and saw her.

'Hello, Moira. It's Elle. Sorry, I didn't mean to wake you.'

'I wasn't sleeping, dear,' she said, and her voice was barely more than a whisper.

'I'm leaving in a few days, so I wanted to make sure I came to say goodbye in case I didn't see you again before I left.'

'Leaving?'

'Yes, I'm off to see a bit more of Scotland before I head home to Australia.' She hesitated before continuing. 'Gran wanted me to bring her back to Scotland after she passed . . . to take her up to Stormeil. Do you remember that story?'

'Aye. Our grandmother used to tell us.'

'Yes,' Elle smiled, remembering how Gran used to talk about her own grandmother. 'She loved that story. So, she made me promise to take her there.'

'Yes . . . Father took her to see it once. Thick as thieves, those two. She was his little shadow.'

'Moira, I hope this doesn't sound strange, but Gran, *Iona*,' she corrected, hoping Moira stayed with her a bit longer until she got through this, 'wanted you to know that she forgave you. That she's sorry you two weren't able to fix things before she passed. It was important to her that you know that.'

For a moment Moira stared at her, then her eyes widened slightly as she stared at a point somewhere over Elle's shoulder. 'Iona?'

The note of hopeful yet shocked surprise gave Elle goosebumps, and she turned to follow Moira's gaze, but the room was empty. Feeling silly, Elle gave herself a mental shake.

'Moira, did you hear what I said?' she asked gently, but the older woman continued to stare at some fixed point in the distance, and Elle began to worry.

As Alice came back into the room, Elle sent her an alarmed look. 'Alice, we were just talking about Gran and her . . .' Elle gestured towards Moira, who sat staring sightlessly across the room.

'Oh, don't fret, love,' Alice said as she set the tray down and came across to put her hand on her mother's arm. 'She's all right, aren't you, darling. She does this sometimes.' Alice looked up at Elle with a quick smile.

*I know how you must have missed Father*, Elle heard Gran say softly, and Moira leaned forward slightly in her chair. *I didn't mean to make him leave. You need to understand that. I never meant to tear our family apart.*

Elle was thinking of the best way to relay Gran's words to her sister, when Moira slowly shook her head. 'I know, dear,' she whispered, as a tear fell from her eye.

'You know what, Ma?' Alice asked gently.

Elle frowned a little as she watched on. Could Moira hear Gran? Surely not.

'I should have been a better sister. I should have stood up for you and I didn't. I allowed them to shame you and drive you away.'

*None of that matters now. I'm home*, Gran said.

'Home where you belong,' Moira added with a sad smile and closed her eyes.

*Home where I belong*, Gran echoed softly.

Alice let out a long sigh as she took her hand off her mother's arm. 'She fades in and out like this a lot more often these days. Having conversations with herself and talking to people who aren't here anymore.' Alice straightened up to return to the tray she'd brought in earlier. 'Sometimes I wonder . . .'

'Wonder what?' Elle asked when Alice let her thoughts trail off.

'Oh, it's silly, really, but my mother said she had a gift—that she could talk to the dead.' She shrugged, but Elle could only stare at her.

Alice glanced up and must have caught Elle's shocked expression, because she quickly amended: 'I don't know if she really could. I mean, she only told me a few years ago and I didn't really believe her . . . at first,' she finished with a slight frown. 'But occasionally, like today, well . . . it makes you wonder. She definitely seems to be having a one-sided conversation. Of course, it could just be part of the dementia process.'

Elle now looked back to Moira. Could she hear voices the way Elle had been hearing Gran?

'How long has she been hearing voices?' Elle asked, hoping she sounded politely interested and not as desperate as she was feeling.

'She said it had been most of her life.' Alice handed Elle a cup. 'Actually, there had been those stories about some of the family having "gifts", being able to predict things and the like, so maybe there's some truth in it. I'm old enough to know there're certain things in life that can't be explained by science, so who knows?'

All those times they joked about Aunty Morag slamming doors and Gran talking to herself . . . Could it be that Gran and Moira shared a special gift? Could *she* have it too?

Elle wanted to ask more questions, but for the remainder of the visit Gran was silent and Moira continued to sleep peacefully in her chair, so there was no opportunity to dig deeper before she had to leave. All the while, however, questions raced through Elle's mind. What if making peace was the thing holding Gran back and now she'd found it, there was nothing keeping her here? Wouldn't she say goodbye before she left, though? What if it didn't work that way—what if she was already gone?

※

*Thank you, my darling*, Gran said later that night as Elle climbed into bed.

She breathed a sigh of relief. 'Did it help, Gran?'

*Yes. I believe it did.*

'But you're still here?'

*Yes.*

'So, fixing things with Moira wasn't the thing keeping you around?'

*Apparently not.*

Elle was glad the sisters had made things right between them, and while she didn't want Gran to be stuck in some kind of limbo, she wasn't ready to say goodbye. Their holiday wasn't done yet and Elle desperately wanted Gran to still be around when they found Stormeil Castle.

※

When the final morning came, the farewells were much more painful than Elle could have imagined.

'If you need *anything*, anything at all, you call us,' Alice instructed through glistening eyes.

'I will. Thank you so much for everything.'

'You're family,' Alice said simply. 'Haste ye back.'

They hugged tightly once more before Elle moved on to the others. When she reached Aila, she was at a loss to find the words she wanted to say. How did you tell someone you'd just met, that you felt as though they were somehow your missing twin?

'I'm a little bit jealous that I'm not going along on this crazy adventure with you,' Aila said, and wiped her eyes quickly. 'You make sure you keep in touch.'

'I will,' Elle said, hugging her. 'I'll check in tonight when I get to where I'm staying.'

'Make sure you do,' Alice said, waving as Elle climbed into the car.

It wasn't easy to leave the little town she had come to love. As she drove past the Portsoy sign, she wiped her eyes and took a deep breath. For the first time since she had arrived in Scotland, she wasn't excited about moving on. But slowly, her tears dried and the countryside began to captivate her once more, and the spark of excitement soon reignited.

Elle followed the same route she and Aila had driven a few days earlier, and she smiled as she recalled how much fun they'd had. Her whole trip to get across to the Isle of Skye would only take two-and-a-half hours, so she had plenty of time to stop and visit Eilean Donan Castle on the way.

As she walked across the bridge that led to the castle—once almost completely destroyed by the English during one of the earlier Jacobite risings, and rebuilt to its former glory in the early nineteen hundreds—she smiled when she saw a pair of young men approach another couple of young female tourists taking photos of each other and strike up conversation. Oh, how she missed having Aila beside her right now. She'd made everything so much more fun. Elle fought back a wave of something that felt like homesickness, which she told herself was ridiculous because she had only just discovered Portsoy and her relations, and she hadn't known either long enough to be homesick over them . . . only, she was.

Elle spent a relaxing hour poking about inside the majestic castle and then found a quiet spot to sketch the loch. The water looked still and dark in places, and silver in others where the sun hit its surface. She drew the gentle roll of the hills across the loch on the opposite side and then leaned back on her hands, feeling the warm cobblestones beneath her as she soaked in the view.

Eventually, she roused herself to head back to the car to complete the final leg of her journey for the day, and as she drove onto the bridge that connected the mainland to the Isle of Skye, her excitement began to build.

'Here we go, Gran,' she said as she felt a grin break out across her face. *Welcome to the Isle of Skye*, the sign said as she came down off the bridge.

It had been an overcast, grey kind of day for the majority of her drive, but somehow it seemed to suit the landscape of mountains that rose and fell for as far as the eye could see, giving the whole landscape a broody, almost lifelike feel that was simply breathtaking.

The heather that covered the almost tree-less scenery was mostly brown, with a few patches of the pretty lavender she had seen in tourist brochures. Green grass was sprinkled across the bare hills and sheep roamed, seemingly free-range, without the aid of fencing. She wondered how farmers managed to keep track of their stock. No fencing was mostly unheard of back home, especially along roadsides.

A light rain began to fall, and Elle had to concentrate as the road width narrowed alarmingly. But still, there was something truly special about this place. Elle had fallen in love with Scotland from day one, which surprised her, and she had marvelled at the landscape as she'd driven through the countryside, but this was different. She wasn't sure what it was, but it just felt special.

*Because this is the home of your ancestors*, Gran said with a happiness Elle could feel radiating around her. *This is the land of the Clan MacCoinnich.*

Goosebumps broke out along Elle's arm as she continued to drive. All those years hearing the story of the castle and the clan suddenly made everything feel very real in a way it never had before. It was like going in search of a mythical creature and suddenly finding signs that it might actually exist. Her mind briefly touched on the fairy incident back at Durn House, but she still wasn't quite ready to dwell on that.

She'd booked into a pub in the small village of Dunvegan, and the view from her window included Loch Dunvegan and the MacLeod's Tables.

*Legend tells*, she read from the information booklet in the room, *that in the sixteenth century, the Chief of the Clan MacLeod boasted at a banquet held by King James V of Scotland that he had a much grander table than the King. Sometime later, the Clan Chief invited the King and his guests to a banquet on the top of the mountain, to prove his point.*

Elle planned to visit the famous Dunvegan Castle tomorrow morning, and in the meantime she decided to take a walk around Dunvegan and look through the cemetery she passed on her way into town. The old graveyard and church sat on the side of a hill on the road into Dunvegan, and as Elle opened the squeaky gate and stepped inside, the sun came out, its silvery rays caught in the droplets of moisture that clung to the trees and flowers growing through the cemetery.

Elle had always loved graveyards, something Gran had instilled in her. They would often visit Pa's grave, and while Gran stood and spent time at his tombstone, Elle would explore. She could spend all day walking around and reading old headstones, but they always made her want to know who these people were and what their lives had been like. The graves in Jessup's Creek, however, did not have dates nearly as old as these ones.

Her mind went back to Moira and her gift for speaking to the dead. The idea was confronting—scary even—and yet somehow also a relief. It meant that talking to Gran wasn't a sign that Elle was going crazy after all. But did that mean she might also have the gift? Her hand hovered briefly on the top of a nearby headstone and she touched it, closing her eyes as she felt the cold, rough stone beneath, and felt her mind go quiet. Instantly she pulled her hand away and rubbed it briskly against her denim-clad thigh. Nope. She was definitely not ready to start discovering whether she had the ability to talk to dead people. One voice was more than enough to deal with. In this particular instance, she was quite happy to live in denial. She moved on, her gaze touching each and every name and marvelling at the dates etched on them. They were so old.

Would people walk around cemeteries in the future, long after she died, and wonder who she was and what kind of life she'd had? It was a sobering and slightly depressing thought. What *did* she have to show for a life?

She'd been born, grown up, left home and started university, then came home to work in a supermarket; she sure hoped she didn't die now or that would be a really boring timeline of her life. What *had* she done with her life so far? Nothing. She came to a stop before a gravestone and paused. Flora MacLeod was the name etched on the stone. There had to be other people with uninteresting lives. What had Flora achieved during her life? Elle wondered briefly before reading on. *Twenty-Eighth Chief of MacLeod. Dame of the British Empire* . . . Okay, that was probably a bad example.

Elle let out a defeated sigh and headed back towards the gate. She had plenty of time to do something with her life. Why was she even questioning it? Hadn't she always said she'd been content with life in Jessup's Creek? She loved her hometown, but there had been an odd feeling creeping its way around her mind lately—she hadn't even realised it was happening—and when she thought about returning home, Elle couldn't quite capture that belief that she was happy to return to the way things had been.

She had flexed her wings and found that she was excited to explore new places. She hated to admit it, but maybe her mum had been right after all. Maybe Elle *did* need to think about the future. It wasn't going to involve heading back to university—that much she knew for sure—but perhaps it was time for her to start thinking a little bigger than Jessup's Creek.

If Elle had ever conjured an image of an eight-hundred-year-old castle in her mind, this would be it, she thought the next day as she sat on a low stone wall in front of the massive old building that was Dunvegan Castle. Sitting here before it, alone and sketching, with the last remaining wisps of early-morning mist still lingering, gave the entire place an otherworldly feel.

The two rounded towers at the entrance, with their narrow, arched stained-glass windows, drew her inside once she'd finished her sketch, and she was greeted by a massive timber staircase that led upstairs. Artwork lined the walls, and at the top of the staircase two wooden doors stood side by side like silent sentinels with a bull's head hanging on the wall above them and the clan motto of *Hold Fast* mounted between its horns.

Hallways led off in all directions with walls full of portraits of the MacLeod family ancestry and framed treasures. Elle stood and admired the craftmanship, taking her time with each one in turn. Would she have been an artist, painting family members of the Scottish clans, had she been alive back in those times? Probably not, she conceded; back then women were pretty much only allowed to breed or work as servants. Then a more sobering thought occurred to her—if she had been alive then and could talk to dead people she would probably have been tried as a witch.

*There were no witches in our family*, Gran reassured her, which was a relief. *At least none that ever got caught,* she added, causing Elle to give a small scoff, making a woman nearby glance over. Elle smiled quickly before turning away.

The chilling stories of the witch burnings and drownings in Edinburgh were still fresh in her mind, so she moved on to the next room, full of beautiful antiques, stopping before a framed piece of tattered yellow silk. Underneath was a sign stating it was the Fairy Flag of Dunvegan. There were, according to the plaque, many tales attached to the flag, but most involved a story about a fairy who had given the flag to the Clan MacLeod to protect them in times of trouble.

'I know we've got the story of Isla and Gavan, Gran,' she said quietly in the empty room, 'but can you imagine having a fairy flag in your family tree? How cool would that be?'

She couldn't be sure, but Elle thought she heard a small unimpressed sniff before she moved on to look through the rest of the castle.

In the grand dining room her gaze settled upon a huge portrait on the wall and she smiled. A grey-haired woman in a tartan kilt with a yellow shawl over her shoulders posed with the loch of Dunvegan behind her. *Flora MacLeod, the only female chief of the MacLeods of Dunvegan*, the plague read. 'Hello, Flora,' Elle murmured, and her smile became wistful. It was strange to see the woman whose grave she had visited only the day before. Flora had known how to live life to its fullest if her mysterious, slightly mischievous smile were any indication.

She moved on to look over the rest of the paintings and artefacts lovingly preserved in the old castle, imagining herself living in a place like this. Elle was sad to leave when she made her way back to the front towers and out into the drizzly weather that had descended once more.

Today she hoped to find Stormeil. Earlier, she had tried to ask Gran more about it, but Elle hadn't been able to hear her grandmother. She'd thought Gran's silence was odd, since this was the main purpose of the trip—locating the mythical family castle—but decided she would just wing it. There was still so much to see, and Elle was happy to simply drive and explore this beautiful island.

Her plan was to head for Kilmuir, the closest village that still existed today to where Stormeil Castle was supposed to be. Gran's description had given Elle a rough idea of the location of the castle ruins, but her googling hadn't offered anything more specific. It didn't help that many village names and places mentioned in research from the fourteenth century no longer existed. Back inside the warmth of her car, she set the GPS to take her towards Kilmuir and decided she would just have to start searching the old-fashioned way—with a little bit of detective work, which included asking locals.

'You know, Gran,' she said quietly, 'I could really use some help.'

The narrow roads had taken some getting used to, but Elle was now quite proud of herself for having mastered the pull-off-to-one-side-and-let-an-approaching-vehicle-pass thing. She looked forward to a friendly wave from passing cars, feeling a kinship with fellow travellers. Once she got used to the fact that *all the roads* looked as though she had mistakenly turned onto a rarely used backroad, she felt a lot more comfortable. But they were incredibly narrow in places. She passed white stone houses, some with traditional thatched roofs, and a gazillion sheep, who, she discovered, were not frightened by cars approaching, and in fact tended to waddle along the road, with their long waggy tails, quite oblivious to the fact they were holding up traffic.

As Elle followed the narrow road, she saw on the map that she was almost at the northernmost tip of Skye, passing through a few tiny hamlets as she followed the coastline towards Uig.

'Is any of this looking vaguely familiar, Gran?' she asked, getting frustrated as a light drizzle started once more and she had to slow down.

*Yes, it is*, Gran finally announced, immediately lifting Elle's spirits and making her tighten her hold on the steering wheel. *I think this is the way.*

'I don't know, I think we've taken a wrong turn somewhere,' Elle said almost half an hour later, peering out to survey the landscape of flat, open paddocks around them.

Gran had instructed her to make a sharp left turn at a road sign about twenty minutes earlier and they hadn't passed a single car or person since.

*Hold on, dear, I'm listening*, Gran said, sounding distracted.

'Listening? To what?'

*To whom*, she corrected.

'Whom?' Elle started to get the feeling she should be concerned.

*My great-grandmother.*

'Your great-grandmother?'

*Must you repeat everything, darling? It's quite distracting. Yes, my great-grandmother, Murdina.*

'What? She's *with you?*' Elle asked, stopping the car. What was this—a freaking progressive ghost tour? Ancestors just jumped on board whenever they felt like it?

'Well? Is this the right way?'

*She's telling me this isn't the place,* Gran finally announced, sounding disappointed.

'Well, if you can summon past relatives, why don't you just ask Isla herself where the damn castle is?'

*It doesn't work like that,* Gran said with a decided snip in her voice.

'Then how *does* it work?'

*I don't know how, Elspeth. I'm somewhat new to this whole death thing myself. She's just here and I can only tell you what she's telling me.*

Elle didn't have the emotional strength to try to figure out the afterlife right now; she was cold and hungry and sick of being lost. Rubbing her fingertips across her forehead as she struggled to get her frustration under control, she asked in a calm tone, 'Are you sure none of this looks familiar?'

*No, I'm not sure. The last time I was here I was nine years old.*

Oh, for goodness sake. How on earth were they going to find this place? Google said it should be around here. Wasn't Google supposed to know everything?

'Look it's already after two, even if we did find it, there wouldn't be much time to have a proper look around. Let's just book into that pub we passed earlier, have some lunch and ask a local where we can find it. We'll start fresh tomorrow morning. Okay?' Her question was met with silence. 'Gran?' Elle sat still, waiting for some kind of reply, but none came.

'Righto, then.' Maybe Gran and Murdina had decided to go and catch up over a cuppa or something. Elle would just carry on with her plan and find a pub. And maybe a stiff drink or two.

# Fifteen

The pub was just like all the other buildings Elle had seen in this region: white stone with a red roof. She parked out the front and walked inside, instantly feeling the warmth from the fireplace that crackled cheerfully up one end of the room. The bar ran along a wall, where a woman in her mid-forties with bouncy blonde hair smiled a welcome as Elle approached her.

'What can I get for you?' she asked in a heavy brogue.

'I was wondering if you had any rooms available for the night?'

'Aye, we do. How many guests?'

'Just the one, thanks,' Elle said, relieved she would be able to put her feet up very soon instead of having to drive back the way she'd come earlier to find somewhere else to stay.

Clusters of round tables filled the centre of the room and at the other end was a square dance floor and small stage.

Around the walls hung flags and tartans as well as the odd enormous deer head. The tantalising scent of something delicious being cooked floated through the air.

'Let me show you to your room,' the woman said, taking a key from the wall behind her and circling out from behind the bar. Elle followed her through a set of doors and up a staircase to a row of rooms on the second floor. The room was basic but clean, and Elle smiled thankfully as she took the key from the woman and sat on the end of the bed to take in her surroundings. It was an effort to get up and head back downstairs to collect her bags from the car, but once she was settled in her room, she gave into the temptation to stretch out on the double bed for a few minutes before going in search of food.

Glenda, the publican, turned out to be a wealth of knowledge about the local area.

'Aye, Stormeil Castle, I remember my granddad talking about that place. Nothing left of it now, though, I'd imagine. It's not a place that a lot of people go. They say it was haunted, you know,' Glenda said in a low voice, as her head bobbed knowingly.

'Is there anywhere in Scotland that *isn't?*' Elle asked doubtfully. So far just about every place she'd stayed was supposed to be haunted, but the only ghost she'd had any problems with was Gran.

Glenda let out a low throaty chuckle and collected Elle's used glass. 'Not many places. So, how did you hear about Stormeil Castle?'

'My gran used to tell me stories about it. She was very proud of her family history. She's a descendant of the MacCoinnichs,' Elle said with a smile.

'Ah,' Glenda said brightly. 'It's not often you hear outsiders use the Gaelic version of MacKenzie.' She nodded thoughtfully as she studied Elle. 'You said she *was* proud. Does that mean your gran has passed on?'

Elle's smile wavered slightly. 'Yes. Just recently. Actually, that's why I'm here. We were always supposed to make the trip over together, but we never got around to it.'

'We all think we're going to have plenty of time to do things, don't we?' Glenda shook her head sadly. 'Well, I'm glad you made the trip. I'll draw you a wee map to help you find your way. Ask for Stuart Buchanan when you get to the house at the end of the road.'

A band had started to play, and Elle noticed a few people moving out onto the dance floor, which she took as her cue to leave. An exhibitionist she was not, and she had two left feet to boot. Although, as she lay in bed and listened to the music and laughter from downstairs, part of her wished she was more outgoing. Aila would have stayed, she thought, suddenly missing her cousin once more.

She tapped out a text to her cousin and took a photo of her room before hitting send. Within a few minutes she had a reply.

*What are you doing in a room alone? Go out and find a willing man . . . or unwilling, it really don't matter!*

Elle gave a small snort, before sending back an eyeroll emoji and reaching over to click off the TV. A few moments later her phone rang and she smiled as Aila's name came up on the screen. They talked for a good half-hour before Elle started yawning, and the two girls said goodnight. It was what she'd needed after the long day—to hear a friendly, cheerful voice to lift her flailing spirits, and she found herself dozing off feeling a little less lonely.

# Sixteen

The map was fine—as far as roughly drawn maps with a couple of stick-figure cows in a paddock and a signpost with an unintelligible road name on it went—but despite searching, Elle failed to spot any signposts or cattle anywhere.

Eventually, with no word from Gran, who could have at least summoned a long-lost ancestor or two for a bit of help with the directions, Elle came to the end of the road. Literally. She'd been following a wonderfully old mossy rock wall for a while on the right-hand side of the road, and as she came around the bend, she discovered it ended abruptly in a driveway to a property.

Maybe she wasn't as lost as she'd thought, then.

Elle drove along the gravel road slowly until she pulled up out the front of a large stone house. As she stepped out of the car, the front door opened and a dark-haired man dressed in a white business shirt and smartly creased dark trousers came out, his face set in a polite but formidable expression. He might have been good-looking in a rough-around-the-edges kind of way if he smiled, she thought as he approached. He stopped a few feet away and looked at her expectantly.

'Hello, I'm wondering if you can help me. I think I'm a bit lost.'

'Look, if you're here for an *Outlander* tour, you're sadly mistaken. This is not the castle where Jamie grew up,' he informed her in a pleasant, perhaps somewhat irritated, voice.

'Oh. No. I'm not here for that.' And hello? I've already been to that castle, Elle thought with an insulted snort. 'I'm looking for Stuart? My name's Elle Kinnaird. I'm sorry I didn't call before coming out, but the lady at the pub didn't give me a phone number, only gave me directions to get here.'

'What lady?' he asked suspiciously.

'Glenda somebody?' she said hesitantly, and swallowed nervously as he continued to watch her with an obvious lack of enthusiasm.

*Go on, dear, ask the nice man*, Gran prodded, making her usual abrupt appearance, her voice sounding like an excited schoolgirl.

'This may sound strange,' she continued, and saw his eyes narrow slightly, so she rushed on before he could call someone to release the hounds on her. 'You see, my gran recently passed away, and she used to tell me a story about some of our ancestors who lived around here . . . the MacCoinnichs.' She saw him tilt his head ever so slightly—possibly in interest, but it could also have been in readiness to throw her off the grounds. 'Anyway, I believe there was a castle around here somewhere, only I can't seem to find it. Glenda said that you'd know about it.'

'I know the place,' he admitted.

Elle waited expectantly for him to continue, only to realise he wasn't going to. 'Could you tell me how I can get to it?'

'I could. But it won't do you any good.'

'Why?'

'It's on private land.'

Gran swore, and Elle gave a small start. 'Gran!'

'Excuse me?' the man asked, frowning.

'I said that's a shame,' she said quickly. 'Can you tell me who I need to speak with to see if they'd let me have a look? It really is a matter of life and death.'

'Life and death, you say? Well, that does sound serious,' he said with a lazy kind of amusement and crossed his arms over his chest.

'You have *no idea* what I've gone through to get this far, mate,' she muttered.

'You're from Australia, I take it?'

She eyed him warily.

'Your accent,' he supplied.

'Oh, yes, I am.'

'That's a long way to travel.'

'For nothing, so it turns out,' she replied, suddenly feeling wearier than she had ever felt before. 'I came here to do something for my gran, but I should have just said no. Sorry to have bothered you,' she said, turning away.

*You can't give up now!* Gran protested.

'Stop it. It's over. I'm done,' she snapped.

'Ah, pardon?' Stuart asked hesitantly.

'Nothing, I wasn't talking to you,' she said, reaching for her door handle.

'Then who *were* you talking to?' he asked.

*You are not a quitter, Elspeth Kinnaird!* Gran said firmly.

'I *am* a quitter! I *always* quit, isn't that what everyone always says?' she snapped again as she reefed open the door.

*Then prove them wrong now. Don't give up.*

Stuart's forehead furrowed. 'Quit what?'

Elle tipped her head back to look up at the overcast sky and gave a frustrated growl.

'Look, you've obviously come a long way,' he said, coming a few steps closer, 'and I wouldn't normally do this but—' he stopped, placing his hands on his hips and looking at her warily before speaking again '—maybe I can help you.'

Elle blinked at him uncertainly. She had been so distracted arguing with Gran that she'd almost forgotten he was still there. 'You will? You know who owns the land?'

'Yes.'

*Well, spit it out!* Gran all but shouted. *Maybe the lad is a little slow after all*, she added uncertainly.

'How do I find them? Is the castle far from here?' Elle asked.

'You found them. This is my property, and no, it's not far. But you won't be able to get there in that,' he said, nodding at her hire car. While she was digesting that bit of news, he glanced swiftly at his watch. 'I'm running late for an appointment right now. Come back tomorrow and wear some good-quality hiking boots.' He looked her up and down quickly before his scowl settled on her bright pink leather wedge-heeled boots.

'Tomorrow?' she echoed dully as he turned and walked back up the steps into the house.

'Ten am,' he called over his shoulder.

He was gone before she could ask any more questions.

*He was nice*, Gran said, breaking the silence. *No Jamie Fraser by any stretch of the imagination, but not too hard on the eye all the same.*

Elle let her gran's observation pass without comment. They were so close it was hard not to feel impatient. All these years she'd heard the stories about Stormeil and it was right here . . . somewhere close by. She wanted to go looking for it right now, but thankfully sanity prevailed and reminded her that this was private property and not suitable for her car. Did she really want to risk a run-in with police for trespassing, or having to call the hire-car people about towing her car out of a boggy paddock? With a reluctant sigh, she got back in the car and closed the door.

*He was rather handsome*, Gran piped up a little later as they drove.

Elle gave a grunt, hoping it sounded noncommittal. He *was* kind of handsome in a grumpy-faced, strong-silent-type way, she supposed. Not that she'd been really looking.

She heard a rather un-Gran-like snort in reply, and shook her head. 'And just where does he think I'll be able to find a pair of hiking boots by tomorrow morning?' she scoffed, just as she rounded the corner to see a mileage sign for the next town ... right beside an advertising board for a hardware–hiking–outdoor store.

'You have got to be kidding me,' she muttered and rolled her eyes. 'Was this your doing?'

*I swear I had nothing to do with it.*

'Uh-huh,' Elle said, unconvinced, as she drove on.

After purchasing a new pair of hiking boots, which technically didn't count as breaking the no-more-boots resolution she'd made with herself after losing her job—Stuart was apparently an authority on these things and said she needed them—Elle spent the rest of the day exploring more of the area.

She came across an outdoor museum—a small village, preserved, to show the traditional way of life for crofters in the past with old-fashioned thatched cottages. Again, she marvelled at the endurance people from earlier days must have had in order to survive, not only all the violence and illness of the time, but also the harsh elements. As she stood outside one of the huts now, the savage winds coming off the ocean seemed to blow right through her. To find a way to live and work in these conditions, with so little, was impressive. Elle realised that this was how Gran's father would have lived as a boy, and his family before him, and was impressed all over again.

'I can't even imagine, Gran. This is how our family would have once lived.'

*Yes, I remember my father telling me about the croft he grew up in—just like this one.*

'Maybe I can find out if there's anyone still around who remembers your dad's family?'

*I doubt it. There might be distant relatives, but my father's line died out with him leaving.*

'I wonder why he stopped talking to his parents?'

*I know you seem to think you're here to solve all our family secrets, darling, but sometimes things happen in the past and no one remembers why.*

'I was just curious.'

'Excuse me, dear, are you talking to me?' a voice asked from behind her, and Elle turned abruptly to find the stocky woman who'd taken her entry payment earlier watching her oddly.

'Oh. Sorry. No,' Elle apologised, embarrassed at being caught talking to herself, and hurried away to escape the woman's confused look.

Leaving the museum, she continued on, visiting some small art galleries and pottery studios along the way, before stopping to sit for a while on a headland that was too beautiful to drive past. She took out her sketchpad and spent a relaxing few hours drawing, more aware of landscapes that caught her eye since Grace commissioned her artwork. Maybe it was because, as a visitor, she knew the kinds of scenery she wanted to capture and take home, like a photo to remember her trip. Or maybe she was discovering she really did have a talent for landscapes, and her art might be something more than just a hobby.

At first, every time she dared think about her artwork selling, her default response was rationality. Don't get your hopes up. Art is very subjective. Not everyone likes sketches. But lately she had started to question herself. Why can't I get excited? What if people really love my sketches? What if art *could* be a career? It had only been a few days, so realistically, it could take some time before anyone actually bought anything, but it didn't stop her checking her phone at the end of each day, hoping to see a message from Grace saying one had sold.

# Seventeen

The next morning, Elle pulled on her hiking boots, and grabbed a coat as she ran down the stairs. She booked another night's accommodation, just to be safe, thinking that after a hike today she would most likely appreciate a bed to fall into later. She was grateful for Gran's envelope, but she would soon need to sit down and make some decisions about how much longer she would stay in Scotland. Accommodation was expensive and her holiday money was being whittled down at an alarming rate. She had overslept and missed her alarm and now she was running late. She didn't think Stuart, dressed in his business shirt and polished shoes, would be terribly impressed by tardiness.

As she pulled up at the house, just as she suspected, Stuart was waiting for her at the front steps, stroking two black-and-white sheep dogs. He was dressed more casually today in a pair of tan-coloured cargo pants and a long shirt, vest and pair of chunky looking hiking boots, similar to the ones she'd bought.

'Morning,' she said, deciding to just jump right in and hope for the best as she climbed out of her car, stuffing her hands into her pockets. 'Sorry, I'm late.'

She watched him stand, gently pushing his two companions aside. 'If you're ready, we'll get started?'

Elle frowned at his abrupt reply. So, she'd guessed right. He was big on punctuality.

'Exactly what are *we* doing?'

He gestured towards an old Land Rover parked nearby. 'I'm taking you to the ruins,' he said, seemingly confused by the question.

'Oh. I assumed when you said I wouldn't get there by car, that you'd give me directions so I could walk there.'

'I said you wouldn't get there in *your* car. *My car*, however, will be fine.'

The dogs sniffed at her curiously, and she gave each of them a pat before Stuart whistled sharply and they jumped up into the back seat of the vehicle.

Elle watched him warily. Glenda from the pub hadn't stopped raving about what a great guy Stuart was, but should Elle really get into a car with a stranger and allow him to take her to what he'd just told her was a hard-to-get-to location of a ruined castle?

*It's all right, darling. We can trust him. He has honest eyes,* Gran said reassuringly.

*So, I take it you have some ghostly self-defence talents I don't know about, in case he turns out to be an axe murderer?*

*We don't need them. I told you, I trust him,* she said with a dainty sniff.

*Well, no offence, Gran, but you're not exactly the one who's in any mortal danger if he decides to rape and pillage.*

*I wouldn't mind being pillaged by a handsome lad like that, I can tell you.*

Elle shook her head and gave up. *Fine. I'll just risk my life in order to find this damn castle for you—happy?*

'If you're worried about travelling alone with me . . .'

'I wasn't worried,' she denied unconvincingly. 'I told Glenda where I was going and when I should be back. So, someone knows where I am,' she added pointedly, in case he had any plans to do away with her.

'That's a relief. She had nice things to say about you too,' he said, walking past her.

Elle felt her mouth drop open. 'You called to check up on me?'

'You could be a serial killer or something. A bloke can't be too careful,' he said with a grin that caught her off guard. Elle wasn't sure if she should be worried that he'd thought she might have been some weirdo and had called Glenda to check, or glad she wasn't the only one who had reservations about strangers.

'Shall we go?'

She settled into the front seat of the old four-wheel drive and glanced over at the two contented-looking dogs waiting patiently in the back, tongues lolling from their grinning mouths. Stuart slid into the driver's seat and slammed his door shut.

'Sorry. You have to slam it,' he explained when Elle jumped. 'We don't get many tourists out this far, and very few have asked to see Stormeil—how is it that you know about it?' he asked as they drove through an open gate into a wide paddock behind the house.

'I was raised on the story about Isla and Gavan,' she said, taking her eyes from the scenery to look over at her companion. 'Do you know it?'

She saw his eyebrows lift slightly. 'I do,' he acknowledged, and she thought once again how much she liked listening to this accent. 'I wouldn't have thought it something well known in Australia, though.'

'It was a family story,' Elle said. 'My gran was told it as a child by her gran, who was told it by hers, and so on.'

'You said your gran had family connections to the castle?'

'Yes, her father was a MacKenzie.'

'I noticed you used the old pronunciation of MacCoinnich yesterday.'

'My gran used to use it when she told the story.'

'She was Scottish, then?'

'Yes, she was, although she moved to Australia when she was fifteen. What about Tàileach Castle? Is it still in the MacCallum family? The ruins?'

'No, the original land has been divided up, and there's nothing left of the castle itself now,' he told her, his thumbs doing a small tap on the steering wheel. 'Estates are expensive to maintain, and a great number of castles have changed clans and owners over the generations.'

'I can't imagine living on a place with so much history,' she said, watching the rolling pastures and cattle grazing contentedly. 'You raise cattle?'

'Aye, and sheep. It's a working property. That surprises you?'

'I guess it does a little bit.' He hadn't looked like a farmer yesterday in his expensive-looking leather shoes. Today, dressed more casually, she supposed he did look a little more farmer-like.

'Not all estates are owned by the National Trust,' he said dryly.

'Apparently not,' she smiled.

'What part of Australia do you come from?'

'The New England region. It's not unlike this place, really . . . except, Scotland's a different type of green. We actually have lots of places named after towns here.' She rattled off a few of the ones she'd noticed on road signs or the map. 'Grafton, Ben Lomond, Glen Innes, Glencoe, Inverell.' There were so many and it made her smile to see the familiar names as she drove.

'I guess they wanted to take a piece of Scotland with them,' Stuart said.

'I guess so,' Elle agreed.

'The ruins are just up ahead,' he informed her a few moments later as they came over a small incline and through a cutting, and there before them was a wide, flat area with a crumbling stone fortress. Elle had seen a lot of castles and old buildings since arriving in this country and she knew it shouldn't surprise her anymore, but it always did. She didn't think she would ever get tired of that first awe-inspiring sight of something so old and majestic as a castle—even a ruined one.

'There it is,' he said.

Elle could only stare.

'It's not in very good shape, I'm afraid.'

It was true, parts of the walls had crumbled away and there was no roof, but this was the fabled Stormeil Castle, where a young girl had run away from her betrothed only to be hunted down and murdered.

'It's just so strange to be finally seeing it. I've grown up hearing the story my whole life, and now, I'm really here.'

*Is this how you remembered it, Gran?*

*Oh yes*, she breathed. *It's exactly how I remember it from when I came here with my father.*

Opening her door, Elle climbed out of the vehicle and walked towards the ruins.

'In its day it would have been an impressive sight. It was a fortress, built to withstand sieges and attacks from even the hardest armies. It went up at least four storeys,' Stuart said from beside her as the two dogs bounded off to explore.

'It's such a shame that it was left to fall apart like this.'

'They built things to last back then, but after eight hundred years they need extensive maintenance to remain intact.'

'I guess it's been like this for a long time?'

'As long as anyone can remember.'

'There's an arch the families built, where Isla and Gavan were supposed to have been buried—do you know where that is?'

'We can drive there on the way back,' he said as they walked towards the ruins in companionable silence.

Elle tried to imagine how the place must have once looked, filling in the missing walls and adding floors and windows, towers at the front and battlements. They walked through a gap where a huge front door must once have stood and Elle looked around, turning to get her bearings.

'How do you know that it had four storeys?' she asked curiously.

'If you look up at this interior wall,' he said, pointing, 'you can see square cuts in the stone at regular intervals. That's where the beams were once in place to support the floor above. It goes up four levels.'

'It must have been massive.'

'It was.'

'You've had your whole life to explore this place. You must know it pretty well.'

'I was only supposed to come here with an adult,' he said, his head tipped back as though searching the craggy rock wall, before he looked back down at her with a grin, 'but occasionally I'd manage to sneak away and come here to explore on my own.'

'I guess it would be too tempting to have your very own castle in your backyard and not come to play,' she agreed, though she hated to think of all the dangers a place like this presented to a child up here all alone.

Elle picked her way across the rocky floor, poking her head into small arch entrances and then climbing a curved section of staircase that led to a landing one floor up. Beneath was a small, ceiling-less room that rose high above her like a tall, narrow chamber into the sky.

'I believe this part of the lower floor used to be the kitchen. The black soot marks on the stone wall would have come from some kind of large open-fire oven.'

'What a shame there isn't more of it left intact,' she said thoughtfully as they continued carefully across the uneven ground.

'So, tell me,' Stuart said, 'what do you do back in Australia?'

Elle looked at him quickly as she picked her way across the rubble. 'Nothing terribly exciting. I work . . . *worked*,' she amended wryly, 'in a supermarket.'

'You don't work there anymore?' he asked.

'No. They put me off in favour of a self-service checkout. Welcome to the era of robots taking over.'

'What are you going to do when you go back?'

'You sound like my mother,' Elle told him dryly.

'Ah, I see.'

'What do you see?' Elle asked, stopping to look at him.

'You have a mother with opinions about your future.'

'You sound like you know how that is.'

'I do,' he said, and she was momentarily distracted by the way he rolled the words off his tongue.

'Yes, well. Mine wasn't too impressed with this trip. In all fairness, it did happen pretty quickly, but, I don't know, I think I just wanted to get away for a while before I had to make a lot of big decisions.'

He nodded. 'Mine's never really understood why I gave up a London office and law degree to become a farmer.'

'But you're still practising?' He lifted an eyebrow questioningly. 'Yesterday you weren't dressed like a farmer,' she said, then wished she hadn't.

He smiled. 'I still have the occasional loose end to tie up, but technically I'm a full-time farmer now. But if you ask my mother, I've lost my mind and given up my career to work with a bunch of smelly cows.'

She grinned at the way he pronounced *coos*.

'So, why did you?' Elle asked, eyeing him curiously. 'Give up a law practice to be a farmer?'

'Because my grandfather was a farmer, and I was tired of living in London doing a job I never really wanted to do in the first place. I guess I wanted a simpler life. This place needed attention, so I moved back.'

'Has it been in your family for a long time?'

'It was my grandfather's. He worked hard to give my father a better life. Dad went off to become a solicitor and I guess it was just expected that I'd follow in his footsteps when my time came.'

'Well, you gave it a shot—at least *you* finished *your* degree,' she said, sitting down on a large rock.

'What were you studying?'

'Accountancy,' she said, finally able to say it without shuddering. 'Anyway, I'm glad you found something you love doing in the end. Maybe there's hope for me yet.'

'I'm sure you'll work out what it is when the time's right.'

'Maybe. Or maybe I'm destined to be a wanderer of the world.'

'You probably need an unlimited bank account for that,' he pointed out.

'Maybe it'll be a very short career as a wanderer, then,' she sighed.

'Is that what you're doing here? Wandering?' he asked with a small smile.

'Not exactly. My gran made me promise to come here, so I guess I'm just keeping my promise . . . and delaying the inevitable once I go home.'

'So, you don't always travel backroads alone and accept rides with strangers?'

She watched him; Stuart didn't seem threatening as he stood, hands in his pockets as he flexed one foot back and forth on a large rock before him.

'Not as a rule, no,' she answered.

'Well, that's a relief, then.' He grinned.

Elle tried not to stare, but the transformation when the man smiled was something quite extraordinary. She looked away quickly, and focused instead on the main tower before her. Not for the first time, she wondered what it had looked like before. Judging by the size of the foundations, the castle was once huge.

'I believe there's a sketch of how it used to look in the library.'

Elle placed her hand on the stone wall of the tower and tilted her head back to look straight up. 'I'll have to go and check it out, but I'm assuming it's the same one Gran had in a frame on her wall.' It wouldn't hurt to see, though, in case there was another one Gran hadn't known about. It was a little disappointing to realise there was nothing else to really look at. Such an imposing castle had been reduced to nothing more than rubble scattered across a field in a farmer's paddock.

Elle jumped again as Stuart suddenly let out a loud, sharp whistle. 'Roy! Jock!' he called and within moments the two dogs came running.

'Shall we go?' he asked Elle, and she nodded and reluctantly followed him back to the car.

Elle was unsure what to make of the man behind the wheel as they left the ruins. Yesterday he'd seemed cold and aloof, but today he'd been quite pleasant. He didn't have to drive her around to look at ruins, he could have just told her to nick off, but he hadn't.

He had a wide face, with nice cheekbones. His nose was straight and didn't look as though it had ever been broken, so not a brawler in his younger years, she decided. He had dark eyelashes that made his blue eyes quite striking, and she liked the way they lit up when he smiled.

Stuart *was* good-looking, she supposed, now that she'd had more time to consider it. His large hands held the steering wheel comfortably as he negotiated the rough dirt road and the small creek they'd just crossed. Everything about him was big. He was well over six feet tall and his physique reminded her of a rugby player, which she presumed he would have been during his university days. It was hard to tell how old he was, but if she had to guess she would say early to mid-thirties.

The track they were on eventually wound over the crest of a hill, and from there looked out across a wide valley surrounded by hills in the distance.

'Rowan trees,' she said with a small smile as she spotted more of the red-berried foliage, the only large type of vegetation growing across the bare hills and gullies.

'You know about the rowan tree?'

'Yes. Gran used to talk about them. She called them fairy trees. They protected against evil magic.'

'This whole area would have been dotted with tenants' homes, and earlier still there was a village just outside the castle. The rowan trees are all that remain where the houses would have stood.'

The fact these trees had managed to survive, like markers, after all this time was both sad and inspiring to Elle. In a way, they were like headstones—for the houses and lives once scattered along the landscape so long ago.

As Stuart drove them down the other side of the hill, she saw rocky outcrops on either side, where large boulders balanced on top of other rocks, and sheep lazily picked at the grass growing in and around them. Then as they came down onto the flat, she spotted it and felt her heart skip a beat.

Ahead of them was a stone wall, divided by an arch. This was the place.

# Eighteen

'Is everything all right?' Stuart asked.

Elle glanced at him and nodded, before opening her door and climbing out. She walked through the stone arch and immediately spotted a cluster of old graves.

'I was imagining only two graves here,' she said quietly as he walked up beside her.

'It was used as a family burial site for a number of generations before the estates both eventually fell apart,' he said. 'There was even a small church here at one point, but it's gone now.'

'What happened to all the families?'

'Wars, taxes.' He shrugged. 'Then after the uprising, over time a lot of Highlands families were cleared from the land.'

'It's such a long history to try to wrap my head around compared to where I come from.'

They came to a stop in front of two of the tallest headstones—and oldest, if the faded engraving was anything to go by. The inscriptions were in Gaelic, but as Elle's gaze slipped over the unfamiliar words, it stopped as she made out the names. Goosebumps broke out along her arms.

Isla. Gavan.

*This is the place*, Gran said in barely a whisper.

'If it's any comfort,' Stuart said gently, 'legend says that they died in each other's arms.'

Elle looked across at him, confused, until she realised he thought she was crying over the two slain lovers before them. She quickly wiped her eyes and shook her head. 'It's not that.' Well, it was, kind of, it was a terribly sad tale, but reality was sinking in. This was the point of the whole trip—to bring Gran home to the place she had always felt she belonged.

'Is it about your gran?'

When she looked at him with a hint of alarm, Stuart hooked his thumbs into the pockets of his pants and shrugged awkwardly. 'You said yesterday that you wanted to do something for your grandmother.'

Relieved he hadn't developed mind-reading skills, Elle nodded. 'She wanted me to bring her ashes to Scotland—' she forced the next words out tightly '—to scatter them *here*.'

'I see,' he said simply.

'I didn't bring them today,' she told him. 'I wasn't sure if we'd find the spot, and I wanted to ask permission first.'

'Of course. But why here?'

'This was the place she visited as a child and she always loved the story of Isla and Gavan,' she said, nodding towards the gravestones. 'It's a story that's been in our family for a long time.'

'Mine too,' he said slowly.

'Really?' she asked, tilting her head curiously.

'My family trace back to the MacColuims through my mother's side, although it translates nowadays to MacCallum.'

'Wow, so your mother's a descendant of Gavan's family. That must be really something, living here, so close, and following on from such a long line of descendants.'

'It's strange how life works out that my grandfather on my dad's side bought the castle next door to my mother's ancestral home.' He grinned.

'That *is* strange,' Elle said slowly as she tried to piece together the complex family history.

'Of course, my mother and her family never lived here. She was raised in London, where she met my father and where they've lived ever since, but I spent a lot of time here with my grandparents, who were as Scottish as you can get, and I inherited this place when they died.'

'I can't imagine having a castle on my back doorstep,' she said, shaking her head.

'Well, it's not exactly a castle anymore.' He shrugged. 'Sadly. At least that would have given me some revenue,' he said with a crooked grin. 'When my grandfather bought it, he built the house you saw as you came in. It's always been pretty modest. They were farmers.'

It was true, the stone house wasn't anything grand, though it was certainly beautiful. Unlike a lot of the houses across the countryside, his wasn't painted white, but had been left as natural stone.

'It's still really special having an estate with this much history attached to it.'

'Yeah, I guess it is,' Stuart agreed.

Elle tried to make sense of the jumble of emotions rushing through her. The story that had been told to her like a bedtime fairy tale had been true. The characters had been real people in a tragic story, and they were buried right here.

A few chunks of rock were missing from the arch, and the stones were black in places where mould had grown, but to think it had withstood the ravages of time so well was truly remarkable.

She tried probing Gran, keen to know what she was thinking, but there was only silence.

A light drizzle started to fall, which brought their visit to an end and had them running for cover as the heavens opened. By the time they climbed back inside the car, Elle was breathless from laughter and from slipping and sliding on moss-covered rocks and mud, in their mad dash to get out of the sudden downpour.

Elle combed her fingers through her wet hair, and inwardly cringed. Her head would be a mass of wild, dark red ringlets.

Stuart handed her a towel from the back seat and she lifted an eyebrow as she thanked him. 'Were you a boy scout?' she asked. 'You know, always prepared?'

He chuckled and shook his head. 'Just necessary. In case you haven't noticed, we get a bit of rain here on occasion.'

She rubbed the towel through her long hair and patted her face. Feeling a little more human, she offered the towel back, and watched as Stuart dragged it roughly across his face and head, before tossing it onto the back seat.

Ah, to be a man, she thought, never having to care about your hair or how you looked.

The rain had shrouded the hills in a low mist, and Elle shivered despite the fact she wore a waterproof jacket over a long-sleeved shirt.

Wordlessly, Stuart reached out and adjusted the car heater, and a gentle rush of warm air blew across her.

When they eventually pulled up outside the house, he surprised her by asking if she would like to come in for a cup of tea.

The prospect of heading back to the pub to sit in her room didn't hold much appeal, so she found herself agreeing, and followed him up the steps to the front door. They entered a wet room, where he kicked his boots off and placed them on a bench. Elle did the same with hers and wiggled her toes in delight at the sudden freedom of escaping her heavy walking boots. She glanced around and saw a hat rack with a few different caps and hats hanging on it, and a long farmer's coat, much like the Australian oilskins back home.

The front hall was almost empty, with just a small table and mirror, and a huge round rug on the floor. Then, as they walked through to the kitchen and dining room, Stuart's tasteful decorating took Elle by surprise. It didn't look like a house he had inherited from his grandparents—unlike at Gran's place, he clearly hadn't been sentimental about holding onto all their old furniture. The artwork and furnishings were modern and sleek. His kitchen looked like it had recently been renovated, with a huge marble-topped island bench the feature of the open room. The appliances shone and a huge oven, double the size of anything Elle had ever seen, dominated the opposite wall.

'I take it you like to entertain?'

He followed her gaze across to the oven and gave another of those lopsided grins she'd liked earlier. 'Not really. I do like to cook, but my friend who oversaw the interior design for me decided it would give the place a better resale value if it had an entertainer's kitchen.'

'That sounds like something my mother would do. Your friend and her would get along great,' she said with a droll glance, and saw Stuart's his mouth twitch in a slight smile.

'Tea or coffee?' he asked, waiting for her decision as he opened a high cupboard.

'Coffee, thanks, if you have it.'

'Not a big tea drinker?'

'Not really. My gran was, but I tend to only have it when I'm sick,' Elle said, still taking in the room around her.

'When you're sick?' he queried.

'Gran would always tuck us up on her lounge if we were home from school sick, with a dressing gown and a hot cup of tea.' She smiled at the memory.

'You and your gran were close,' Stuart said, more pointing out a fact than asking a question.

'Yes, we are . . . were.' It was complicated.

'I was close to my grandparents too. Probably a lot closer than I am with my parents, actually.'

'Do you have any brothers and sisters?'

'No. Just me. How about you?'

'I have three. Two brothers and a sister.'

'Wow, big family.'

'Yeah, I guess.'

'I always wished I could have siblings. It was kind of lonely most of the time. That's why I liked coming up here as often as I could. It never felt as lonely here as at home.'

An image of Stuart as a little boy instantly came to mind, making Elle smile before she pushed it aside.

'I sometimes felt lonely even with my brothers and sister around,' she said, trying to sound offhand but realising it was true.

'How so?' Stuart asked, after he'd finished organising their cups and turned around to lean back against the bench to face her.

'I've always been the odd one out. The others loved doing the same kinds of things and I always seemed to be off on my own involved in something else.'

'I admire people who can stand up and be themselves. I always seemed to be doing what made everyone else happy for most of my life.'

'Not now, though,' she said with a smile. 'Now you're a farmer.'

'Yeah,' he said, returning her grin. Elle was once again struck by how different he looked when he smiled. 'It took a while, but I finally made the leap.'

'Has it been harder than you thought?' she asked.

Stuart turned back as the kettle switched off. 'It's been a pretty steep learning curve,' he said. 'I always thought I had a fairly decent handle on farming—I'd been following my granddad around ever since I could walk—but there's so much more to learn. More than I was expecting, to be honest.'

'Do you have other workers?'

'Yeah, when it's busy I get in some extra help, and I kind of inherited my granddad's foreman, Old Geordie. I don't think I could do it without him.' He walked across the kitchen to a set of doors off the side. 'I thought we might sit out here,' he said over his shoulder as she followed him curiously.

The doors opened out into a glass conservatory, and Elle let out a small gasp, her eyes widening at the unexpected find.

'Wow, this is beautiful,' she said as she stepped out from the house. Glass surrounded her on all sides and stretched right out to a beautifully maintained garden accessed via large glass doors. It was a spacious room with glossy tropical plants that even Elle realised couldn't be found outside in any gardens here in Scotland.

'My granny always wanted to build a conservatory, but they never got around to doing it. When I moved back, I decided it was the first thing I was going to do.'

'I imagine you spend a lot of time out here?'

'I do. Not that we get as many sunny, warm days as I'd like, though.'

Elle glanced at his hand, seeing no sign of a wedding ring. She couldn't help but wonder if it was a significant-other kind of *we* he just mentioned, or a more general one.

She took a seat on a comfy-looking outdoor settee and looked up at the glass ceiling. The rain had lightened, but a fine drizzle continued to fall and she watched as the raindrops gently fell and trickled down the outside of the glass surrounding them.

'Tell me more about what you do back home . . . for fun,' he asked.

'Not that much, really. I work and then I go home.' Her smile slipped a little as she remembered she wouldn't even have that once she went back. 'I like to sketch,' she added, then wondered why she'd blurted that out.

'You're an artist?' Stuart asked with interest.

'Well, not really. I mean . . .' Well, she did have a couple of sketches in a shop waiting to be sold . . . but she didn't mention that. Saying those words out loud still sounded too strange. 'I just like drawing.'

'Is that something you'd like to do as a career one day?'

Elle shifted uncomfortably in her seat. She'd dreamed of it, sure, *but it wasn't a career.* She could almost hear her mother saying those exact words and she momentarily faltered before saying, 'I don't think it would be a steady-income kind of thing.'

'You never know,' he said, shrugging.

'Actually, I was wishing I had my sketchpad with me today. I'd love to draw the castle.' She pictured her art supplies, tucked into her suitcase back at the pub, and kicked herself again for sleeping in and forgetting to put them in the car. In all the flurry to get here on time this morning she'd gone without them.

'Bring it out tomorrow and I'll take you back there.'

Her eyes widened at the unexpected offer, before politeness intervened. 'I can't take up another of your days, I'm sure you've got plenty of other stuff to do.'

'Nothing I can't fit around dropping you out there for a while. It'll be fine. I have some livestock to check on in that area. I can drop you at the ruins and come back to collect you once I'm done.'

'Really? You wouldn't mind?'

'Not at all.'

Elle immediately began to consider the idea and found herself excited by the thought of being able to spend the day sketching. 'Thank you, Stuart. I'd really like that.'

'That's settled then,' he said, sipping his tea as he sat back and looked out over the green garden before them.

Time slipped by as they talked easily about everything from the state of the English government and the equally mind-boggling state of the Australian government to the royal family and which of their countries had the worst reputation for drinking. Elle was pretty sure Australians would be a strong contender for the trophy, but then again, the Scots loved their whisky . . .

When she glanced down at her watch she was shocked to find how late it was. 'I'm sorry, you probably have work to do and I've been holding you up,' Elle said, getting to her feet.

'Not at all, I've really enjoyed the day. I'd forgotten how peaceful it was out there. Sometimes it takes seeing something through somebody else's eyes to remind you to appreciate what you have.'

Elle smiled and found it hard to drag her eyes away from Stuart's for a moment. 'Well, I better get going. Thanks again for today . . . and the coffee.'

'I'll see you tomorrow.'

'What time?' Elle asked, as she hovered at the front door.

'How about you take my number and call me when you're about to leave? That way I can make sure I've finished up whatever I'm doing so I'm ready when you get here.' He slid his wallet from his back pocket and handed over a business card.

She looked down at the card in her hand. 'At least I know who to call if I need a solicitor specialising in banking and finance.'

Stuart did that crooked-grin thing again and she suddenly had a weird little flutter of nerves.

'I'll call you tomorrow,' Elle said quickly, before abruptly turning to head down the front steps to her car. She saw him in the rear-view mirror, standing on the steps, watching her with his hands in his pockets as she drove away, then she forced herself to get her mind back on track.

'Gran?' Silence greeted her. Elle wished she knew how this thing was supposed to work. She'd last heard from Gran back at Isla and Gavan's memorial. What did this silence now mean?

There had to be more to all this than just ticking off places they had always wanted to see. After all, plenty of people died with regrets. Gran had mended fences with her sister, and they'd found Stormeil Castle. There was really only one last thing to do—but now that the time had come, Elle really didn't want to do it. Was Gran feeling the same way? Is that why she disappeared so often?

'It's okay, Gran. We don't have to do anything until we're ready.'

Elle had no idea what, if any, control they had over whatever it was that connected them, but for now she was going to do a Gran and simply not deal with it.

---

Elle listened to the dial tone as she waited for her parents to pick up the phone. It rang a few more times before a recorded voice cut in to announce that the person she was trying to reach had not answered and asked her to leave a message.

'Hi, Mum and Dad, just me, checking in. I've just spent a really exciting day walking through Stormeil Castle, well, the ruins, but we . . . I mean, *I* found it. Anyway, just wanted to let you know. It was pretty exciting. I've sent you through some photos, so go check Facebook . . . And I guess I'll talk to you both later. Bye. Love you.'

She hung up and sat the phone beside her on the bed, feeling her shoulders slump a little. She'd been looking forward to telling them about her day.

The phone vibrated on the bed, drawing Elle's gaze and a smile as she read the name on the screen.

'Hey, you.'

'Are you sitting down?' Aila said, not bothering with a greeting.

'Yes. Why?' Elle asked slowly.

'Your sketches sold.'

'What!' Elle said, leaping from the bed.

'You just sold three freaking sketches!' Aila screamed on the other end of the phone.

Elle froze.

'Elle? Are you there? Oh God, you haven't fainted on me, have you?'

'I'm here,' Elle said, finally managing to find her voice. 'Are you serious?'

'I am! You just had your first sale. Congratulations.'

'All three sold?'

'Yep. To the same buyer. She loved them all.'

'Oh my God. I can't believe it.'

'Grace wants more. When are you heading back?'

'I don't know. I mean ...' She still had to talk to Gran. Instantly her excitement faded. 'I still have some things to do here.'

'Oh, right. Sorry. I kind of got a bit carried away and I forgot why you went up there for a minute.'

'No, it's okay. It's great news,' Elle said, as she ran a hand through her hair. 'I still can't believe it.'

'Well, believe it. We want to put more in the shop.'

Elle's mind flicked through her recent sketches and knew exactly which ones she would give Aila and Grace. 'Can I get back to you about the others?'

'Absolutely. Another few days won't hurt, but the buyer was keen to see more, so don't leave it too long.'

'Okay, no, that'll be fine, I think I just need to let it all sink in for a minute. I honestly didn't think they'd sell.'

'I did. I may not have an artistic bone in my body, but I know good art when I see it. Okay, I need to go, I'm heading out tonight . . . on a date.'

Elle instantly perked up at this piece of news. 'With whom?'

'Steven,' she said, before the rest came out in a rush. 'He dropped into work and asked me out on a date. A real date—dinner and all.'

Elle couldn't help but smile as she pictured her usually cool cousin practically squealing with excitement. 'That's so great, Al. I'm really happy for you. Make sure you tell me everything tomorrow.'

'I will, gotta go. Love you. Bye.'

Elle sat on the edge of the bed and stared at the wall across the room. She itched to call her parents back. She wanted to scream it from the rooftops that someone had liked her artwork so much they'd bought three sketches. Elle took her sketchpad out of her bag and carefully flipped through the pages, her thoughts racing. Maybe she did have talent. Maybe art could be something more than a hobby. Her future suddenly looked less clear but also a little brighter.

# Nineteen

With slightly shaky fingers, Elle dialled the number from the business card Stuart had given her and listened as it rang on the other end.

When he answered, his curt tone surprised her.

'Uh, hi, Stuart. It's Elle.'

'Elle.' The abrupt tone dropped and he was back to yesterday's friendly, non-threatening-Stuart tone.

'I was thinking about coming out now, but if you're busy, I can wait.'

'No, now is fine. Sorry, I was just doing some paperwork and I was a bit distracted.'

'Okay, see you soon.'

As she drove to the farm, she was looking forward to a morning of sketching, especially because the day had dawned with sunshine for a change, but part of her was even more excited about seeing Stuart again—and she wasn't sure at all about that.

Elle came to an intersection, and after a quick check for errant sheep, she turned onto the road that led to the castle, and to Stuart. It had been a long time since she'd had to work out the male psyche. Was he into her? Was she picking up on the right signals? Was she just being an obsessive woman who heard voices in her head? And what about the voice who *wasn't* speaking in her head right now? She still hadn't heard from Gran and she didn't know what to make of any of it. As these thoughts battled for prominence, Elle suddenly slammed the brakes on hard and felt the seatbelt go taut across her chest as a mob of four-footed woolly beasts wandered across the road, completely oblivious to the fact it was a road for cars, *not* sheep. With a brief prayer of thanks that once again she didn't have to use her accident insurance, Elle continued on her way, her heartrate still erratic after her near-death-by-sheep experience.

When she pulled up in front of the house a few minutes later, Stuart was walking down the steps towards his vehicle, his faithful companions Roy and Jock hot on his heels.

Today he definitely looked like a farmer. His jeans were well-worn and his jumper had a small hole in the hem. There was nothing of the man in the white shirt and trousers she'd met on that first day. He carried two thick coats over his arm and had a pair of gum boots in his hand, which he dumped into the back of the old four-wheel drive.

'Morning,' she said, as she opened the boot of her car and

lifted out the canvas bag with her supplies. 'The sun's out for a change.'

'Must be a sign,' he said, reaching out to take the bag from her to carry to his car.

Elle eyed the smaller backpack in the front seat of her car as she chewed her lip thoughtfully. She didn't know what to do. She'd tried to talk to Gran last night and again this morning about how she wanted Elle to go about the whole ashes thing, but there had been no reply. Not a single boo. With a reconciled sigh, Elle took the backpack and locked the car. She wasn't sure if she was going to do it or not, but on the off-chance Gran decided to make an appearance, she wanted to be prepared.

'How's the accommodation at the pub?' Stuart asked as they bounced along the track retracing the previous day's route.

'It's fine. The beds are super comfy, and the food's great,' she said, looking out the window. 'I've been meeting some of the locals over the past few nights. They seem like a nice bunch.'

'That would have been entertaining for you, no doubt?'

'It's been very informative,' she said diplomatically. 'There's a lot more to sheep farming than I expected.' Somehow, no matter what the topics discussed, the conversation always seemed to come back to sheep. It shouldn't have been surprising—the community was largely made up of crofting and farming, after all—but Elle felt under-prepared to weigh in on the finer points of breeding and the debate on whether bolus or drenching was the better way to go, pre-tupping.

'That there is,' Stuart agreed with a slight grin.

'What are you doing today?' she asked.

'I'll be assessing the tups, checking feed,' he answered.

'Oh. I see.' Elle nodded as though she had a clue what any of that was. 'So, what exactly is a tup?' she asked after a few moments when the curiosity became too much.

He sent her a slightly amused sideways glance before answering. 'A tup is a ram . . . a male sheep,' he added.

'I know what a ram is,' she assured him. She *was* from Australia, after all—sheep were their thing too . . . just not exactly *her* thing.

'Right, so at the moment we're well into tupping season.' He paused once again before adding, 'Mating season.'

'Got it,' she nodded more confidently.

'In another few weeks we'll separate the ewes from the rams and then a few more weeks after that scanning will start.'

'Scanning?'

'We scan the ewes to check how many are pregnant and how many lambs they're carrying.'

'You give each sheep an ultrasound? Like a human mother?'

'Yep,' he agreed. 'I thought you came from a farming community?' he asked, hitching an eyebrow curiously.

'I do, but I don't necessarily *farm*. I'm learning quite a lot on this trip.'

Stuart grunted in an offhand way. 'It gets fairly busy. We have a contractor who comes out to do it. Then we sort them into their groups—singles, twins and triplets and sell off any barren ones.'

'Do you get many twins and triplets?' she asked. Who would have thought sheep could be so interesting? She'd never really given them much thought before.

'Aye. Ideally we like twins—the ewe has two teats, so we get maximum benefit. But we get a few triplets too.'

'Wouldn't that be hard? I mean, if they only have two teats, what happens to the third lamb?'

'They're not ideal,' he agreed. 'We generally leave them on their mam for the first twenty-four to thirty-six hours so they get some colostrum in them and then we try to put one onto a single, or with an ewe that might have lost its own lamb.'

'How many sheep do you run here?'

'Around four hundred.'

That was a lot of roast lamb.

Her gaze once more travelled to the hilly landscape around them. Stuart had mentioned that this was considered low-lying country, but it seemed a Scots version of low-lying and hers were two very different things. There were areas of flat land, but then so many ridges that led down steep gullies into flowing streams or that dropped off into cliff faces that bordered the coastline. There was a harsh beauty to the place, but in no way did it look as though it should be even remotely hospitable to livestock, and yet it was.

She spotted sheep now, grazing on the sides of hills and seemingly immune to the wind that was blowing despite the sun shining. 'They must be incredibly tough to survive out here,' she said, still watching the sheep in the distance.

'They're a hardy breed.'

'They look happy enough,' she said. She wasn't quite sure what an unhappy sheep might look like, but these ones definitely looked content.

Stuart's low laugh made her feel warm all over. 'Happy sheep—that's our aim.'

When they arrived at the ruins, Stuart unpacked her gear from the back of the Land Rover, as well as a fold-up chair.

'Oh, thank you,' she said touched by the gesture.

'Will you be all right here, then?' he asked, looking down at Elle with a concerned expression as though suddenly having second thoughts about leaving her.

'I'll be fine,' she assured him with a wave.

'Phone reception's not that great, you might have to head for a hilltop,' he said. 'But I won't be too long. When I come back, I thought we could have some lunch?' He tapped his hand on a large basket in the back of the vehicle.

'You brought along a picnic?' she asked, surprised.

'Since it was such a bonnie day and all, I thought it might be nice.'

'Sounds great, thank you.' She smiled, and a little jump of awareness spurred a ridiculous rush of shyness through her. As she realised how close she was standing to him, she quickly looked down and took a small step back.

'All right, then, I best be off,' Stuart said after clearing his throat a little awkwardly, and he walked back to the driver's-side door.

As the engine noise faded into the distance, Elle stood at the edge of the ruins, and could almost feel the descent of silence like a soft veil draped over her surroundings.

*Take Me Home*

Today the castle had a different feel about it. Maybe it was because she was here alone with only the wind in the treetops nearby to keep her company. She took her time walking through the ruins, trying to see it as it had once been—the tall walls reaching up to the sky above, once divided into floors, now just gaping roofless towers.

There was a sadness hanging around this place. It could very well just be her over-active imagination, but lately with everything that had been going on, Elle had started to wonder about her heritage. Scotland had always been shrouded in all things mystical, from fairies to monsters living in lochs and everything in between. Its landscapes inspired stories of old, and only added to the legends that were handed down from generation to generation.

She came from a long line of Scottish men and women, and if Moira were to be believed, perhaps they had passed down special gifts as well as strong genes and uncontrollable red curly hair. She wished Gran had told her more about all that. Why hadn't she? Maybe there was still something forbidden about it, even now. Or maybe, more likely, Gran never knew that Elle had any special abilities—after all, until Gran started talking to her, Elle didn't even know herself.

She leaned back against the wall of the tower, soaking up the warmth of the sun on her face as she imagined how she might feel if this had been her home and she had come back to see what had become of it. How Isla would feel if she had found herself standing right here in this moment looking upon the castle of her childhood. The pain that sliced through Elle felt real. She felt abandoned and devastated.

Elle gave herself a small shake. She'd obviously been watching too much *Outlander*. Time travel wasn't real, any more than the Loch Ness monster was. Although, she supposed talking to your dead grandmother could also be considered unlikely and yet . . .

'Stop it,' she scolded herself. 'You came here to draw, not daydream.' And Stuart could be back at any time.

Sitting on a rock nearby, she took out her sketchpad. The first few drawings were made with quick strokes and lines, capturing the harshness of rock and rubble, but when she turned the page and began another, this time her pencil skimmed across the paper as if of its own accord, a quick mark in one section, a long, deliberate line elsewhere, the lead pencil building up on itself, creating a gradient of shading that gave depth to the shapes she had created on the paper.

She wasn't sure how long she sat there for, but the page quickly filled up and the first faint lines took shape and grew into something that seemed to leap from the page.

When she finished, Elle leaned back, feeling the muscles in her back protest as she straightened, but she didn't pay them any attention, she was too busy staring at the picture on the page in her lap. It was almost as though she'd been working in a trance. She didn't remember consciously deciding to draw the castle that now stared back at her—not as the ruins that were before her, but as a fierce yet beautiful castle standing proud and magnificent in all its glory. It was as detailed and lifelike as if it had really been standing there for her to sketch, only it wasn't and somehow she'd known exactly what it looked like despite the fact it was all but rubble and one crumbling tower now.

The gently shaded areas and intricate stonework made the drawing feel as though she could almost step through into the picture and touch it, and she felt a shaky breath leave her chest as she blinked back tears.

Stormeil Castle had once looked so beautiful, and the shock of seeing it as it was now felt like seeing a loved one sick and ill, and a mere shadow of the person they once were.

*I always said you had a talent, my darling girl*, Gran's voice whispered from close by. *Just beautiful.*

'I don't even know how I knew what it looked like . . . not really.' Sure, Gran had that old drawing on the wall, but it wasn't very detailed. Somehow today, sitting here, Elle could feel it all around her.

*Because you just know. The same way I knew, when I was a little girl. There are some things the soul never forgets.*

For a long while Elle sat and listened to the quiet, feeling a contentment and peace she had rarely experienced before.

'I'm not ready to do it yet, Gran . . . to say goodbye,' she finally said.

*I know, my love, but it has to be done. We came here for a reason.*

'But our trip isn't over yet. There's more to see.'

*I've seen everything that was important to me. You brought me home.*

'But are you sure this is where you want to be?' Elle looked around at the lonely ruins. 'Who'll visit you here? You'll be alone.'

*I'm not alone*, Gran said with such contentment that Elle had a sudden rush of emotion. *And you don't need to visit me here to know I'm still with you. Your father needs to know that, Elle. He doesn't trust enough to open his mind and believe. Make sure he knows.*

'I'll tell him, Gran.'

The sound of a vehicle approaching made Elle turn, and she found herself grateful for Stuart's arrival. 'I know we have to do it, Gran, but not today,' she said.

She knew that she wouldn't be able to put it off much longer, but today wasn't that day. This much she knew for certain.

# Twenty

'Did you get much done?' Stuart asked as he set out a picnic blanket.

'Yes. A bit. Did you finish what you needed to do?'

'Mostly. There's always more. Work never seems to end around here.'

'Where did you get all this? There's enough to feed an army here.' Elle laughed as he put out containers of food from a seemingly bottomless basket.

'Well, I wasn't sure what you liked, so I got . . . all of it.' He shrugged, looking a little bashful, which made her smile more.

It was obvious he had made a special trip into town. The question was why. Did he do this kind of thing for everyone he entertained? Was this even really classed as entertaining? It seemed like a very generous thing to do for someone he hardly knew.

'I'll pretty much eat anything . . . except black pudding.'

'No?' He sent her a look of horror. 'You dinna like black pudding?'

Elle always found it amusing that he seemed to slip in and out of his Scottish tongue. 'I just can't.'

'You don't know what you're missing,' he said, shaking his head slowly.

'I'll live with the regret,' she assured him.

'Well, we have plenty of other things on offer,' he said, opening the containers and handing her a plate.

There were sandwiches and pastries, a selection of cold meats and cheeses, fruit and a couple of local ciders to wash it all down with.

As they sat and ate, Elle listened to him tell her about his day and some of his plans for his property. She loved the lilt of his words as he spoke, sometimes finding herself so caught up in just listening, that she forgot to actually take in what he was saying and had to clear her throat quickly to ask him to repeat the question.

'I asked if I was boring you with all the farm talk.' He chuckled and Elle was once again distracted, this time by the tanned column of his broad neck.

'Not at all. I think it's great that you've found your passion.'

'What about you?' Stuart asked, leaning back on one elbow as he watched her lazily, popping a strawberry into his mouth.

'Me?' she asked, flustered. She swallowed an uncomfortable lump of sudden, inappropriate thoughts as she watched him bite into the ripe berry.

'*Your* passion?'

She stared at him guiltily, wondering if he'd somehow read her thoughts.

'The other day you mentioned you would have to return home and find another job,' he continued. 'Have you given any more thought to what you want to do?'

'Oh.' She breathed a relieved sigh. That. 'No, not really.' In truth she was trying very hard *not* to think about returning home. In fact, the idea of staying in Scotland had begun to grow on her, and after a conversation in the pub the other night, an idea had been sitting in the back of Elle's mind, slowly fermenting away.

'I'm thinking about maybe looking for work somewhere over here for a while,' she said, deciding to test the waters and see what it sounded like if she spoke the words aloud to someone.

'Really? What kind of work would you do?' he asked.

So far so good, at least he hadn't laughed at her idea. Maybe it wasn't so crazy after all. 'I don't know. Maybe I could do some bar work. Or there's a woman who owns a place somewhere near here who advertises for help with general cooking and cleaning and some farm work. She said she gets people from all over the world staying with her. I thought I might check it out.'

'But it's not paid work?' he asked slowly.

'No,' she conceded, 'it's food and accommodation, but at least I wouldn't be paying to stay at the pub anymore.'

'Sounds interesting,' he said, reaching for another sandwich.

'You should look into it for some help around this place. Free labour,' she added, following his lead and selecting another sandwich. She had no idea what they put in the mayonnaise around here but this chicken-and-mayo sandwich was amazing.

He made a small sound that was a cross between a grunt and a *hmmph*, which could have meant anything really, and continued chewing his food.

After they'd finished eating, Elle helped pack the leftovers away and then lay back on the blanket.

Looking up through the treetops above, she smiled sleepily at the pretty lace-like pattern the leaves made where they connected high above the ground, filtering the warm sunlight down on them.

'It's so peaceful out here. There's not a sound,' Elle said as he stretched out beside her, leaning back on his elbows. 'You really don't come up here often?' she asked, turning her head to look at him.

She saw Stuart shake his head slightly. 'I guess it's not as special until you show it to someone else,' he said, looking down into her eyes. This time when they shared the look, Elle didn't turn away. She saw his eyelids lower slightly, almost lazily, before he leaned across and lowered his head.

Elle held her breath for just a moment before their lips touched, then let it out as the warmth of his mouth touched hers. She could feel the tentativeness behind his kiss, as he slowly, lightly moved his lips and a burst of butterflies exploded inside her, spurring her on to deepen the kiss. Winding her arms around his neck, she pulled him closer and felt him finally lower whatever guard he'd been holding firmly in check.

It had been a while since she'd had a decent kiss—too long, if her reaction to this one was anything to go by. Maybe it was just the distant memory of the last one, but Elle was fairly certain this kiss was like nothing she'd ever had before. Stuart made the other guys she'd kissed seem like mere boys compared to this gentle yet rather masterful way of his. Maybe it was a Scottish thing? Did they teach classes up here in the Highlands on *how to kiss a lass thoroughly until she forgot what her name was*? They probably did.

She could feel the slight rub of his stubble against her face but it wasn't unpleasant. Elle realised at some point that he'd been bracing himself on his arms either side of her head, but as the kiss deepened, she felt more of his weight across her and she slid one leg up along his to move closer still.

She ran her fingers through his hair at the base of his skull and smothered a groan as Stuart lifted his lips to run them along the side of her neck, sending shivers of hot, biting lust to all points south. If this *was* a skill they taught the men, how on earth did Scottish women ever leave their beds?

A few moments later, Stuart rested his forehead against hers and she felt his breathing was as unsteady as her own. When he eased back slightly, she opened her eyes to find him looking down at her, his gaze blurry with unsated desire.

'Not that it wouldn't be great, but if I'm going to bed you, I'd rather do it in the comfort of an actual bed.'

'Bed me?' She laughed. 'I think this castle is growing on you. What century did you say you were from again?'

'I dinna ken about old-fashioned, but I'm definitely *feeling* old, lying on this hard ground.'

Elle had to admit she'd been trying to ignore the rock under her back, which had been surprisingly easy to do while she was being distracted by the man beside her kissing her senseless only a few minutes earlier, but now she was definitely feeling it.

'Would you mind if we stopped by the arch just for a few minutes on the way back?' she asked, accepting his hand to pull her up from the blanket. He didn't immediately step away when she stood and she found she had to tilt her head back to look up at him.

'I was planning on picking up where we just left off when we got back to the house,' Stuart said and his deep voice sent a shiver of excitement down her spine.

'I should hope so,' Elle told him with a slow smile, 'but I'd really love to capture the arch with this afternoon sun behind it. I'll make it quick,' she promised.

'Fine,' he sighed, but his slow grin made everything tingle and she was pretty sure it would be the fastest damn drawing she'd ever done in her life.

In the car, she couldn't help but watch him as he drove. It seemed so bizarre that earlier this morning they were still at that two-polite-strangers point, and then suddenly, over the course of a meal, they . . . weren't.

'If you keep looking at me like that, I'm going to rethink the whole outdoor recreational thing and pull over right here,' Stuart warned lightly, without taking his eyes from the road ahead.

Elle leaned back in her seat a little and studied him with a curious smile. 'Exactly how *old* are you?' she asked.

'Thirty-one,' he said, then sent her a quick glance, maybe to try to gauge if she was horrified by the announcement.

'I was expecting you to say forty,' she scoffed lightly.

'You think I look forty?' he asked, and she laughed at the slightly higher key he used.

'No, I just assumed by the whole *too old for outdoor sex thing*, you were maybe older,' she clarified.

'I have old rugby injuries that play up in the cold and during certain activities,' he said with only a touch of defensiveness.

So, she'd been right about the rugby thing. 'Hey, I'm not judging,' she said putting a palm up in surrender.

'If you really want the outdoor experience, I can put up with a bit of discomfort,' he offered.

'No, it's okay, but I appreciate the sacrifice you were willing to make,' she added, hiding her smile. She actually couldn't think of anything worse than trying to look seductive with twigs and leaves stuck in her unruly hair, or the insect bites she would find in unmentionable places for days afterwards.

They pulled up in the same spot he'd parked the day before at the arch, and again the significance of the place stole her breath away.

The afternoon light was just as beautiful as she'd imagined, the gentler glow casting a golden filter across the stone and making everything look magical.

She climbed out of the car and walked across to find the perfect vantage point, leaning against a smaller rock wall that she assumed had been built to keep animals out of the cemetery behind it.

As she sketched, she felt Stuart behind her, but she was so eager to capture the image before her that she didn't worry about an audience. Nor did she consider that he was the very first person she had ever let watch her draw. Not even Gran had been allowed to see any of her sketches until they were finished.

As Elle pencilled in the last stroke, she suddenly realised the sun had begun to drop low in the sky, and as time once more became relevant, she turned to look up at Stuart with a concerned frown. 'I'm so sorry, I didn't realise how long I'd been drawing for. You should have said something.'

He glanced up from the page and looked at her with a strange look that she found hard to read. 'I had no idea when you said you enjoyed drawing you meant like this,' he said with a slow smile. 'It's amazing.'

A blush crept up her neck and she quickly packed away her pencils and closed the sketchbook. 'Thanks,' she murmured. She thought about telling him about her sketches that had sold, but it was too new, and it felt a little like boasting—and part of her still found it hard to believe the sales had actually happened.

When she turned back to look at the arch once more, Elle felt Stuart's hands slip around her waist and she was pulled gently back against his chest. After a moment of surprise, she felt herself relax against him and realised how nice it was to share a sunset with someone like this.

'It's such a beautiful spot,' she said after a few moments, feeling the first icy tentacles of cold begin to creep up across her skin as the sun disappeared slowly.

'It is. There's something incredibly peaceful about it, despite what the legend says took place here.'

'Do you think it really happened?' she asked, tilting her head slightly and realising it only came up to his collarbone. 'I mean, the way the story's told?'

'Hard to say. It crossed my mind to have an archaeological survey done of the area, but I could never bring myself to have a bunch of strangers come here and dig everything up. I think I'd rather just leave things as they are.'

Elle looked back at the twin headstones and nodded slowly in agreement. She preferred to believe in the story the way it had been told for generations, without some scientist or historian deciding to muddy the waters if they found any kind of inconsistency.

'Come on, let's get you out of the cold,' he said when she couldn't suppress the small shiver that went through her.

Turning away after one last look, Elle slipped her hand into his much larger one as they walked back to the car. Stuart gently pulled her in front of him and kissed her, and once again she was amazed by her spontaneous reaction to the man.

She was certain he had only meant the kiss to be a playful reminder of what was to come later, but all of a sudden it turned from playful to something a lot more. Behind her, his large four-wheel drive held her up, while in front of her, Stuart's solid body pressed against her hungrily.

Elle had no idea where this wantonness she was experiencing had come from. She'd never reacted this strongly to a man she'd just met before—or ever. She couldn't get enough of him, despite the fact they'd already discussed the downside of outdoor recreational sex, she was fairly sure unless one of them put a stop to this soon, that's exactly what they would be doing.

'Your war wounds,' she managed to breathe against his lips as she pulled away slightly.

'I'm fine,' he murmured, taking her mouth once more, sliding his hand up under her top. Elle yelped, jumping and banging her forehead against his, which instantly brought tears to her eyes.

'Son of a bi—'

'Far—'

They both muttered expletives, stepping apart and rubbing their heads.

'Jesus, do you have a steel plate in your head or something?' she asked, frowning up at him.

'I was about to ask you the same thing,' he groaned. 'What the hell happened?'

'Your hand was freezing,' she told him, carefully probing her forehead with her fingertips to check for blood, certain there must be a huge cut there but thankful there wasn't.

'Let me take a look,' he said gently moving her hand away. 'You're going to have a bruise there,' he said with a shake of his head. 'I'm sorry.'

'It's okay. How's *your* head?' she asked, looking up at him and kind of hoping he had something similar just because she was always snappy when she was in any kind of pain.

'Just took me by surprise,' he said somewhat cheerfully. 'Come on, I'll put some ice on it back at the house.'

He opened the door and helped her in the car, before climbing in his side.

'Well, that was one way to kill the moment,' Elle said, tipping her head back against the seat.

Stuart's slightly guttural *hmm* was, she discovered, becoming a thing. He seemed to be able to convey a wide range of emotions through that grunt-like sound. When they reached the house, he sat her down on a comfy-looking lounge and disappeared into the kitchen before returning with a packet of frozen peas and a tea towel.

'Lie back,' he instructed, and she did as she was told. Drawing sometimes took it out of her, but today's sketching had been a whole other level of emotional exhaustion. Or maybe it was a mix of that and newly awakened passion, with a touch of concussion on the side.

Sitting next to her, Stuart carefully placed the frozen peas on her forehead and held them there, gently moving a few loose strands of her hair away from her face. His touch was comforting and gentle and Elle let out a small sigh as her body began to relax.

'That'll be the kettle,' he said as a click sounded from the kitchen. 'I'll be right back,' he said, leaning forward to kiss her nose. *Her nose* . . .

While she was coming to terms with how sweet that gesture was, Stuart reappeared with a cup of tea and sat it down on the table beside her. 'I ken you're not exactly sick, but I thought maybe this might be an occasion for tea.'

'This is *exactly* the occasion for tea,' Elle said, pushing herself into a sitting position. 'Ah,' she added with a small sigh, 'just like Gran used to make it.'

'I wasn't trying to remind you of your granny,' he said with a grave twist of his lips.

'Well, you don't . . . she never headbutted me.'

'Not one of my finer moments,' he agreed. 'I really am sorry.'

'I'm okay, it's just a bump.' He looked a little perturbed by that, and she felt sorry for him. 'Seriously, I'm fine. It hardly even hurts. See?' she said, touching it with her finger and biting the inside of her cheek stoically.

Stuart moved her finger away from her forehead, holding her hand in his and bringing it to his mouth to kiss gently. Elle found his steady gaze almost hypnotic as she held her breath and waited out the flutter of butterflies that had once more started up inside her.

Slowly he leaned in, and Elle felt her breath come out in a shaky rush. This time when his lips met hers, it was a slow, tender kiss—one that was both new and yet familiar. He smelled of the outdoors—windswept and clean with a hint of hay and the faint scent of leather. With gentle pressure Stuart eased her backwards until she reclined on the big sofa, and he followed her down.

The annoying throb at her temple dulled as new and more urgent feelings began to unfold. Her hands moved to the hem of his jumper and he leaned back to roughly tug it over his head, followed swiftly by the shirt he wore beneath.

Elle let her gaze wander across the newly bared skin, taking in the wide, lightly haired chest and following it down to where it tapered into a narrow line that disappeared beneath the band of his jeans. His skin felt warm beneath her fingers as she traced a path from his neck, across his collarbone and down his sides before sweeping across his flat stomach and slipping beneath the button at the top of his jeans to deftly unfasten them.

Her smile widened slightly as she heard the sharp intake of breath her cool fingers against his hot skin evoked. She watched him, his eyes heavy with stirring arousal as she touched him.

When he reached the limit of his patience, a low frustrated sound escaped from the depths of his chest and he hastily took over the removal of his jeans, before coming back to undress her.

'You're truly beautiful,' he murmured, looking down at her with a mix of awe and desire.

Elle had never considered herself beautiful—for so long she'd always looked different, with her bright copper hair and long ringlets. Growing up she'd just wanted to look like everyone else, with brown or blonde hair that hung straight and behaved itself, not the riot of curls that did whatever they felt like doing on any given day and tiny freckles that covered her skin like a tan. As she'd got older, she'd grown into her freckles and didn't notice them as much. Gran had always told her they were unique, and that she carried the genes of her ancestors, but there were times she'd wished she looked a little more boring, and not so unique for Jessup's Creek.

Now, though—here, with this man staring down at her as if she were some precious gem sent from the gods—she was glad for whatever genes she'd been passed.

The fire Stuart had made earlier cast a gentle glow over their bodies, and as their lips met once more, she felt a roar of heat rush through her veins.

Sliding a leg along his, Elle tipped her head back with a low groan as his lips trailed hot, slow kisses down along the sensitive skin and a quiver of desire ran through her as he worked magic with his hands and lips upon her body long into the evening.

# Twenty-one

The fire popped and crackled as Elle lay with her head on Stuart's chest, feeling content as she watched the red flames dance lazily in the open fireplace.

She couldn't recall ever feeling this relaxed in the presence of a man, and she was trying to work out the reason why.

'What's going on in that head of yours?' Stuart's deep voice rumbled through his chest against her ear after a while.

Her fingers stilled from their lazy circling through the hairs on his chest. 'What makes you think there's anything going on?' she murmured lightly.

'Because I can practically *feel* your mind working overtime.'

Slowly Elle lifted her head and looked up at him, folding her hands beneath her chin. 'Maybe I'm just going over your performance to see where improvements could be made,' she said with a grin.

'Now, we both know that's not true. It was faultless,' he said without any modesty at all.

Elle chuckled at his slow, smug grin and had to admit, he could be right. It was pretty damn good.

'So, truly, what are you thinking about?'

'I'm wondering how this could possibly feel as comfortable as it does when we're practically strangers.'

Stuart made a deep sound once more, which felt a lot like agreement. She was getting the hang of decoding his grunts. He used them in a variety of situations and they all had a different meaning depending on the occasion.

'Maybe it's the other part of the legend coming true?' he said after a while.

'What other part?' She eyed him doubtfully.

'You haven't heard the other one?' he asked, while his hands were idly doing little swirls along her back.

She kinked an eyebrow, waiting for him to go on.

'It's said that one day Isla and Gavan will meet again, for a second chance to be together.'

'Meet again. As in . . . ?' She wasn't quite sure where he was going with the story. Elle's eyes narrowed slightly as she watched him. 'What? Come back . . . reincarnated?' she asked.

Stuart shrugged and grinned lazily. 'I'm just telling you what the legend says.'

'You're making that up,' she said, shaking her head. Gran would have known about a second part to the story if it were true. It sounded like a second-rate version of one of the *Mummy* movies, and they'd been bad enough.

'That's what people around here believe, anyway,' he said.

'You don't seriously think that you and I—' She stopped before shaking her head. 'What? We're Isla and Gavan?' She grinned.

'Well, you were drawn here searching for a long-forgotten castle,' he said matter-of-factly.

'Because of my gran,' she pointed out.

'Maybe. But how do you explain the coincidence that my mother's side of the family were drawn back to this place through my father's family? They didn't even know each other until they met at university, and in turn I, having MacColuim blood, now own the land? The land that *you* found your way to from the other side of the world, no less.'

'Well, it's a nice story, and I know my gran would have loved that to be true, but I think you're grasping at straws here. It *is* a happy coincidence that your family found its way back to living on your ancestral land after all those years, but I'm pretty sure I'm not Isla. I'm just plain old Elspeth Kinnaird from Jessup's Creek,' she smiled with a shake of her head.

'There's nothing plain about you, Elspeth Kinnaird,' Stuart said softly as he gently tucked a wayward strand of hair behind her ear, then moved his fingers along her jawline as he held her gaze steadily. The heat in his look sent a warm flush through her body in response. 'I don't care what brought you here, I'm just glad it did.'

Wordlessly she lifted up and leaned closer to meet his deep kiss, which grew quickly into something hungry and needy and once again they were dragged with urgent demand to find fulfilment.

※

'I had better get back,' Elle said after they'd roused themselves long enough to make something for a late dinner.

'It's late, stay here tonight,' Stuart said, catching her hand and bringing her forward to stand between his thighs as he sat on the bar stool at the counter.

'I don't have any clean clothes, they're all back at my room,' she protested but feared it sounded pathetically weak.

'We can wash these ones. I have a dryer. Besides, you won't be needing them tonight anyway,' he said with that intoxicating little half grin he did that made her heart lurch.

She didn't really *have* to go to the pub. All she'd be doing there would be sitting alone and staring at the walls inside her room.

'Stay,' he urged, nuzzling at her neck until she could barely remember what they'd been talking about.

'Okay,' she heard herself agree in between kisses, before finding herself back upstairs in an enormous bed.

※

Elle opened her eyes slowly, and took a moment to recall her whereabouts. Something heavy lay across her waist and she turned her head to find Stuart asleep next to her. In sleep he looked a lot more relaxed. He always seemed to be taking everything in when he was awake, studying the situation before he spoke and measuring his words; at least he had before they'd come back to his house late yesterday afternoon. After that, she'd seen a different side to this man. He was gentle and considerate and had the uncanny ability to make her feel as though he were in total sync with her every thought and need. There was a playful side to him she would never have imagined on the first occasion they'd briefly met. He'd seemed so aloof that day, but then again, he'd thought she was some lost tourist, which, she supposed, she had been.

While she'd been busy thinking about all this, the man in question had woken up and was now watching her.

'Morning,' Stuart said with a lazy deep brogue that sent her insides flipping. She really needed to work on how easy it was for him to set her off; he barely had to do more than speak. Curse that sexy Scottish accent.

'Morning,' Elle replied, feeling unfathomably shy.

'Do you ken you snore?'

'I do not,' she scoffed.

'You do,' he countered with a slow grin. 'But it's a cute wee kind of sound.'

'I do *not* snore,' she told him firmly.

*Actually, dear, you do*, Gran said, and Elle jumped, scrambling for the sheet.

'Gran!' she yelped.

Her startled movement caused Stuart to sit upright in bed and search the room for some kind of danger worthy of her reaction.

'What's wrong?' he demanded, looking confused.

Oh dear God, he was going to think she was crazy.

*Gran, you can't be here now*, she said silently, horror-struck by the fact her gran had decided *now* was a perfectly acceptable time and place to re-enter her life after mysteriously vanishing for days.

*Oh, stop being so dramatic. I'm under no illusions that you're still a virgin.*

Elle squeezed her eyes tightly shut and felt a blush creep up her neck. *Gran, you need to leave right now. Come back later.*

She heard her gran give something between a scoff and a chuckle. *Darling, you seem to assume I have any say whatsoever in where and when I turn up.*

*Gran!* This was so humiliating.

'Elle, are you all right? What's wrong?' Stuart was now looking at her with a great deal of concern.

'I'm fine. I just remembered . . .' Now she was stammering like a fool as she searched wildly for some kind of explanation that didn't make her seem like a lunatic. 'I forgot to put my clothes on to wash last night and I haven't got anything to wear,' she finished lamely.

He seemed to relax a little after that, though he was still watching her a little oddly. 'Is that all? I put them on after I got up through the night. They'll be done by now.'

'You did?' she asked, momentarily surprised by his thoughtfulness.

'Well, it was the least I could do after I was the one who distracted you from doing it earlier,' he pointed out.

'Oh, well, thank you. That was really sweet of you.'

'Christ, woman, you almost gave me a heart attack when you jumped up like that,' Stuart said, with a chuckle. 'I thought you'd seen a ghost or something.'

'Ha,' Elle managed with a shaky laugh. She wasn't game to even think about Gran in case she was still there, but the mood of a few moments earlier had certainly gone now. 'How about I go downstairs and make breakfast?' She was out of bed before Stuart could protest, and grabbed a T-shirt off the floor to pull on.

'Wait a minute and I'll come down with you,' he said, throwing back the bed covers. For a moment Elle stopped and stared at the masculine beauty of the man now standing before her. She itched to grab her sketchpad. He would make a great subject; she could already see the lines appearing on the page, long and sleek before shading and defining his abs, and that particularly enticing little hollow between his hip and his . . . She cleared her throat and dragged her mind away from where it had been trying really hard to go.

'Are you sure you're okay? You seem a little jumpy.'

'No, no. I'm fine.' She waved a hand carelessly and forced out a laugh, which sounded a little less convincing than she'd hoped for, judging by the eyebrow he raised in response.

'Have I done something to make you feel uncomfortable?' he asked.

'No, not at all,' she said, relieved that this time she sounded almost normal. 'I guess it's just a little strange. I don't have a great deal of experience with the whole morning-after thing,' she admitted, and that much at least was true. It *was* a little strange. What *was* the protocol for this situation, anyway?

He looked relieved at that and smiled, moving across the room to take her hand. 'Just be you,' he said, lowering his head for a kiss that, as usual, took very little to turn it into something more. Before she realised what was happening he was walking her backwards to the edge of the bed and she was too distracted to worry about her wayward gran's whereabouts.

***

After breakfast, and dressed in clean clothes once more, Elle went out with Stuart to check on the livestock.

'Are these the same kind of sheep and cattle your grandfather used to run?' she asked as they passed a hilly paddock dotted with white sheep.

'He used mainly black-faced,' he said, looking out over his herd, 'but I decided to run North Country Cheviot.'

As they got closer, she could see the sheep more clearly. Their heads and legs were covered with short glossy-white hair and they had black hoofs and long-ish noses and were big compared to other sheep she had seen throughout the Scottish countryside. As far as sheep went, they were quite pretty, she thought. 'Are they used mainly for their wool?'

'They're a meat sheep, generally, but their wool is used a lot by hand spinners. Though it isn't worth much at the current wool price. We usually shear as soon as the weather warms up—sometimes it's a bit of a gamble, spring is renowned for throwing you a curve ball now and again and delivering a cold snap when it's supposed to be hot. So, we try to judge the best time to bring them in for shearing. Usually it's a few weeks after lambing finishes.'

The countryside was stunning. So different to the farmland back home. Elle let her eyes wander across the hills and valleys before her, and in the distance she saw that it went right down to the rugged coastline beyond.

'What type of cattle are they?' she asked as she spotted the black shaggy-looking animals happily grazing among the clumps of heather and native grasses beside a craggy stone fence.

'They're Highland cattle.'

'I thought Highland cattle were red?'

'Those ones are the Kyloe breed. Highlands were traditionally black. It was only later that the red was selectively bred into them.'

Elle, like every other tourist who came to Scotland, had been on the lookout for the shaggy red Highland *coos*, as they were lovingly called, in every gift shop and tourist centre she visited. She'd taken a few photos of some she'd found along the roadside but hadn't yet seen one up close.

'The mainland Highland breed are bigger, but they do better on pasture and quality feed. I have these because they're a lot hardier and they're better suited to the landscape here where it's mostly hill ground. There're plenty of native grasses and flora for them to forage, which helps lessen the damage to habitat for the wildlife.'

'Is that your thing?' she asked, interested in his decision to give up a law practice to become a farmer. 'To turn your property into something of a conservationist-type farming venture?'

'Yes and no. I mean my ancestors, and yours,' Stuart added with a grin, 'have been managing their land for generations. Agriculture has been happening here for something like six thousand years. I think farmers, particularly Scots, have always been conservationists at heart—managing farming and nature hand in hand. But I guess, in a way I just wanted to go back to more traditional roots with the livestock.'

Elle watched him as he drove, his hands big and capable on the wheel, his eyes constantly searching the land for his livestock, and checking any fences they came across. She could get used to this, she thought contentedly, before pulling herself up quickly as reality barged its way into her peaceful little fantasy. She would have to leave one day soon. This was not something she would ever have a chance to *get used to*.

The sooner she remembered that and stopped romanticising this whole thing, the better off she'd be.

But she didn't have to leave just yet.

# Twenty-two

The first streaks of daylight breached the sky and filtered into the conservatory as Elle listened to the dial tone on her phone.

'Hi,' Elle said when her friend answered. 'I was hoping I did the maths right and you'd be waiting for Rose to get out of school.'

'I am, actually,' Lilly replied brightly. 'And I was just thinking about you earlier. We got the postcard yesterday. Rose loved the cow.'

Elle hadn't realised how much she missed hearing her old friend's voice until now and felt her throat tighten unexpectedly. 'Oh good. I was wondering if it'd turned up yet.'

'I thought maybe you'd beat it home. How's the trip?'

'It's great. I've been seeing so much. Met the rellies.'

'You were about to head up there, you said in the postcard. How did that go?'

'Great. It was incredible, actually. Lilly, I finally felt as though I fitted in somewhere. One of the cousins is an artist—an honest to God, real artist. She's had her artwork hung in galleries in Paris.'

'No way,' Lilly said, surprised.

'I know! And you're never going to believe this, but . . . I sold three of my sketches,' Elle blurted, covering her mouth with her hand to stop herself squealing into the phone like an idiot.

'You did not!' Lilly gasped. 'How? When? Who to?'

'My cousins have a gift shop, and Grace, the cousin who's an artist, put three of my sketches up before I left—and someone bought them. Like, a real customer.'

'Elle, that's so freaking amazing. You're amazing!'

'And they have red hair, just like me.'

'Sounds like you really hit it off.'

'We did,' she smiled. 'I wasn't really expecting to, since Mum and Dad had organised it, but I'm really glad I got to meet them.'

'So, where are you now?'

'I'm still on the Isle of Skye.'

'Have you found the castle?'

'Yes. A couple of days ago.'

'And Gran? Is she still . . . with you?'

Elle kind of wished she hadn't mentioned the whole Gran-talking-to-her thing before she left. 'It's complicated.'

'Oh?'

'She hasn't been around as much,' Elle hedged.

'Have you scattered her ashes yet?' Elle heard the slight frown in her friend's voice at the question.

'No, not yet. I've kind of been busy.'

'Doing what?'

'Well, I sort of . . . met someone,' Elle said, reluctantly.

'*What?* Who? What's his name? What's he like?'

Elle briefly closed her eyes and again wished she'd kept her mouth shut. But this was Lilly. They told each other everything. Only, this time it was different. She wasn't sure how to answer.

'His name's Stuart,' she said eventually, 'and he owns the land around Stormeil. He's . . . nice.'

'Nice?' Lilly repeated doubtfully.

'Yes, he's nice. Really nice,' she added.

'It sounds like he's more than just nice if you've delayed the whole Gran thing. Is it serious?'

'No, of course not. I mean, that would be ridiculous.'

'Why?' Lilly asked bluntly.

'Well, because . . .' Elle found herself floundering. 'It just would be.'

The line went suspiciously quiet for a moment and she could imagine Lilly narrowing her eyes thoughtfully on the other end. 'You sound pretty flustered over something that's supposed to be nothing.'

'I'm not flustered! It's early over here and I haven't had coffee yet. I just rang because I was missing you.'

'We miss you too. Nice topic change, by the way, but okay, I get that you're a bit nervous.'

'Of what?'

'The possibility of a relationship. I mean, you've avoided them up to now because you've never been able to find anyone you think your mother will approve of.'

'It's not a . . .' Elle let out a frustrated huff. 'What do you mean? Why would I be worried about that?'

'Oh, come on, Elle. Let's face it, your mum hasn't approved of pretty much anything in your life lately. Your job, your career choices, your friends,' she stressed. Although her parents had always been polite to Lilly, they had never approved of her life choices. 'Have you told them about selling your sketches?' Lilly asked, but it sounded more like a challenge.

When Elle didn't answer, she heard Lilly make a knowing little sound under her breath and let out a frustrated sigh of her own.

'Why not?' Lilly asked.

'I called but they weren't home,' Elle replied defensively.

'I'm willing to bet you wouldn't have mentioned the sketches even if they had been.'

Oh, it's easy to be smug, Elle thought irritably.

'Elle,' Lilly sighed, 'if *you* don't even believe in your talent, how do you expect your parents to? You've always played it down.'

'No, I haven't.'

'*Yes*. You have. And I know why.' She softened her tone as she continued. 'Your mum's never been backward in coming forward when it comes to her definition of what makes a career and what doesn't, but if you think art is where your heart is, then you need to stop putting yourself down all the time. You *are* an artist. It's time to take it seriously, because if you don't, then no one else will.'

Trust Lilly to say it like it was.

'I'm sorry, Elle, but you need to hear this and it's no wonder you've avoided having a serious relationship. Unless the guy's a doctor or a lawyer, I hate to say it, but he's pretty much screwed if he's after your mother's approval.'

Well, at least he had *that* going for him, she supposed, before quickly shrugging off the thought. It didn't matter if her mother approved of Stuart—there was nothing serious about their relationship that needed approval.

'I say if you've found someone you really like, you should enjoy it for as long as you can.'

'Well, that's kind of the problem, isn't it? Time. I don't really have much of it.'

'You've got your UK passport,' she reminded her, 'So, use it. Find a job and stay for a while. See where it goes.'

Maybe this was why Elle had felt a need to call her best friend—to have someone she trusted tell her she was doing the right thing. 'I've been thinking about that,' she said.

'Good. Do it.'

'Well, I'm glad you won't miss me or anything,' Elle said dryly.

'Of course I will. But I want you to do the right thing *for you*. Until this trip came up, you hadn't been happy for a very long time, Elle. I could see it even if you couldn't. Take this opportunity. I think you'll regret it if you don't.'

'I'll think about it,' she promised, slightly surprised that Lilly had been more perceptive than she'd given her credit for.

'Keep me updated. I want to hear all about this Stuart guy. I might do some Facebook stalking tonight. Text me his full name.'

'I promise I'll keep you in the loop.'

A loud bell rang in the background. 'I gotta go, the animals have been released from the zoo,' Lilly said as the sound of high-pitched yelling and noise drowned out normal conversation. Elle had done the school pick-up occasionally when Lilly had been sick or stuck at work, and a shudder of fear ran up her spine as she recalled the utter bedlam those first few moments of freedom from classrooms created.

They said their goodbyes and Elle ended the call, staring out the glass windows at the pretty garden before her. It was cold, and she wrapped the woollen throw rug she'd grabbed from the bottom of the bed on her way downstairs around her shoulders tighter, before heading into the kitchen to make coffee.

The thought of staying on longer had really only been a back-up plan, but now, the more she thought about it, the more it seemed like it might happen. It was kind of scary. But it was also a little bit exciting. Coming to Scotland for a holiday was very different to coming here to stay and work. To live. When she first arrived, it was simply to see some sights and bring Gran home, but since then Elle had found family, and found a place for her art. It was all still new and tentative, but she wasn't sure she was ready to give any of it up just yet.

# Twenty-three

For two days Stuart and Elle played hermit and practically never left the house. After the first night, Stuart had driven her into the pub where she checked out and thanked Glenda for all her help, collected her bags and handed them to Stuart to load into the back of his car.

She'd made a quick stop at the post office to pack several more sketches into long canisters and send them to Aila and Grace to be framed.

'Why didn't you tell me you'd sold your sketches?' Stuart asked, when she told him what she needed to do at the post office.

'I don't know.' She shrugged, feeling that damn red flush beginning to warm her cheeks once more. 'I guess I was still in shock. And, I mean, it's not like I've made a fortune or anything,' she said, trying not to feel like a traitor to herself. She didn't need to hear Lilly to feel her disapproval and realise that she'd been right. Elle *did* put her art down. It had become a habit, and one she needed to break. 'Actually, now that it has sunk in, I'm really excited about it. Which is why I'm sending more sketches up there.'

'Congratulations,' Stuart said, before he disappeared into the pub and came back out with a bottle of champagne, which they opened when they got back home.

'Do you have any plans?' Stuart asked now as they sat together at the kitchen bench, eating pancakes.

Plans. She sighed. There was that ugly word again. 'Not really. Why?'

'I thought you might be having sketching withdrawals and you'd like to take a look at another old ruin not far from here.'

'Really?' Again with the whole intuitive thing. She *had* been feeling like she wanted to grab her pencils and draw something.

'If you want to, that is,' he added.

'I would. That sounds great.'

The ruins of Duntulm Castle, perched on the edge of a cliffside overlooking the ocean, were barely more than a handful of rocks that only vaguely resembled what would have once been a very impressive, fortified castle. But the moment Elle saw the site, she was mesmerised.

*Look at that, Gran*, she said softly in her head, but there was no response. Elle liked to imagine Gran wandering aimlessly; exploring somewhere on her own whenever she went silent for long stretches, something that was becoming more and more frequent.

While there were countless beautiful, awe-inspiring castles scattered across Scotland, there was something about ruins that spoke to Elle. Maybe it was the way they made her use her imagination to conjure up an image of what it would have once looked like, or maybe it was the lingering ghosts that seemed to remain about the site. Not actual ghosts, more memories. Whatever it was, there was definitely *something* she could feel around ruins, and Duntulm Castle was no different.

'This was once an early castle of the MacLeods,' Stuart told her. 'Until the castle was taken over by the MacDonalds of Sleat in the seventeenth century. Apparently it even had a royal visit from James the fifth in 1540.'

'I don't think I'll ever get used to the history and age of everything over here.'

'I guess we take it for granted; at least I always did when I was younger. It's only been since my grandparents have both gone that I've really started to appreciate it.'

As they strolled along the narrow sheep track that led to the ruins, avoiding sheep poo as they went, Stuart held her hand securely and she felt an unexpected contentment settle inside her. The wind blew her hair around her face and stung her cheeks, but inside she felt as gooey and warm as melted chocolate. How had this man become so important to her in such a short time? Was it real? Maybe what she was feeling was just a trick, a happy afterglow of good sex. She didn't have a great deal of experience in these kinds of things, so perhaps it was a completely normal side effect. But it felt like more. She knew enough to realise that a casual one-night stand didn't make you want to spend the next day, and the next, with a person. It kind of defeated the point of having a one-night stand, if it went longer than one night.

But what was she supposed to make of it? This hadn't been on her itinerary. Mentally she went over it: *complete Gran's bucket list, meet her long-lost relatives, see some castles, take Gran to Stormeil and go home.* The list had definitely *not* included: *have a bit of fling with a sexy Scotsman.* And yet here they were.

They stood for a moment to take in the breathtaking view of the coastline before them. The hilltop where the castle stood had been separated on the land side by a deep trench, but that was no longer there and so the steep hill that ran down from it fell into a rugged stretch of rock that now, being somewhere between low and high tide, was a scattering of rockpools, before dropping into the sea beyond it. The views were phenomenal.

'What's that land out there?' she asked Stuart. The long line of mountains seemed to stretch forever as a faint shadow in the distance.

'That's the hills of Harris.'

'This place is beautiful.' Every time she thought Scotland couldn't get any more amazing she found another view that took her breath away.

'They certainly knew how to choose the best real estate,' he agreed. They found a spot on the grass to sit and Elle took out her sketchpad. Stuart braced his back against a rock, and settled her in front of him. For a moment she found herself distracted by the warmth of his body behind her, but as soon as she put her pencil onto the paper, everything else disappeared and she found herself concentrating on the image forming on the blank page before her.

As she stopped drawing, she tilted her head critically.

'That's impressive,' he said from behind her, and she smiled over her shoulder at him.

'Thank you.' She was happy with the landscape she'd drawn, capturing the ruins in the forefront with the ocean stretching out beyond.

She got to her feet and took more photos for inspiration later in case she wanted to do some more sketching, but she knew the image of this place would stay with her for a long time without the need to look at photographs.

They walked back to Stuart's four-wheel drive slowly, hand in hand, and Elle savoured every minute, tucking the memories into a safe little corner of her mind to reflect on later. She didn't want to waste time analysing everything now—when she knew that very soon she would need to make some big decisions.

In order to stay in Scotland, Elle needed to secure a job—she couldn't live on the leftover money from Gran indefinitely, and the United Kingdom was a very expensive place to live. What she didn't know was whether staying on meant staying on . . . here.

That evening as she and Stuart cooked dinner in his beautiful kitchen, inside his even more beautiful house, Elle knew she had to bring up the subject they had both been avoiding, but as she went to open her mouth, Stuart spoke first.

'Do you have any plans for tomorrow? If not, I was thinking maybe you might want to come along and help me with some sheep work.'

'Sheep work?'

'I need to move some stock up before the cold weather sets in, and there's a few other jobs I need to take care of. I could use a hand.'

'Oh. Sure,' she said, surprised by his request. 'I mean, I'm not exactly experienced, so I'm not sure how much help I'll be, but I'd like to give you a hand.' How could she say no? It was her fault he was falling behind on his jobs because she'd been holding him hostage in the bedroom for the past few days. And then there was all the tour-guide work he'd been doing. She owed him at least a day of labour for all that.

'I was thinking I should probably get back on the road soon,' she said, reaching for another carrot to chop as they worked companionably across from each other at the huge island bench.

'Where were you planning to go?' he asked, after a moment passed in silence.

'I'm not exactly sure. I've got a few more things I'd like to see, but I'm thinking I'd like to stay on in Scotland a bit longer, so I'll need to find a job. I thought I'd probably head back up to where my family are in Portsoy.'

'I see.'

'I was originally flying home in a few more days, but the longer I think about it, the more I'm just not ready to go back yet.'

'You could stay here,' he offered, holding her gaze for a moment, before Elle dropped hers to take another carrot.

'I can't,' she said with a sad smile.

'Why not?'

'Because you hardly know me. It's been unexpected and . . . incredible,' she said, lifting her eyes back to his with a smile. 'I wasn't expecting any of this when I set out on this trip, but I can't just stay here indefinitely.'

'What if you worked for me?' he suggested, concentrating a little too hard on the potato he was slicing.

'Worked for you, how?' she asked suspiciously.

'Nothing dodgy,' he added quickly. 'I mean *here*, with me. It got me thinking the other day when you were talking about the woman who got backpackers to help out. I could use some help; you're looking for a place to stay and a job . . .' He let the sentence hang in the air as he watched her face expectantly.

'But I don't know anything about farming,' she said slowly.

'I'm not sure many backpackers would come with farming experience either,' he said with a smile. 'It wouldn't have to be farming work. You could do some cooking, help out with the house . . . whatever needed doing.'

'I don't know, Stuart,' Elle said with a wary shake of her head. 'I'm not sure I'd feel right about it.'

'You were going to work for food and board with the other place, how is this any different?' he asked.

'Well, I wouldn't be *sleeping with the boss* at the other place,' she pointed out.

'Which is why *this* offer is much better,' Stuart countered.

He did have a point.

'It was just a thought,' he said after a while, when she didn't readily reply. She sensed he was a little hurt that she hadn't jumped at the idea. 'I know you have other places you want to see.'

'It's not that I want to leave this area. I love it here. It's beautiful. I guess it's just this whole thing with us . . .' She tried to explain, but the words were all sticking together. 'I mean, we've never really talked about . . . what this is between us. We kind of just fell into it without really thinking everything through.'

'What do *you* think it is?' he asked slowly, careful not to look at her.

Elle wasn't sure. She'd been trying to work it out since day one. 'I guess it was just a happenchance kind of thing that we met and hit it off,' she said with a small shrug.

She heard him give a quiet scoff-type grunt as he continued to gather the ingredients for their meal.

'I mean, I came here looking for Stormeil, and I found you,' she said lightly. 'I wasn't expecting that.'

He looked up and the gentle expression on his face made her heart thud slightly out of rhythm. 'Neither was I.'

'I've loved being here with you, Stuart,' she said softly.

'I've loved having you here,' he replied. 'I never realised how quiet this place was before you got here. This has been the first time in, I don't know how long, since I've taken time to stop and appreciate the moment. I've been so busy trying to end my old life and start a new one that I forgot what it was like to just enjoy someone's company.'

'You've had a lot to do. You've got a lot invested in the success of your farm.'

'It's been good to stop and take stock of things for a while.'

'I'm glad you have.'

A quiet kind of peace fell between them for a moment and the soft *thunk* of slicing and dicing on a chopping board was the only sound in the kitchen.

'Think on it a bit,' he said when they'd finished. 'There's no hurry to decide.'

Elle did think on it—she couldn't stop. It would be so easy to take Stuart's offer and let things continue as they had been, but she worried that she would simply be putting off making a hard decision down the track. This wasn't real life—even if they did have some miraculous future together, it wouldn't be like this forever. Reality would step in. The farm would need Stuart's full attention and eventually stress and long hours, bills and the demands of a farming life would change what they had right now and make it, well, ordinary. At the moment it was fun and exciting and new, but what if they didn't like each other when reality replaced what they had now? It would only end up messy and complicated. Maybe it was better in the long run for both of them to have *these* memories . . . memories of a beautiful holiday romance that was brief, but perfect.

# Twenty-four

'Morning, sleepyhead,' Stuart said, kissing Elle's nose as she came to stand beside him at the kitchen bench the next morning. She took the mug he was holding out to her and sighed as she tasted her first sip of coffee and then noticed the plate of bacon and eggs he'd placed before her.

'Eat up, you're going to need all the energy you can get today,' he said cheerfully. Too cheerfully for this early in the morning.

By the end of her first cup of coffee Elle had at least stopped yawning, and after coffee number two she managed to string together a few words. But it was the fresh air which greeted her like a slap across the face as she walked outside that really woke her up. She was definitely having second thoughts about a career as a farmhand. What would Claire do? The *Outlander* heroine had managed to overcome plenty of unpleasant hurdles after being sent back in time in the books. If Claire could survive

Scotland in 1743, then surely Elle could handle this. Suitably fortified, she embraced her inner Claire and headed outside.

'Here, you're going to need these,' Stuart said, handing her a pair of black gum boots at least two sizes too big.

'I've got my sneakers. These kind of look a bit big.' She eyed them warily.

'Trust me. Wear the boots,' he told her, before putting them next to her.

Elle trudged as quickly as she could behind him, around the back of the house and through the gate in the low stone wall. She hadn't ventured out this way before and now she saw that there were three huge sheds. Two were newer, much like the large farming sheds back home made of Colorbond-type tin, but the other older one was built from stone. Between the sheds stood a combination of old timber and newer steel stockyards, and as the two of them sloshed towards the yards through ankle-deep, smelly mud, Elle saw why she needed gum boots.

Bleating noises grew louder as they entered one of the newer sheds and Elle found herself looking at a complex system of stockyards—called, Stuart informed her, a fank—set up inside.

An older man with a salt-and-pepper beard and dark green beanie covering his shaggy grey hair was already working and glanced over as they came in, giving a brief nod.

'Elle, this is Geordie,' Stuart introduced her.

'Hello, Geordie,' Elle said with a smile that wavered a little when the man barely glanced at her. 'Hard at work,' she added cheerfully before he turned his back on her to continue whatever it was he was doing.

Stuart hid a grin as he took her arm and led her away. 'Don't mind him,' he said in a low tone. 'He takes a while to warm up to people.'

'Hmm.' Somehow she didn't think there was going to be enough time for Geordie to get around to warming up to her. If this were *Outlander*, then she'd just found her Murtagh, Jamie Fraser's stony-faced godfather. She tried to imagine him in a kilt with a sword, and surprisingly had no trouble doing so.

'Wow, this looks very professional,' she said as they walked towards a gate that led to the outside yards. Stuart gave a loud whistle, and within moments the two black-and-white border collies appeared and began to push the mob of sheep forward, who rushed into the first, largest yard inside the shed. When they were all in, Stuart shut the gate behind them and moved through the sea of woolly sheep to come back to her side.

'Do you think you can work the gates for me?' he asked, waving her over to the end of a long race where a small gate divided two separate yards. 'Geordie'll open the one at that end to send them in, and then you'll be up the other end to let them out as I'm done with them.'

'Okay,' she said a little warily. It sounded simple enough.

Elle heard a little snicker, and Gran's voice in her ear: *Good luck, darling.*

*Gran! Where have you been hiding?* Elle asked, relieved she could still hear her.

*Oh, here and there,* Gran replied breezily. *I must say, I never thought I'd see you doing farm work.*

*That makes two of us,* Elle answered dryly. *Thank goodness no one back home can see me now.*

There was no time for further musings as she watched Stuart put on a backpack attached to a long hose with a nozzle on the end. 'I'll worm them, then send them down to you, okay?' he called as he leaned over the side of the narrow race.

'Okay,' she called back nervously, taking hold of the long bar that would open the gate.

'Open,' he called and she pulled the lever. Immediately sheep began to push through the narrow opening as the dogs barked at the back of the crowd, holding them in a tight formation, unable to run back the way they'd come.

Elle stood by the lever, waiting as Stuart stuck the drench into the sheep's mouth and Geordie sprayed them with a coloured tin of paint. 'Open,' he called as he let that one go and grabbed the next. The sheep heading towards her suddenly looked much bigger than she'd been expecting. It was running quite fast. She pulled the handle quickly and closed her eyes as the animal shot by and into the open yard beyond. By the fifth or sixth time, she'd almost got used to it and could open the gate without closing her eyes.

They worked surprisingly quickly, and Elle found herself admiring the strength it took to hold each animal still enough to insert the nozzle into its mouth. She was also impressed by the way the dogs worked, very much like two more employees, but far cuter with their long lolling tongues and big brown eyes.

The queue seemed never-ending as she looked over at the yard of sheep yet to be wormed, despite the fact the other yard behind her was filling up.

It took a couple of hours to finish the job. Every now and then Elle had to run back down the other end of the lane and open the gate to let the dogs bring up some more sheep from outside when Geordie got stuck helping Stuart, and then run back to the other end of the race to let out the sheep that were waiting to be released. When the men eventually stopped, Elle wiped her brow and sent a proud and relieved smile across at Stuart. Despite the fact that the weather had been getting noticeably cooler each day since she'd arrived, she'd managed to work up a sweat.

'We'll make a farmhand out of you yet,' he said, dropping a kiss on her lips as she came to a stop beside him.

'I bet you say that to all your backpacker helpers,' she scoffed.

'Only the good-looking Australian ones.'

The light-hearted banter made the rest of the morning pass quickly, and Elle found herself truly enjoying the work. She took time to play with the dogs, rubbing their heads and cooing to them affectionately, before Stuart sent them back to work.

'You've even made my dogs fall in love with you,' he complained, then froze, sending her a startled look that made her own heartrate pause uncertainly. Time seemed to stop. Surely he hadn't meant . . .

She quickly forced a grin to her face and brushed past the remark. 'They're so cute. Did you train them yourself?'

'Yeah, it's a bit of a passion of mine,' he said with a smile that looked a little bashful. 'My granddad used to have show-quality sheepdogs he took to compete in trials. As a kid, I had a couple of dogs I helped train and entered in a show here and there. I decided to get back into it.'

'That's so cool,' she said, watching the dogs as they headed off to do their work. It was amazing to watch the communication between man and dog as they worked intuitively with one another.

Geordie walked past and muttered something, making Elle glance across at Stuart for a translation.

'He's going to head off and finish some other jobs.'

'How on earth did you understand that?'

Stuart chuckled. 'I've grown up around him. He does warm to you after a while.'

Later, as they ate lunch on a wall outside in the sun, Elle let her gaze roam across the busy farmyard. Chooks clucked and pecked as they scratched around the yard and garden, noisy sheep bleated, wanting out of the yards they were being held in, and the dogs lay by their feet, snoozing in the warm sun, their ears flicking the odd insect away as they rested between jobs.

'I can see why you made the switch to farming,' she said after she finished her sandwich and dusted her hands off. 'You really were born to do this.'

'You think?' he asked, looking at her.

'I do,' she said firmly. 'I think certain things are in your blood and you just know that's what you're destined to be.'

'And what about you? Have you discovered what your destiny is yet?'

'No, not really,' Elle said with a small sigh.

'You don't think your calling is in art?'

'I'm not sure it's something I could make enough to live on,' she said finally, after mulling the answer over in her mind.

Elle hadn't immediately dismissed the idea as she normally would have, but she was trying to be practical about it. If only her mother could hear her now.

'It could be,' Stuart pointed out reasonably. 'There's got to be lots of ways you could turn art into some kind of career path.'

This was true, and when Elle had been at uni she had considered all the possible avenues she could take with art in order to find something that might convince her parents that switching to an art degree would be beneficial to a lifelong career. There had been nothing with the kind of job security they would be happy with—not like the good old reliable degrees like accountancy, medicine or law.

'No, I think art is just my escape, my happy place to go to when I need to get away from everything else for a while.'

'Maybe,' Stuart said. 'Or maybe you're one of those lucky people who can turn their passion into a job they actually love. Not too many people get a chance to do that.'

His words filled her with a warm glow that rose all the way up into her cheeks. 'Who knows,' she said, ducking her head. 'I never imagined I'd be a farmhand, and look at me now, smelling like sheep and covered in mud.' She grinned across at him.

'And it's a complete turn-on,' Stuart told her, leaning over and giving her what she suspected was only supposed to be a playful kiss, until it turned into something else. By the time they were done, she'd ended up covered in even more mud, with bits of hay stuck in her hair and down her top.

# Twenty-five

'*Finally*,' her mother said when she answered the phone.

'Hi, Mum,' Elle said dryly. Even this far away she still managed to annoy her mother, it seemed. That afternoon when Elle and Stuart had headed inside, grubby and sweaty and smelling like sheep, her phone began to ping as it connected to the wi-fi, and message after message came through, reminding Elle that she had missed her agreed-upon check-in call.

'We've been trying to call you since last night.'

'Why? Is everything okay?'

'Everything's fine. It's just been three days since we heard from you.'

'I'm fine. I've just been out of reception on and off.'

'Where are you?'

'I'm still on Skye. I've found a bit of work for a few days,' she said, then instantly regretted mentioning it when both parents started to shoot questions at her on speaker.

'Hi, Dad,' Elle cut in.

'Work?'

'Well, of sorts. There're lots of backpacker-type jobs. Working for food and board kind of thing. I thought it might be fun and it saves on accommodation costs.'

'What kind of work?' Caroline asked.

'Farm work, actually. Today I helped worm sheep,' Elle said cheerfully, though cringing at her mother's response as she waited for it.

'Farm work?'

'Yes, well, I thought I'd give it a go.'

'That sounds interesting,' Alister said, and Elle could almost picture her mother's disapproving glare.

'It was.'

'Are you short of money?' her mother asked briskly.

'No,' Elle assured her quickly, 'I just thought it couldn't hurt to save some since the opportunity came up.'

'I'm not sure I like the fact that people are using you for that kind of labour.'

'It's not as bad as it sounds. I liked it.'

'So, you're a farmer now?' Her dad chuckled.

'I've heard all kinds of horror stories about people taking advantage of foreign backpackers overseas, Elspeth. I really don't like this idea.'

'It's okay, Mum, really. This is a nice, normal kind of place and the people are lovely.'

'It's a family?' Caroline pressed.

Elle didn't think it would help her cause to mention she was working for a good-looking Scotsman with whom she happened to be sleeping. So, she opted for an abridged version of the truth. 'It's just a small family farm.'

'Make sure you allow plenty of time to get back to Edinburgh for your flight,' Alister warned. 'In case something goes wrong. Don't cut it too close.'

'I won't, Dad.' She paused, then figured that now was as good a time as any to bring it up with them. 'But I was thinking I might extend my stay a bit.'

'Extend?' Caroline repeated.

'Well, yeah. I can work—get a job for a while and explore some more. I don't have anything to get back to.'

'Certainly not a job,' her mother snapped.

'Exactly,' Elle said, forcing herself to stay calm. 'So, I may as well make the most of the time I have.'

'It could be a good experience,' her father said, surprising her, and her mother too, judging by the unusual silence on the other end of the line.

'I think so,' Elle agreed. 'It's such a long flight over here, it's not practical to come back another time to do it, so I may as well do it while I'm here.'

'I can't believe you're serious,' Caroline broke in. 'You can't bring yourself to look for a job here, but you're willing to do it on the other side of the world?' Her voice was laced with a healthy dose of disappointment.

'It's an experience I can't get back at home, Mum.'

'I sometimes wished I'd taken a year to travel overseas after I finished university,' Alister said, sounding a little wistful.

'Only, you were married and had a career to think about,' Caroline added pointedly.

'Yes, well, maybe in hindsight we didn't have to rush quite so much. We could have taken the time to travel before we settled down,' Alister said, and Elle raised an eyebrow at her father's candid reply.

'Hindsight is a fine thing,' her mother said with an impatient sniff.

'Oh, come on, Caroline,' Alister said. 'Tell me you didn't say exactly the same thing when we went on our first trip to Greece. Remember we were doing a tour of the islands and we got talking to those backpackers who'd just finished university?'

'I don't remember that at all, Alister.'

'You must?' Elle could hear the teasing grin on his face from all the way over here. 'You said, you wished we'd gone and done something so spontaneous before we decided to open our own practices and start a family.'

'I'm sure I said no such thing.'

'Oh? So, you've probably also forgotten how we spent the remainder of that night then?' Alister countered with a decidedly suggestive tone, and Elle quickly stepped in to put a stop to hearing anything remotely traumatising about her parents' past sex life.

'I should go. I'll call in two days' time and I'll make sure I've got reception,' she promised. 'Love you. Bye.'

Crisis averted, she thought with a relieved sigh as she walked back inside. Then she was momentarily distracted by Stuart coming downstairs in just a pair of jeans.

'How are your parents?' he asked.

'Relieved I wasn't dead in some ditch, apparently.'

'It's what parents do,' he said with a grin. 'It must be a bit of a concern to have kids so far away from home.'

'Yeah, I know,' she said. 'I told them about changing my flight. They took it better than I expected. Dad actually stood up for me.'

'Well, that's good.'

'Yeah,' she said, less than enthusiastically.

'Isn't it?' he asked as he came to a stop beside her.

'I still don't really know *what* I'm going to do.' It was all well and good to just play it by ear, but the reality was, it was as expensive as hell over here. She couldn't just get in the car and drive and see where the road took her. Fuel cost an arm and a leg, and before she knew it she would eat through all her money and have to end up calling her parents to help bail her out of trouble. A small shudder ran through her at the thought of *that* phone call. This was not what she thought having an overseas adventure would be like, stressing over money and having to budget everything. Where was the carefree, fun-loving backpacker life in that?

'I can give you a few suggestions,' Stuart said helpfully.

'Your suggestions usually end up with us in bed,' Elle replied with a grin, and thought again how lucky she had been to have stumbled upon this man so unexpectedly.

'But they're good suggestions,' he added, sliding his arms around her.

'I smell like sheep,' she protested, trying to wriggle from his hold. 'You're all clean.' *And you smell so good*, she added silently.

'It's a good thing I'm rather partial to sheep then, isn't it?'

'That's probably not something you should go around advertising,' she teased, escaping his arms to head for the stairs. 'I'm going to wash off all the sheep smell and come back down to help with dinner.'

'Or,' he said, following her up the stairs, 'now that you've got me all smelly and in need of another shower, I could come with you.'

'You know, sometimes you *do* come up with really good suggestions,' she said, as he took her hand to lead her to the bathroom.

✿

For the next few days, Elle worked alongside Stuart and they found themselves settling into an easy routine. Even the early starts began to feel not so bad, and the reward was more than worth it. Elle loved watching the sun as it crept its way into the sky from behind the craggy hills and ridges of the farm. But her favourite place was the rugged cliff face where the paddock dropped off into the ocean. The view, standing there and looking across the endless expanse of water, stretching as far as the eye could see, filled her with so much awe and . . . peace. She often took her sketchbook and found time to sit and draw at some point in her day; at these moments she realised that this was the most content she had ever felt with life.

They would share a packed lunch if they were out working in the paddocks, or she would make their lunch and bring it out if they had been doing yard work in the sheds. They were together every hour of the day and it should have started to feel stifling, but it didn't. Each day she felt herself falling a little more deeply for Stuart Buchanan.

As they lay together one night, Stuart's body curled behind hers and his arm securely across her waist, she felt the deep, rhythmic rise and fall of his breathing against her back.

'Are you happy, Elle?' he asked quietly.

His question was unexpected, but she found herself smiling in the dark. 'I am.'

'Good,' he said after a while, and she heard his breathing change as he drifted off to sleep.

But Elle stayed awake as she thought over his question. It was true, she was happier here than she had been in a very long time. She loved everything about this place—the farm, the land, the island—and she felt connected to this place in a way she couldn't explain. But now she understood why Gran had fought so hard to come back. She'd had no choice. She was drawn back here by that same connection. And yet, that previous feeling that warned Elle not to get too settled had begun to stir again.

*It's time, my love. Time to say goodbye.* She didn't hear Gran's words in her head like she had before. This time she felt them, in her heart.

Elle had been trying not to think about why she had come here. Partly because Stuart was mixed up in it all, but mostly because she just couldn't face the moment when she would have to say goodbye to Gran. Deep down she knew that warning she kept hearing was her conscience reminding her that she wasn't here for herself. She was here for Gran, and she needed to make good on her promise.

It was time.

# Twenty-six

As they cooked breakfast side by side, Stuart's phone rang and he handed Elle the spatula while he took the call.

'Hello, Mum,' he said, and Elle glanced up. 'No, I haven't forgotten,' he continued, then looked across at Elle with a grimace that told her that he possibly *had* forgotten whatever it was his mother was calling to remind him about. 'Yeah, all right. I'll see you then. Bye.' He put the phone back down on the bench with a long sigh. 'I forgot about my parents coming up for the weekend,' he groaned.

Elle stopped moving the scrambled eggs about in the pan.

'They'll be here tomorrow.'

His parents? Here?

'Elle?' His question snapped her attention from the pan she'd been staring at.

'Sorry?'

'Are you all right?'

'Of course,' she said, putting a bright smile on her face. 'That's great your parents are coming for a visit.'

'It's not exactly ideal timing,' he said, and she watched as Stuart rubbed a hand over the back of his neck, looking somewhat uncomfortable.

'Oh no. It's fine. I should have probably left days ago,' she said, setting the spatula on the counter and stepping away from the stove. 'It's fine,' she babbled on.

'What?'

'Seriously, it's no big deal. I need to go anyway.'

'What are you talking about?' Stuart asked, his accent becoming thicker as his frown deepened.

'Your parents are coming,' she said.

'Yes, but what's that got to do with you going?'

'Well, it's not like I can stay.'

'Why not?'

'Because . . . your parents are coming,' she said, eyeing him pointedly.

'That doesn't mean you have to leave.'

'I don't think they'll want to be stuck here in the same house with a stranger—especially one they weren't expecting.'

'You're not a stranger, and it's my house.'

'You can't tell me you're not uncomfortable with the idea?'

He'd looked more than a little flustered when he'd got off the phone.

'I was worried you'd think I was rushing you into the whole meet-the-parents kind of thing.'

Stuart was right, it wasn't exactly ideal timing. And she *was* freaking out a little at the idea.

'I don't want you to leave,' he said, when she didn't answer immediately.

'I think I have to.' Sadness poured into the space where, before, happiness had been. 'How can I meet your parents and explain what this is, when *we* don't even know?'

'I haven't had to explain anything to my parents about my personal life for a good few years now,' he said.

Elle took a step closer to him and pushed past her growing misery. 'Stuart, these last couple of weeks have been so great. It's the happiest I've been in a long time, but the fact that we're back to this same point again, only makes me realise that all I've been doing is putting off the inevitable.' He went to speak but she kissed him to stop the argument she knew he was going to put forward. She couldn't let him talk her out of this again, and she knew he so easily could if she let him. It was just all too easy to imagine herself staying, but it wasn't real. It was just a break from life—a brief, beautiful interlude that one day reality would barge in and ruin.

'I came here to do something for my gran and it's time I finished what I started,' Elle said softly when she pulled away from the kiss, biting her lip against the tears that had already started to fall despite her best intentions to stay strong.

She turned away and headed back upstairs to pack her suitcase, which didn't take long, since she'd never unpacked anything, despite Stuart leaving her two empty drawers and hanging space in the closet for her things. It hadn't been an accident. Deep down she'd known that if she unpacked her suitcase, she would never want to leave.

Coming back down with her bags, she saw Stuart, arms crossed and staring at the floor of the kitchen as he leaned back against the bench. She didn't want to see him so wretched; Elle needed him to be strong because she wasn't sure she was going to be able to walk away from him by herself.

'Can I borrow your car to go back to the ruins before I leave?' she asked, forcing the words out.

'I can take you,' he said calmly, without looking at her.

'I think it's something I need to do on my own,' she said, holding up the backpack with the urn inside. 'I've put it off for too long.'

Stuart looked up and she swallowed over the lump in her throat as he walked towards her, coming to a stop to stare down at her bags.

'Don't go, Elle,' he said, and it almost tore her heart in half.

'I have to. The longer I stay, the harder it'll get.'

'Then why leave at all?' he said, searching her eyes.

'Stuart,' she almost groaned his name, miserably.

'I mean it, Elle. Stay. You said this was the happiest you'd been in a long time. Well, it's the same for me. I know you think this doesn't have any future, but it could. I can see a future with you, Elle.'

Elle cursed the stupid tears that began to flow like a river down her face at his words. It was crazy. People didn't fall in love this fast. It was a holiday fling, two people thrown together, spending every minute of the day with each other—it just amplified things and made it seem as though they'd known each other forever. The reality was they *didn't* know each other. It was just something unexpected and a little bit exciting.

'I care about you, Elle.'

'I care about you too,' she said, wishing she could have a conversation with him calmly, instead of while she was crying. She never cried, certainly not in front of people, and yet here she was, blubbering like a baby. 'But this was never supposed to be permanent.'

'Maybe not, but plans can change.'

He was killing her with his honest, heartfelt arguments. 'Stuart, I need to figure out where I'm going. I think that's why I came on this trip, with Gran. I thought it was just to bring her back to where she wanted to be and heal a few old wounds, but it's more than that. It's about me and finding out who I am and where I'm headed. It's something I need to figure out on my own. I can't do that if I have someone else in my life to think about.' She hated that it sounded so selfish, but it was the truth. She knew she was at one of those crossroads in life that, whatever direction she chose, was going have a major impact on her future.

'I get it, Elle. I know all about following your dreams, but I also know that sometimes life leads you to places you weren't expecting and gives you a different option to get to where you were meant to be.'

'That's the problem,' she said helplessly. 'I don't know where that place is yet.' She shook her head. 'This wasn't part of your plan either.'

'Doesn't mean I'm not glad it happened.'

'I'm so happy that I got to spend this time with you. I will treasure these last few weeks forever, but right now I don't see how this can be something permanent. I can't stay here forever, I live on the other side of the world.'

'Maybe the answer to your question is staring you right in the face,' he said softly.

It sounded so simple. How easy would it be to just forget everything else and unpack her suitcase? But somehow it didn't feel right. It felt like she was taking the easy way out. Something deep inside was telling her that until she worked out the rest of her life, even what she had with Stuart right now wouldn't end the uneasiness she carried.

Wordlessly, she buried her head against his chest and felt his arms tighten around her. They stood like that for a long time, both lost in their own thoughts, taking comfort from each other. There was nothing left to say.

---

As Elle drove the now familiar track to the ruins, she brushed away the odd tear that continued to leak from her eyes and tried to concentrate on where she was going.

Pulling up at the site, she sat for a long while in the car, staring at the stone and rubble of the once-imposing castle before her.

'Well, here we are, Gran,' she said after a while.

Silence greeted her.

'Seriously?' she said, looking at the backpack beside her on the passenger seat. Where the hell was she? Of all the times *not* to be here. Elle tipped her head back against the seat and closed her eyes. She had been fighting against this moment since before she even left Australia. She didn't want to reach this point, the end of the journey. Once this was done, her promise would be fulfilled, and Gran would really be gone.

Slowly, she climbed from the car and walked through the large opening of what remained of the front wall, and into the rectangle room in the centre of the ruins that would have once been the heart of the castle.

This was where Isla's wedding feast had taken place the night before she was supposed to marry the Baron. It was hard to imagine that the hall—now with a grass floor and decayed tatters of stone, and barely one standing wall remaining—had once been somewhere people gathered to dance and dine, but as she closed her eyes she could see it perfectly.

The raised platform at the end of the hall where the family sat, reeds and hay on the stone floor beneath her feet, soaking up all the spilled mead and wine. Cats and dogs roaming beneath the tables looking for scraps. Music filled the room, and voices mingled in happy conversation all around her, but in heavy accents and a language she didn't understand—Gaelic perhaps? She saw the long wooden pews and tables groaning under the weight of food, and bright, colourful tapestries hanging on the tall stone walls. When she opened her eyes it all faded away and she was standing alone once more, in the stillness and rubble.

'Gran, are you sure this is what you want?' she asked as she crossed to the only remaining window—a lone arch with no walls or roof to support it, just a small row of stone holding it together. She looked through it now, towards the hills in the distance it framed. It didn't feel right. She couldn't imagine

Gran being left here all alone. This wasn't her. Gran had loved company and family, and this place was too quiet. Too lonely.

*You know, I think maybe you're right after all, dear.*

Elle blinked back a fresh set of tears. 'Where have you been?'

*I've been here*, she said calmly. *I'll always be here.*

Elle swallowed hard, and blinked back the sting in her eyes that her grandmother's gentle words stirred, still looking out over the mountains in the distance. 'I don't want to leave you here, Gran.'

*I know, dear. But it was never about where I'm left, you know*, she said in that calm, soothing way she had always had. *It was about the journey.*

'Then why would you bring me here if you didn't really want to stay?'

*One day you'll realise why.*

Elle let a long silence fill the space between them before making her decision. 'I think we should go back to Portsoy. I know it holds a lot of sad memories for you, but I think it's time you stopped your own ghosts holding you back.'

After an even longer silence, Gran's words were quiet, and filled with emotion. *I allowed my guilt and sadness to destroy any chance I might have had to find my family again. I punished myself for all those sins people blamed me for as a child, and allowed them to keep me alienated from where I truly belonged. I lost so many precious moments in my life because of it. You're right. It's time to stop being angry at myself and the past.*

'Will you be happy there, Gran?'

*Darling, I'll be happy wherever I am. I'm home again. That's all that matters.*

'Will you still . . . be around?' Elle asked hesitantly. As strange as all this was, it was hard to imagine life without Gran being with her anymore.

*Not like this. We've reached the end of our little adventure.*

'What are you talking about?'

*Our quest is over.*

'Our *quest*?' Elle scoffed. 'Gran, seriously, you are such a drama queen.'

She heard her gran's soft chuckle and a wave of grief rolled over her. Gran was saying goodbye. For real this time. 'I don't think I'm ready.'

*Yes, you are, darling. You don't need me anymore.*

'I'll always need you,' Elle said brokenly.

*You've got your life to live. It's time you went out and lived it. No more hiding. No more stalling. Go and find your purpose.*

Gran knew her better than she even knew herself. 'I love you, Gran.'

*And I love you, my beautiful, talented darling. Thank you for giving me the most wonderful gift I could ever ask for.*

Elle felt the gentle stir of a breeze against her skin and closed her eyes against it.

*It's time*, she heard Gran say, and then the breeze was gone, and the soft chirp of birds in the trees was the only sound that remained.

'Goodbye, Gran.'

With one last look around her, Elle farewelled the castle and walked slowly back to the four-wheel drive.

When she reached the house, her car was parked out the front and her bags had been placed in the back. A note on the windscreen made her hesitate briefly before she reached for it.

*I can't say goodbye again. If you change your mind, the front door is open.*
*S.*

Elle wiped her eyes and took a deep breath, tucking the note into the pocket of her jeans and opening the car door. She wished things could be different—she wished she could be someone who could be happy with the easiest road instead of the right one.

She didn't look back in the rear-view mirror as she drove away. She couldn't. She didn't want the last thing she saw to be a chance of happiness fading into the distance behind her. She focused instead on the road ahead and tried not to worry that she had just made the biggest mistake of her life.

# Twenty-seven

'Hi, Mum. It's me,' Elle said as she curled up on the hard bed of the pub room she'd found late that afternoon.

'How are you?'

She opened her mouth to answer, but nothing came out.

'Elle?' Caroline asked. 'Elle, what is it?'

'I couldn't do it, Mum,' she said, unable to hold back her sob. 'I couldn't spread her ashes at Stormeil.'

'Oh, sweetheart,' her mother said softly, which only made Elle cry harder. 'I knew it would be harder than you thought,' she said gently. 'Letting go always is.'

Elle knew her mother was talking about Gran, and maybe that's what this *was* really about, but part of Elle knew it was also about Stuart and what she'd just given up.

It had been the worst day. She'd stopped so many times to give in to the tears that she'd tried so hard to control as she left Skye, feeling as though part of herself were being torn away and left behind as she finally reached the bridge that took her back to the mainland.

'Just come home,' her mother said.

'I can't,' Elle said. 'Not yet. I'm not ready.'

'What are you going to do?' Caroline asked, and for the first time in far too long, there was no criticism or judgement in the question.

'I'm heading back to Portsoy. I think Gran would like it there. It'd be nicer to have family around.'

Elle hadn't called Alice yet to tell her she was coming; she wanted a day or so to herself before she would have to muster a believable smile.

After saying goodbye to her mother, she put on the TV and cuddled her pillow as a sitcom played, the recorded studio laughter breaking the silence of her room. As her tired, gritty eyes grew heavy, she imagined the soft touch of a hand on her head, brushing back her hair, and the soft hum of an old lullaby as she let herself fall into an exhausted sleep.

※

'It's so good to see you,' Alice said, wrapping Elle in a tight hug two days later when she arrived in Portsoy.

'It's good to be back,' Elle said, and found she actually meant it. She hadn't realised how much she'd missed the family—even if they were only recently discovered family.

'Come inside, Peter's gone to—' she stopped abruptly, causing Elle to raise an eyebrow curiously at her, before she continued '—pick something up, he'll be back soon,' she finished. 'And the girls will be coming over later.'

Elle followed her into the kitchen and sat at the table while Alice put the kettle on and went about making tea.

'I think it's a lovely idea, to bring Iona home,' Alice said, bringing over two cups and placing one down in front of Elle carefully.

Elle smiled briefly and thanked her for the tea. It was funny how this was exactly what she needed right now. It seemed heartache also fell under general sickness, and what tea was good for.

'I think she'd be happy back here with her family,' Elle said. 'She never really got over leaving.'

'No,' Alice said patting her hand gently. 'I don't think she did either. I know Mum always wished Iona had come home again. Now she has, in a way.'

Elle swallowed hard and took a sip of her tea to stall any further tears. She hadn't cried this much . . . well, ever, she was sure.

The sound of the front door opening drew the two women's attention and Alice got up quickly, a huge smile on her face. Wow, Elle thought, it was nice to see that even after all this time married, Alice could get so excited to see her husband—even if he had only just ducked out to pick something up.

'Come on, dear, Peter's home.'

Elle put down her tea cup carefully. She liked Peter just fine, but rushing out to meet him seemed a bit enthusiastic. Still, it would be plain rude not to get up and greet him.

As she walked out into the hall behind Alice, Elle stopped in her tracks, staring at the doorway in shock.

'Surprise!' Alice said, almost giggling.

'Mum. Dad?' Elle managed to squeak out, frozen to the spot.

'Hello, darling,' her mother said, and Elle found herself wrapped in her parents' arms. If she'd thought she had managed to cry herself out over the past few days, she'd been sorely mistaken as a fresh rush of tears fell unchecked. She had missed them so much, far more than she had expected to, and her mother's familiar floral perfume floating around her instantly brought with it a flood of memories.

'Mum,' Elle said, pulling away briefly, unable to believe that Caroline was really standing there. 'What are you doing here? When did you leave?'

'Almost straight after your phone call. Your father and I decided we needed to be here. We should have come with you in the beginning instead of letting you shoulder all the responsibility alone.'

'We should have listened to what Gran wanted,' her father said with a sad smile, 'instead of what made us feel better.'

'I'm so glad you're here,' Elle said, hugging them both tightly again. 'I've missed you.'

'Come in out of the hallway,' Alice said, breaking up the reunion and wiping her own eyes.

Once they were in the living room, Elle introduced Alice to her parents and watched as Alice grabbed her father in one of her famously warm, engulfing hugs.

'We can't thank you enough, Alice, for looking out for Elle while she's been over here,' Caroline said, holding the other woman's hand in between both of her own.

'It's been a pleasure to get to know her, all of you, in fact. We've been so excited for you to get here.'

'It was very last minute,' her mother apologised and Elle bit back a grin at how funny it was for her obsessively organised mother to have decided to spontaneously jump on a plane to Scotland. But as the afternoon wore on and melted into early evening, Caroline and Alister relaxed into their new surroundings, and the front door continued to open and close as more family arrived.

Elle grinned as she hugged her cousin Aila, and was grateful for the friendship they had forged over the past few weeks. It was strange to think they had only known each other for a short while; she felt as though they had been close their whole lives.

Seated later with Aila and Grace, the girls caught up on everything that had been happening while she'd been away.

'I can't wait to see your new drawings,' Grace said, rubbing a hand over her now enormous belly. 'Aila said you'd been doing a lot while you were away. The ones you mailed came up a treat.'

Elle mentally skimmed through her sketchpad and hesitated before answering. She had sketched more in the past few weeks than ever before, but there were a lot of drawings that were far too personal to sell. 'I've been doing a bit. I'm sure we can find one or two you can have, but some of them are . . . special.'

Her older cousin eyed her with a small smile. 'Aye, sometimes it's just good therapy.'

'How are you and baby doing?' Elle asked, feeling a little too raw yet to open up to her cousins about her time away.

'Fine. I'm more than ready to meet this wee one, though. Another three weeks to go.'

'She should be at home resting, but she's too stubborn to listen to anyone,' Aila put in, coming back with a piece of cake.

'The shop's busier than ever,' Grace said with a shrug. 'Someone had a great idea to put us online,' she added, looking directly at her sister.

'It *was* a great idea,' Aila said with a wide grin, before putting a forkful of cake in her mouth.

'Well, if you need a hand, I'm thinking I'll stay around for a bit longer,' Elle offered, and the sisters swapped glances.

'That would be brilliant,' Aila said excitedly. 'You can move in with me, I've got a spare room.'

'I'm not sure how long I'll stay, but I'm happy to help out where I can.'

'We can definitely work something out,' Grace said. 'I wouldn't mind being able to put my feet up a bit more than I have been.'

'Let me know when you want me to start,' Elle said, finding herself excited by the prospect.

After everyone went home, Alister and Peter went out to bring in the luggage, and Elle had a chance to sit with her mum over coffee.

'You and the girls look like three peas in a pod,' her mother said.

'I know. I couldn't believe it when I was surrounded by redheads over here,' Elle grinned.

'You think you'll still stay longer?' Caroline asked.

'I think so, Mum. I know it's not what you want me to do, but I . . . I'm happy here. I'd like to spend some time with the family here, and explore more of Scotland. I'm just not ready to go back home yet.'

Her mother reached out to stroke Elle's hair. 'Just remember you have family back home too, who miss you,' she said gently, and Elle once again realised how long it had been since she and her mother had been able to talk like this. Without the frustration and arguments.

'I know. It's just something I feel like I need to do.'

'Grace mentioned earlier that you'd sold some of your drawings,' her mother said after they'd sat in silence for a while. 'Why didn't you tell us?'

Elle traced a finger along the seam of the couch before answering. 'I knew what you'd say,' she said, then looked up at her mother. 'That selling one or two pieces of art didn't mean anything—it wasn't enough to make a career of.'

'But it did mean something,' Caroline replied. 'To you. I hate that you don't feel like you can share those kinds of moments with us—the things that make you happy.' She smiled sadly. 'You have a talent, Elle. I should have told you that a long time ago.'

'Why didn't you?' Elle asked. She didn't want to spoil their newfound truce, but her mother's announcement surprised her.

'I guess I was worried that it would encourage you to give up completely on finding a career and you'd only focus on art,' Caroline said wearily.

'Mum, *you* were the only one who hadn't given up on me finding a "career". You just weren't listening to me.'

'I know. I just wanted what was best for you.'

'I just wish you'd been able to see that I *was* doing what was best for me. I'm not cut out to be an academic like everyone else in the family, Mum. I'm just not. I'm sorry that I'm a disappointment to you, but that's just how it is.' Elle shrugged.

'You have *never* been a disappointment to me,' her mother said, causing Elle to look over at her when she heard her urgent tone. 'I think I was always just a little bit jealous of you, if you want to know the truth.'

'What?'

'You *are* talented, Elle. You always have been. You're like a ray of sunshine. I often watched you in the park when you were little—running up to other children and dragging them over to me saying, "Look, Mummy, this is my new best friend."'

Elle gave a small groan.

'You light up a room when you walk in. There's something very special about you, Elspeth, and I used to wish I had even a fraction of that specialness—your . . . I don't even know how to describe it . . . your *glow*,' Caroline said finally, with a slight, almost bewildered, shake of her head. 'I don't know where you got it from. My childhood was very different to yours, and I know that in a lot of ways, even though I thought I'd been able to move on and put it behind me, I let it become a wedge between you and me. I just wanted to make a better life for all of you. Better than I had,' she said simply.

'And we did. We had two parents who loved us, and a home,' Elle said. 'I know it was important to you that all your kids went to university and found careers, but that was *your* dream, Mum.'

'You were the only child of mine who refused to stick to what I thought was the best path for you,' Caroline said with amused tolerance. 'It took you leaving for me to realise I'd pushed too hard and as a result pushed you away. I'm ashamed to say that I was also a little jealous of your relationship with Iona. You two were so close. I wanted us to be that way, but I didn't know how.'

'Oh Mum,' Elle said, biting her lip against the sadness of her mother's words. 'I always loved you as much as I loved Gran.'

'I know you did. I just always seemed to be the bad guy, though, and I didn't know how to fix it.'

'I'm sorry you felt like that,' Elle said, hugging her mother tightly. She'd never really stopped to think that maybe her mum had felt left out. Caroline was always so busy and Gran had always just . . . been there.

Her mother pulled away and hastily wiped her eyes, composing herself once more. 'It was my fault, nothing that you or Gran did. I should have realised a lot sooner what it was that I was feeling, and tried to do something about it. I guess it's only since I've got older and life seems to have slowed down that I'm able to sit and see things differently. Anyway, it's all in the past now.'

'That doesn't mean we can't start over and make things better now,' Elle said.

'Exactly,' Caroline said, and this time when she smiled Elle saw something that looked a lot like relief in her mother's eyes.

'Now, I don't suppose you've heard Malcolm's news?' Caroline asked.

'No. What?' Elle replied, wondering what amazing thing he'd done now. Probably engineered a cure for the common cold.

'He's moved in with his new girlfriend,' Caroline said in a dry tone.

'What girlfriend?' Elle asked, taking an eager sip of her coffee as she waited for the gossip.

'Becky Sloan,' her mother said crisply.

Elle gasped, inhaling her mouthful of coffee and almost choking. Once she had herself back under control, she stared at her mother incredulously.

'Yes, I know. Quite a surprise.'

Elle bit back a smug little smile as she recalled how Mal had protested that day at Gran's will reading. *Just mates my arse—*

'Called to tell us a few days ago. Just dropped it into the conversation like it was nothing special.'

'So, Becky moved to Sydney?'

'Apparently.'

'Ha,' Elle said. 'Well, I hope it works out for them. I like Becky.'

Her mother gave a short huff. 'Yes, well, I guess time will tell.'

'Give her a chance, Mum,' Elle urged gently. 'Malcolm could have chosen anyone, but he wants Becky. He deserves to be happy.'

'Yes, I know.' Caroline leaned forward to place her cup on the coffee table in front of her. 'Your father's already given me the lecture about not butting in. I'm trying,' she said with sardonic little grin.

'I have faith in you, Mum,' Elle chuckled as Alice returned to join them. Elle took this as her cue to excuse herself so she could call her brother and get the rest of the story. Maybe things really were changing for the better.

# Twenty-eight

Elle stood between her mother and father on the small headland that overlooked the ocean, trying to contain her emotions. In just two days Alice had managed to pull together a simple but poignant farewell to Gran, and standing on the headland with them was a crowd of more than forty family members and friends.

After listening to some beautiful words from a celebrant friend of Alice's, followed by a hauntingly beautiful bagpipe solo that Peter had arranged, Elle couldn't help but feel relieved that in the end Gran had decided against being left behind at Stormeil. This was what Gran deserved—to be surrounded by her family.

As the last stirring notes of the song faded, Elle passed the box she cradled to her father at the edge of the cliff and watched as he gently released the contents. The wind picked up some of the lighter particles and a small cloud of almost invisible ash was swept upwards, until it disappeared completely.

Elle felt her mother's arm around her and she rested her head against Caroline's as they stood silently for a moment, lost in their thoughts of the woman they had come so far to farewell.

She missed Gran's presence desperately. What she wouldn't give to hear her voice in her head just one more time.

A slight movement from the corner of her eye caught Elle's attention and she looked across at a small grassy knoll just off to the side of the crowd. A teenage girl stood holding a baby, her dress blowing around her knees as she smiled happily across at Elle.

*Gran.* Elle's breath caught as she recognised Gran from photos of her as a fifteen-year-old girl. Holding a baby.

Elle managed a watery smile, but her heart swelled with love. Gran was fine. She had found the baby she thought she had lost forever, and she was finally at peace. Elle watched as the image faded, blowing away with the wind, out across the ocean.

'Bye, Gran,' she whispered before turning away slowly, knowing this time, she was really gone.

※

They went back to Alice's house for the wake. It was a hastily put-together event, but one that was filled with so much love and kindness that Elle knew Gran would have appreciated it.

She found Moira in her usual chair, a cup of tea sitting beside her untouched.

'Can I get you another tea, Moira?' she asked, touching the old woman's hand gently.

The time away from Portsoy and everything that had happened since had erased the last of her anger for the part Moira had played in Gran's sadness.

'No, thank you, dear. But could you sit for a while?'

Elle smiled and sat on a fold-out chair that had been brought in to accommodate the extra guests.

'She's not here anymore, is she?' the old woman asked quietly.

'No,' Elle said, wondering if Moira was fully present or not.

'But you saw her, didn't you? The last time we were here. You saw Iona.'

Elle opened her mouth in surprise, unsure how to answer. 'Did *you* see her?' she finally decided to ask.

'Of course,' Moira smiled faintly.

'I couldn't see her . . . not then,' Elle said hesitantly. 'I could hear her, though.'

Moira nodded, her pale eyes holding Elle's as she reached out and clasped her hand. 'I knew you were special,' she said softly. 'So much like Iona.'

'Moira, what is it—why could I hear Gran?'

'A gift,' Moira replied solemnly. 'A very special gift. Treasure it—don't be like me. For years I tried to ignore and deny it. Be grateful that the ancestors trusted you enough to bestow this gift upon you.'

'But . . . what do I do with it?' Elle asked.

Moira gave a fleeting smile before she closed her eyes.

Elle bit back her frustration. What was the point of having a gift like this if no one told her what to do with it? Maybe other than helping Gran, there *wasn't* any point to having it. Maybe that had been her purpose and it was now done with? Either way, it was clear she wasn't getting any more answers from Moira today. And at this moment, she didn't really mind. That part of her journey was complete.

Her parents spent another three days with her before heading to London and then on to Paris, making the most of their unexpected trip. They were happier than Elle could ever recall seeing them; her mother seemed more relaxed, and her father so enjoyed the time with his Scottish relatives that Elle was positive there would be follow-up visits from both sides of the family in the future.

Their farewell was a little sad, but not tinged with the same frustration as the first time. Elle wasn't sure when she would see them again as she had no real plan set in stone, but she knew that things had changed for the better.

Later that same day, she moved in to Aila's cottage. For a long while Elle sat on the end of the bed in her new room and stared at the set of empty drawers, which were waiting for her to unpack her belongings, trying to force the image of another set of empty drawers from her mind.

She'd found a soft woollen jumper that belonged to Stuart in her bag when she'd been digging through it to find something to wear. She'd buried her face into its softness and breathed in his scent, and felt the tentative melding of her fragile heart unravel once more. It was still too raw to think about, and she wondered when it would ever begin to feel better. In time, she reminded herself.

Staring at the drawers, she knew she had no reason not to unpack now. She'd started working in the gift shop and Grace was officially on maternity leave, so she had a full-time job and a wage for at least the next six months.

In her free time, she planned to do some more sketches of the local area and put them up for sale. She had also seen an advertisement for an art course she'd decided to enrol in, so it seemed she would be pretty busy for the foreseeable future. Standing up, she unzipped her suitcase and carried the first pile of clothes across to the drawers. This was a new beginning. Small steps, she told herself firmly.

---

Elle put her pencil down at the familiar sound of the incoming video call, and smiled as her sister and niece appeared on the phone screen.

'Hello. This is a nice surprise,' Elle said.

'Hey,' Lauren said, struggling to keep Lucy on her lap. 'Say hello to Aunty Elle.'

'Hey, Lucy. Look how much you've grown,' Elle said, surprised by the change. The chubby baby cheeks were gone and in their place was the face of a little girl. She listened as Lucy babbled something unintelligible before climbing down from her mother's lap and wandering off to play.

'I was just talking to Mum and Dad and thought I'd give you a call too. I'm a bit jealous everyone's overseas and having a great time,' Lauren said.

'It's pretty terrible,' Elle said with a grin. 'How're Mum and Dad going?'

'They're happier than I've ever seen them. What did you do to our parents?' Lauren asked in mock horror.

'I guess I was destined to break them eventually,' Elle said.

'How are you?' Lauren asked, and Elle heard the genuine interest behind the question.

'I'm really good. Better than I've ever been,' she added.

'I heard you're an in-demand artist nowadays,' Lauren said, smiling.

Her first instinct was to deny it, but then she stopped and smiled. 'I don't know about in demand just yet, but my sketches are selling.'

'That's so exciting, Elle. I'm really proud of you.'

Elle took a moment to reply as her throat felt unexpectedly thick at her sister's praise. 'Thanks.'

They went on to discuss Malcolm's latest bombshell, talking for the first time in ages more as friends than as older sister lecturing younger sister.

'Have fun, but remember to stay in touch,' Lauren said as they wound up the call.

'I will. I'll give you a ring next week.'

After they hung up, Elle found herself thinking about how much had changed since she'd left home. Maybe everyone in her family had been taking each other for granted a bit too much lately, and it had taken Elle leaving to bring them all closer. She had a feeling they would all be better for the experience, and a tiny bit of confidence began to unfurl inside her. Maybe she wasn't the family disappointment after all.

It was quiet in the afternoons at the shop, and today Elle found herself looking for something to do. She'd cleaned and dusted the shelves, and admired the beautiful giftware and craft her cousins had on display. She smiled as she rearranged the collection of *Outlander* books on the shelf—this was the second time she'd restocked them in the past few weeks, and Aila always made sure they had plenty on hand for the tourists.

Elle loved her job in her cousins' quirky little shop. Working here had given her the opportunity to meet a lot of the locals, and she looked forward to the daily pop-ins and hellos. She also loved walking through the co-op, the only supermarket in town, though occasionally it brought on a bout of homesickness as she reminisced about her happy years at Brown's. She'd kept in touch with Pat on Facebook and was informed that business had been picking up lately with the unexpected closure of the big new store in Hentley, which had gone into receivership practically overnight. She hadn't seen that coming at all.

*You'll be able to get your job back no worries at all*, Pat had written.

Once, that would have been a relief. Now, she wasn't sure. She did know that she still wasn't ready to return to Jessup's Creek. She'd been in Scotland for three months and the time was racing past. Her artwork had taken off in a direction she could never have anticipated; her local sketches especially were one of the shop's biggest sellers, and now that the store was online they were selling all over the United Kingdom.

Elle had taken to using watercolours, and spent most of her free time in her makeshift studio-cum-bedroom at Aila's cottage, perfecting her technique and often working for hours without noticing the time. Through the community art course she had made friends with a group of women and loved their weekly get-togethers exploring the nearby surrounds, where they would find places to sketch or paint. She felt as though she had found her tribe at long last—people just like her. For so long she had hidden her art away, seeing it more as an escape from reality than something she truly needed to be doing, and now that she had freed herself, she wondered how she could have possibly lived without it for so long.

Elle went along to evenings at the pub with Aila and her friends, and though Andrew had asked her out, she'd turned him down, knowing she wasn't interested in accidentally finding romance again. Sabrina and Joe had shocked everyone by splitting up—for all of a week—before getting back together again and announcing their engagement.

She was happy for Aila and Steven, who had finally stopped dancing around their attraction for each other and done something about it, but seeing them together made her miss Stuart. She kept telling herself she had made the right choice by leaving, but she also felt like she'd left a piece of herself on Skye, and she didn't know what to do about it. She was happy since coming back to Portsoy, but she missed him. More than she'd thought it was possible to miss someone she had only known for a handful of days. They sent occasional text messages and he kept her up to date with what was going on at the farm, but as much as she looked forward to hearing from him—it only made her realise what they'd had and what she'd walked away from.

She also missed Gran.

There were still times Elle found herself staring out to sea, longing to hear her grandmother's comforting voice. She often went to the headland to sit and unwind—Gran's place, she now called it. But she didn't hear her anymore.

Sitting there now, Elle closed her eyes in the late-afternoon sun and let the wind whip her hair about her face as she turned it up to the sky. Only moments later, though, she opened them at the sound of approaching footsteps on the rock steps behind her, and she stifled a moment's irritation at having her precious solitude broken.

She turned, and her forced smile wavered slightly as she met two dark eyes and a hesitant expression.

'Stuart?' Oh God, she hoped she hadn't resorted to conjuring up visons now instead of voices.

'I went to the shop and your cousin told me where I'd probably find you.'

His deep voice sent a stab of longing through her, and as she let her eyes roam over the broad chest beneath his woollen jumper and his strong denim-clad thighs, she had to admit she had missed all of him.

'What are you doing here?' she asked, too stunned to try to form a less direct question.

She watched as he shuffled forward and lowered his gaze before looking at her once more. 'I missed you.'

His simple, honest words made her bite the inside of her lip as her heart melted.

'I know I should have asked if it was okay to come and see

you, but I was afraid you'd say no,' he said with an uncertainty she had never seen in him before.

'I wouldn't have said no,' Elle said quietly.

Her reply seemed to make him feel a little more confident, and he walked across the remaining distance between them to sit beside her. They didn't touch, or speak, but the silence wasn't uncomfortable. They both seemed to be weighing up their next words.

'I'm sorry—'

'Elle, I—'

They both spoke at once and then stopped, each with a shy smile. It was like they were two strangers all over again.

'You go,' Stuart said gallantly, lowering his head, as if to brace himself in case whatever she said was going to hurt.

'I'm sorry about how it all ended so . . . unexpectedly,' she said.

'I am too. I wish I'd done things differently.'

'There's nothing I would change about our time together. It was all just . . . perfect,' Elle said gently. And it had been. A perfect, unexpected surprise.

'I didn't want to leave it the way we did,' Stuart said.

'There wasn't much else we could have done,' she said, looking back out across the ocean before them.

'I could have told you to go and that I'd follow. That I'd do whatever it took to make it work,' he said after a few moments, making her look back at him uncertainly.

'We still have the same issue,' she said with a helpless shrug. 'I'm not sure what I'm doing or where I'll be in three months' time; six months' time. How can we plan anything around that?'

'Plans are overrated.' He shrugged back at her with a smile. 'You know, you really need to loosen up a bit.'

She laughed and gave a long sigh.

Stuart reached over and took her hand in his gently, and the contact immediately sent a tsunami of memories through her. She blinked quickly and swallowed hard as her throat clogged with emotion.

'I missed you too,' she said, once she was sure she could speak without falling apart.

'We don't have to plan anything, Elle. I'm not going anywhere. I can wait for you as long as I have to. I just need to know you want to give us a chance, that there's something to wait for,' he said softly. 'Nothing's the same since you left. The house is too quiet, and even the sheep seem miserable,' he finished with a grin.

'That's kind of low, using the sheep as emotional blackmail,' she said, shaking her head and unable to hide her own smile.

'If I have to play dirty, so be it,' he said simply.

'Stuart, I—' She cut her own words off helplessly. She what? The time apart had done nothing to ease the hole in her heart. He was often the last thing she thought about at night before she went to sleep, her traitorous mind wondering how he was and what he was doing. Whether he was thinking of her too. 'You live all the way over in Skye,' she said finally.

'All the way?' he taunted lightly. 'Wasn't it *you* who scoffed at the distances to anywhere here? Miss I Come From Australia Where We Drive For Days Before We Reach The End Of Our Driveway.'

God, she'd missed that accent. The man could read the phone book and she would never get tired of listening to him.

'What's three hours or so?' he dismissed.

'I took the hire car back. I don't have a car anymore,' she said, realising he was once again using her own words to make his case.

'I do,' he countered.

'You have a farm to run,' she pointed out.

'I also have new employees.' He shrugged.

'Did you come prepared with arguments for everything?'

'Absolutely. What kind of solicitor would I be if I wasn't prepared to defend my case?'

Her smile turned serious. 'What happens if, after six months I decide to go back to Australia?' It hurt enough to say goodbye last time after only a handful of days, she couldn't imagine how painful it would be after that long.

'Elle, I'm planning on making sure that by that time you've fallen so madly in love with me you won't be able to say goodbye,' he said simply, but his eyes held a probing, almost pleading look that managed to crumble the last of the barrier she'd hastily tried to build around her heart.

'It's too late,' she said and saw the hope in his eyes start to fade, before reaching up to place her free hand on the side of his face. 'I'm already madly in love with you.'

She saw his throat work briefly, and his eyes darken with a look so full of tenderness that her own eyes stung with the fresh sheen of tears. When his lips took hers, she felt all the broken little pieces inside her begin to repair themselves as the missing parts came back together.

# Epilogue

*Long ago in the Highlands of Scotland, a girl from the clan MacCoinnich and Stormeil Castle fell in love with a boy of Clan MacColuim and Tàileach Castle. Their deaths would end a bitter war and reunite their clans. But their love . . . oh my darling, their love would transcend time.*

# Acknowledgements

Jaki Gardner, John Scrudis, Rosie Robertson, Jade from Jez Art for her insightful help with all things arty. Morven Steen and her mum in Scotland, Anne Lane, Joyce Campbell. A big thank you to Ilana and Sylvia from the Haunted Palace blog for their help creating the family legend of Iona and Gavan, and the MacLeod Estate team at Dunvegan Castle.

Like Elle and Gran, I also have a long-term love affair with *Outlander*. I read this book over twenty years ago and I'm pretty sure it was the fire that lit my desire to start seriously writing after years of dabbling. Jamie is the man that has shaped every male hero I write—there aren't any redheaded Scottish warriors from 1743 in my books, but his core values and his ability to love so wholeheartedly stuck with me long after I read that first book.

I was so lucky to finally get a chance to live my dream and visit Scotland, and it was an experience I will always treasure. As with many people, I have a family link that leads back to Scotland. I'm lucky enough to have Scottish ancestry on both my mother's and father's side of the family, but for me, the stories of Dunvegan on the Isle of Skye, where my father's side descend from the MacLeods of Dunvegan, has the strongest pull.

We were brought up on stories of raids and castles, feuds and fairies and they've always stayed with me, much like Gran's family stories she told to Elle. So, I went on my own little quest in search of our family legacy and found Dunvegan Castle, which I'm happy to say was in much better shape than poor old Stormeil Castle.

While Australia is where I was born and bred and I have at least five generations' worth of family, visiting Scotland made me realise just how deeply a place can come to be buried within a person, because part of my heart will always belong to that beautiful, wild country that my ancestors came from.

Many of the places featured in the book are where my husband and I spent time on our trip to Scotland and can be visited or stayed at. Feel free to add them to your own Scotland bucket list.

Please note that although I researched and asked advice on certain aspects of sheep farming in Scotland and other general bits and pieces, all mistakes are my own, or were changed to suit the plot!